ONCE UPON THE CONGO

CHAP HARPER

This is a work of fiction, and is produced from the author's imagination. People, places and things mentioned in this novel are used in a fictional manner.

ISBN: 978-1-7348196-2-5

Library of Congress Control Number: 2015937541

Acknowledgements

I would like to thank Nancy Gibson, Bill Schuler , Gene Forsyth, Carole Fox, Gail Paul, Carole Katchen , Patricia Hanard, Susan Harper, Nannette Crane-Post, David Rose, Taylor Foss, Leslie Foss, Madelyn Young, Kerry Lockwood Owen, Kim Everhart, and Diane Daniels for suggested changes, encouragement, and edits. No one completes a project like this without the help of many good friends. Thanks to all!

My editor, Claire Applewhite, earns special thanks for her diligent review of each and every chapter. She always encouraged me to create the best book possible.

The cover and interior design was done by graphic artist, Lois Mans, who created the unique and outstanding African design for my book. Hopefully, it will attract those who love a good adventure. To them, I say, "Pick up ONCE UPON THE CONGO and start reading!"

Chap Harper
April, 2015

Dedication

I dedicate this book to my late mother
Freda Earle Lewellyn Harper

When I was a kid, I would come home from school and find my mother sitting on her feet in a large stuffed chair reading a book. She loved to read and because of her membership in every "Book of the Month Cub" known to mankind, our home was pretty much a storage facility for books. Every room except for the kitchen and bathroom (does a magazine rack count?) had at least one bookcase. She encouraged me to read and helped me to write short stories. When I was in high school, I signed up for The Famous Writer's School with her support. I had to drop out though, since I couldn't continue the eighteen dollar monthly tuition. I'm not sure the books I have written so far would have been her type, but someday, I would like to write a book she might have ordered from her book club and enjoyed.

Starvation was so great just before we left that the native slaves seized one of their comrades, who had gone some distance to draw water, cut him in pieces, and ate him. In conclusion, I may mention that Captain Nelson and myself did everything we could to preserve a good feeling with the Manyuema chiefs and people, and we parted on friendly terms.

T.M Parke

To H.M. Stanley, Esq., Commanding E.P.R. Expedition.

(Excerpt from Henry Stanley's *In Darkest Africa*.)

Chapter 1

**Oct. 9, 1887 – *Aruwimi River, the Congo,*
West Africa**

The early morning mist beside the river had burned off, only to
be replaced by wet, thick and sticky air. The air did not move, and
appeared to have been put in place a thousand years ago. The village
next to the hanging tree sat on the banks of the Aruwimi River in the
Congo basin. A foul smell emitting from the settlement suggested the
natives' latrines were fresh and ripe. Combined with the heat, it was
difficult to breathe.

The skinny porter stared without emotion or expression into
Henry Stanley's eyes. Stanley stood with his arms crossed, occasionally
wiping the sweat from his face with a dirty handkerchief. He had an "I
take no pleasure in this" look on his face, while he slapped his ears in
a vain attempt to kill attacking insects.

In the shade of a large mahogany tree, the stoic Zanzibar native
waited, his hands bound behind him. Stanley asked him if he had
anything to say. He shook his head. Death was sometimes a reason to
rejoice when starvation and sickness are the payments for shouldering
sixty pounds of supplies every day. Stanley's men placed the noose
around his neck.

Giving the signal with a wave of his hand, forty sweating wide eyed
porters pulled on the other end of the cord and hoisted the black man's
body high beneath a large limb, until he no longer jerked and kicked
at the air. He had drawn the short piece of paper distributed among
three of his fellow bearers who had deserted with their Winchester
rifles. Their crimes had been discovered when neighboring tribesmen

delivered them that morning bound with ropes. The Zanzibar porter was told he would be the first of three to be hanged. The others would meet their fate on subsequent days.

Actually, Stanley wanted to set an example. Later, he set the other two men free, and called it an act of God. Stanley walked to the front of the line of emaciated bearers. Holding his handkerchief over his nose to filter out their ferocious body odor, Stanley instructed the men to tie off the body to the tree with rattan vines and save the rope. "Guns are the soul of our expedition," he said as the porters dispersed and picked up their loads. In fifteen minutes the entire expedition, except for some rear guards, marched under the body hanging in the tree and made good time to their next camp.

Stanley's expedition to Africa centered on the rescue of Emin Pasha, governor of the Egyptian province of Equatoria, four hundred miles farther upstream. For reasons known only to Stanley and King Leopold of Belgium, the expedition traversed one of the most difficult inland passages in the world. Stanley had decided against using a much easier route leading inland from the east coast of Africa. He was truly in the wilds of the Dark Continent, traveling through the unexplored jungles of the Congo basin. Crude maps shed little light on this region of West Africa. Stanley was killing his men the way fire burns up kindling, and reaching the Ituri River and Lake Albert Nyanza appeared all but impossible. His men were dying of starvation, poisoned arrows, disease, and accidents; when Stanley was really pissed, by hanging to set an example for the natives.

The next day, on October 10th, a hundred men volunteered to swim across the river to a huge island in search of food. Stanley went upriver by boat while one of his officers, Captain Robert Nelson, went downstream to see if he could raid a village of hapless natives for food. Other men stayed close and hunted the nearby forest in search of wild fruit and forest beans. The men who looked for food in the jungle ran the risk of getting stomped to death by herds of forest elephants.

Two of Captain Nelson's tent boys, Baruk and Abdalla, tagged along with the group who swam to the island, if for no other reason than to get away from their white European masters. Most of the boys assigned to the British explorers ranged in age from twelve to seventeen years old. They cooked, carried water, set up camp, and in general, were personal servants to expedition officers. Without a "boy," the officers would be close to helpless and would lose a great deal of status as bona fide African explorers. Henry Stanley carried it a step further, since he also brought along a personal manservant. How ignoble it was to have to pitch your own tent, get your water, cook, and dress yourself. The agony was obvious. Along for the ride was Dr. Thomas Parke's main boy, Binza, and Stanley's cook, Zikomo.

Binza was on his second expedition in the service of a doctor. He estimated his survival rate was about ten times greater than the average native load humper. Binza had observed that Dr. Parke was an avid naturalist. When given a little freedom, Binza collected samples of anything he thought would please his master. On this day he was more intent on getting plant and rock samples than looking for food, so he stayed with the other boys who were not taking the hunt seriously. As the older men turned to the left of an outcropping, the boys headed directly up the side of the escarpment using their youthful energy and monkeylike climbing skills. None of the men stopped the climbing youth since a boy had an invisible halo of protection, based on their connections to the British. This tie kept the older men at bay, and in fear of their safety if they bothered one of them.

From atop the high bluff, which was about five hundred feet tall, the boys watched the men break into groups and disappear into the wooded sections of the island. The boys began to explore the rock-strewn landscape. Captain Nelson's tent boys, Abdalla and Baruk, headed to the left where a path went around the edge of the bluff. After a while they stretched out, exhausted, and fell asleep from the cumulative effect of hard work and little nourishment to sustain them.

Binza and Zikomo took an opposite route. After climbing farther up the rocky bluff, they found a wooded area that appeared unnatural. The vegetation was so thick with wet ferns, vines, trees and large leafy plants they had difficulty getting through it. Binza thought these trees might have been planted, since the trees were so close to one another. After an hour of fighting the dense jungle, they noticed the growth was in a depression, perhaps trapping water and creating an environment for plants to grow in great profusion.

Zikomo kept looking back over his shoulder. "Binza, don't you think we should go back now?" he said. His voice sounded shaky.

Binza also felt the jungle was too thick, and as he was about to turn back he noticed a change in the forest. "What is that strange darkness ahead of us?"

They could see a large object through gaps in the trees. "In the name of Allah, what type of place is this?" Zikomo said. He rushed to Binza's side and began to fight through the last of the jungle foliage.

After hurrying out of the forest, they came to a shallow clearing between huge date palms that encircled a stone wall. They strained their necks to behold a twenty foot-high, expertly constructed wall that did not belong on this bluff. Only the finest mason could have cut the stone so precisely that no seams appeared between the huge blocks of black lava.

Binza and Zikomo raced around the wall to a gate with massive ironwood doors. Enormous bronze hinges coated with an olive patina held the open doors in place. They entered slowly, their eyes drawn to the sparkling water of a large blue hole in the middle of the fort. The pool was about a hundred feet across, surrounded by giant piles of moss-colored soil. Heaps of rust-colored soil stood behind sea-green rocks. Near the walls, silver-gray ore was stacked, pyramid style.

"Binza, what is this place?"

"I don't know what they were digging for, but I will take some soil to Dr. Parke."

They walked about two hundred yards to the edge of the crystal-clear blue hole. Along the way, snakes sunned themselves, and a few hissed as the boys passed by, yet Binza ignored them.

"Binza, did you see that cobra right by you?" Zikomo whispered as he tugged at Binza's shirt sleeve.

Binza didn't answer; instead, he approached a small stone cottage on the far side of the blue hole. The house, adjacent to the water's edge, had steps leading down into the water. A door above the steps was sealed with stones and mortar. A forest cobra slid off the steps into the water and quickly swam to the opposite shoreline, where it coiled its wet and glistening body next to a green pile of soil. Zikomo's gaze followed the cobra, but Binza ignored the snake and circled the house, finding the windows and doors sealed with stone. The one story structure had four stone columns in front that made a porch-like edifice supporting a sloping roof. Binza said more to himself than to Zikomo, "All the cracks and crevices have been sealed around the doors and windows. It looks like a tomb."

Zikomo nodded and began to look over his shoulder again, which was his signal for, "We need to get out of here."

Strange vegetation grew in patches and appeared mutated, stunted, and displayed sickly green leaves. Tiny miniature palm trees with a toy-like appearance dotted the enclosed area. Binza pulled from his knapsack cloth bags he used to collect plants, small animals and rocks for Dr. Parke. He scooped up moss-colored soil and emptied it into a bag. He did the same with soil and ore from other sections of the quarry. One area had rusty-orange colored ore, while heaps of a silver-gray, crystalline were next to the walls. Light green soil extended down the sides of the blue hole and into the depths of the pool. Zikomo collected colored soil, brought it to Binza and helped him fill the bags, but he was anxious to leave. Again, he was looking back over his shoulder with a painful look on his dark face.

Dr. Parke had given Binza paper and a pencil. The boys sketched the dimensions of the cottage and the blue hole. Zikomo called out the number of steps he took to measure the length and width, to Binza, who wrote down the numbers next to his drawings.

"Binza, let's go—we are going to be in trouble!" Zikomo knew they had been away too long and feared that their white masters would not be pleased. Punishment could range from a beating all the way up to being shot.

They scaled down the cliff. Their friends had already left to return to Captain Nelson, and both boys felt they had better hurry back to help prepare a meal in case the others had found food worth eating.

Dr. Parke scolded Binza for being gone so long and put him to work scraping wood beans and preparing plantains for dinner. Binza sliced a few banana-shaped fruits into thin pieces and deep-fried them into chips, a treat the doctor enjoyed. After dinner, Binza told the doctor about their find. Impressed, Dr. Parke studied the drawings that young

Binza had made and marveled at the colorful ores he had recovered. He suggested that Binza may have happened on to an ancient quarry which might have been mined and abandoned. With no time to examine the ore samples, because the expedition members were so ill, the doctor made notes in a small journal including their approximate location of south latitude 1 degree 24 minutes and 22 degrees 35 minutes east longitude. He placed Binza's drawings carefully inside the journal. Eager to save the men Stanley was killing at a steady pace, Dr. Parke tucked the journal and bags of ore samples into a pocket of his leather valise. He zipped shut the expensive piece of luggage and hurried off to tend to his patients.

That night, several men stole items from their expedition. One of the thieves, Wadi Adam, stole Dr. Parke's entire luggage kit and headed into the forest. He was never to be seen again by the expedition.

Chapter 2

The Luggage

The four black men decided not to stay close to camp after dark. Two of them had stolen whole cases of Winchester 44.40 ammunition. One had the doctor's luggage. The other one had run off with hiking boots. All risked possible death in the jungle, instead of more probable death by starvation while carrying sixty pounds of gear on their backs. If Henry Stanley caught them, they had little doubt they would be hung. They hadn't packed out a rifle but planned on stealing one after dark. Porters didn't take care to hide rifles at night and hated lugging around the extra ten pounds per weapon. After careful consideration, the four former expedition porters chose to flee downriver, where they could trade with natives who had stolen rifles, but lacked ammunition.

Wadi Adam was a Somali, hired both as a porter and a back-up mercenary fighter. The real warriors on the expedition were the Sudanese, who carried only their rifles and ammo. Many Muslim men were called "Wadi," a first name as common as Joe or Bill among the English. Wadi Adam was more experienced with firearms than the Zanzibar natives, who, according to Stanley and his officers, were not much help in battle. The two men who had stolen crates of ammunition were Bull Neck Uchungu and Kajeli from Zanzibar, slaves of the wealthy Arab trader, Tippu-Tib, who rented them out to Stanley. Lives of natives were considered cheap and a tradable commodity in Africa. Salim, one of the few Swahilis on the expedition, from the British East Africa Protectorate, had grabbed a leather kit that contained three pairs of expensive hiking boots. Two were Stanley's and one was a custom pair for the Emin Pasha, who apparently expected this expedition to rescue him. A fifth porter fled about the same time as the other four. His name was Swadi, whose country of origin was a mystery. Swadi had dropped what he was carrying and disappeared into the jungle. At this point, the expedition had lost over sixty men by desertion or death. More than thirty rifles had been stolen or lost.

After pushing through steamy forests for several hours, the four men stopped to rest by an elephant trail that paralleled the Aruwimi River. Rope handles on each end of the ammo boxes made it possible to share the load, if necessary. Each crate had twenty boxes of fifty rounds for a total weight of about sixty pounds. Porters used thick pads on their shoulders to keep the rough wood from cutting their flesh. In addition, the men had their own private kits, usually small home-made knapsacks or sometimes a roll attached around their waist. Everyone knew the ammunition was valuable. One fifty-round box of rifle ammo would bring $2.00 in the States and twice that halfway around the world. Remington repeaters sold for only $17.00 in America and of course more in Africa, but still much less than a case of ammo. The four men expected to trade one case of ammo for two lever action rifles. But first, they must survive, at least until they found a trading partner.

After resting a few minutes, the men moved slowly along the jungle path. The men's stomachs growled with hunger when they resumed their trek, as the berries and fruit along the trail lacked protein and did not provide real substance. Although they could hear monkeys overhead in the tall trees, there was no hope of bagging one for dinner, unless they threw some bullets at them.

Wadi Adam held on proudly to Dr. Parke's kit, hoping it contained something of value. He was reluctant to open the bag in front of the others, in the fear they might steal the contents for themselves. The satchel was heavy and soft, yet very thick, and made of beautiful polished leather. Rare and recently invented brass zippers enclosed numerous compartments and pockets. The kit must have cost a fortune!

While Wadi Adam caressed the bag and traced the indented monogram with his finger, his other hand felt something hard behind an outside pocket. Carefully, he passed his hand over the object and discerned a round and cylindrical item that felt unmistakably like a gun barrel. He stopped walking, as did the others. He knew he must find the end of the zipper. His hand slid into the outside pocket, and the pistol's cool metal brushed against his fingers. Next, he moved his hand down to the pistol grip and gently pulled out the gun as though he was giving birth to it. The eyes of his fellow travelers grew large. In Wadi's hand, was a loaded Enfield .476 revolver. At the base of the grip, a lanyard ring had kept the gun attached to the officer while he bounced around in battle. A few years later, this powerful handgun would be dumbed down by the British to a .45 caliber. This was the same model gun Wadi had trained to use in Somalia. The British had been bringing this pistol to Africa since 1880 and had left a few lying around from Egypt to South Africa. Watching the others pass around the weapon, Wadi Adam surmised they had never shot a pistol. He also found a box of fifty rounds in that same compartment along with a cleaning kit, holster, belt, and leather cord.

The small group realized they could protect themselves if they met up with a tribe who attacked with spears and poisoned arrows. If they got close enough, they might be able to shoot game. Smiling and confident for the first time since escaping the wretched expedition, the four men started down the elephant trail. Every few steps, Wadi Adam reached down and felt the cool steel in the holster, and checked the cord tied to the lanyard ring. He felt happier than he had in years.

Chapter 3

The Elephant

They had been on the path about half a day when they heard bellowing in the woods. Actually meeting an elephant had just not occurred to the four men—yet. Wadi Adam and his three companions saw piles of elephant dung on the trail and noticed footprints in the mud. Rainforest elephants, smaller than those found on savannas, make up for their size by fearlessness.

A young rainforest elephant emerged from the thick jungle, charged, faced them, and stopped. This bull appeared to have gone into musk with gallons of testosterone surging through his body. He was either going to find a female elephant to mate with or stomp anything he saw into an unrecognizable pulp. Wadi Adam stood directly in front of him, frozen, his buddies scurrying into the forest like squirrels running from an oncoming garbage truck. Wadi pulled his pistol from the holster and cocked the hammer. The large .476 caliber might not be a match for the creature's thick skull and large tusks, but Wadi knew the gun was his only chance.

Wadi had never shot an elephant, lion or anything large. A springbuck was his claim to fame, requiring four shots to kill the moving target. This elephant was fairly still, except for pawing the ground and raising his head in a threatening manner. The initial charge—head down and tusks in the kill position—came. Wadi took aim and started firing—first in the skull—second shot dead center— same for the third and fourth. When the fifth shot struck, the elephant stopped and shook his head side to side as though he was trying to dislodge the bullet. He was wounded but not done, dazed, standing in front of Wadi, not thirty yards away. Wadi carefully reached in his pocket and found more rounds. Slowly and methodically he clicked the cylinder out, ejected the spent shells, and put in the new loads without taking his eyes off the elephant. No sooner had he pushed the cylinder back in the firing position, than the elephant started his final charge. Although the injured beast wobbled from side to side, he was well enough to kill Wadi. Taking a standing firing position, Wadi fired round after round. Finally one shot penetrated the skull of the giant. He fell, almost at Wadi's feet.

Wadi's companions crept from their hiding places. They would have elephant meat for quite a while. With their knives they carved off pieces, started a fire, and cooked many pounds of meat. Once they were full, they packed as much cooked elephant flesh as they could carry and hurried to make time on the trail. This was the first meat in weeks and their digestive systems made strange sounds, but eating protein was worth the occasional stomach ache and bowel uproar. Since he didn't have a heavy load, Swadi agreed to carry the tusks. Tusks were another valuable item to trade, in some cases worth a man's life.

Two days later, they found a small village, but no one had rifles. Although the villagers spoke a different language, everyone knew a little Swahili, so communication was possible. They spent the night sharing elephant meat with the villagers, and telling the amazing story of how Wadi killed the elephant, which would be told for generations to come.

The following day, the four travelers started downstream along a path cut by Stanley's men only days before their arrival. At times, they would pass the bodies of bearers left to rot in the jungle after they died from exhaustion or disease. The villagers had told the group how many days' walk to expect before reaching the big settlement where several stolen rifles were located. Ugarrowwa, an Arab slave and ivory trader who worked for Tippu-Tib, controlled the village named for him. Wadi knew Henry Stanley had left over fifty of his sick and injured men in Ugarrowwa to receive care. An agreement had been reached for Ugarrowwa to provide food for the men, but instead, some of the men had to trade their weapons to keep from starving. Stanley had hung one bearer nearby for selling rifles for food, yet it's unlikely his officers would suffer this same fate. If Wadi and his three friends were caught by the Arab slave traders, they would be turned over to Stanley when he returned. Their best hope was for Ugarrowwa to be out of camp trading with chiefs in outlying areas of the Congo. At the end of the day the four men rested and ate elephant meat along with ripe plantains they had found along the way. Before dark, Wadi decided to further explore Dr. Parke's luggage. He started at the top and worked his way down, opening each section zipper by zipper. The top enclosure held shirts, socks, and underwear. Also there was a raincoat and a sweater. "Why a sweater?" Wadi asked himself. Next he found a personal care compartment with shaving gear, along with medicines and bandages.

Wadi was able to read only a few English words. His home country of Somalia, being Muslim, used an Arabic script that Wadi didn't know well. Swahili, on the other hand, had a written language part Arabic and part Bantu which Wadi knew better than Arabic. He recognized a bottle of morphine from helping hold down a porter while the doctor gave an injection from a similar container. Near the middle of the kit, Wadi found identification, money, and trade items. A single sheet paper passport listed the doctor's name as Thomas H. Parke, Army Medical Doctor. Inside the folded paper passport was money…more money than Wadi had ever seen. Over one hundred U.S. dollars and one hundred and fifty British pounds were neatly pressed, mostly in small bills. This was more money than most native Africans would see in a lifetime. On the other hand, most natives didn't live very long.

Trade items in the kit included beautiful cowrie shells. Native chiefs loved the seashells so much they accepted them in exchange for natives they sold into slavery, called Maafa or "the great disaster" by the slaves. Wadi also found beads and jewelry for trading in the luggage. Finally he reached the bottom zipper. Inside were Dr. Parke's personal journal and his collection of native plants, feathers, rocks, small skulls, and three cloth bags tied at the top by a cord. Wadi removed the cord on one to discover green soil and ore containing glass-looking objects. He tied the cloth bag closed and returned it to its place. In the luggage were books, writing materials, boot polish, wash rags, towels, combs and brushes, and more medical supplies. Feeling assured he had explored the suitcase well, Wadi wanted to capitalize on his newfound assets, but first he needed to be well armed.

The next morning, the small band of porters, on the lam, headed downriver with a sense of urgency. Wadi told his companions he had many more items to trade for guns. Obtaining four rifles and a canoe would be desirable. When he told this to his companions, they looked at him as though a new head had grown from his shoulder. He stopped on the trail and asked to see their slave marks. Uchungu and Kajeli had been branded. The two raised their left arms and revealed a "T" burned into their flesh right below the arm pit; the mark of ownership by Tippu-Tib. The two men were a small part of the ten thousand slaves Tippu-Tib owned in Zanzibar. Wadi knew slave owners usually branded their slaves because tattoos took longer and didn't show up well on dark African skin.

Wadi addressed the men in Swahili, their common language.

"We will try to bypass the Ugarrowwa station at night in a canoe. We cannot count on the Arab settlement being willing to trade with us. Most likely they will rob us of everything we have. While I hope Ugarrowwa is off hunting ivory, we will approach the settlement as though they are fully manned."

Wadi took on the role of leader. No one opposed him.

"We will look along the trails and in the small villages on the way since other deserters may have been wary of the Arab town," Wadi said.

During the next two days, they picked up one other deserter who was almost starved to death. Swadi had left the Stanley expedition with only his meager gear. In his possession was a stolen rifle loaded with three rounds of ammo that so far he had not needed to use. Wadi checked on the still intact firing spring. Stanley had removed firing springs from some of the weapons, so the rifles would be useless in a trade and also to prevent shooting at birds and wasting ammunition. Swadi had seen some of the deserters on various trails and was surprised Wadi had not run into them. Three deserters, carrying both rifles and crates of ammunition, let Swadi know they did not want him in their group by firing a round over his head and motioned him to stay back.

The village that lay ahead was near a trail that led directly to the Aruwimi River. The five men noted several canoes on the river banks. The village chief greeted them, offered food, and was quite friendly. Wadi got right to the point and asked what he would want for two canoes. The chief would consider only one canoe, saying he would take ivory in exchange. Wadi offered a tusk and a few cowrie shells, which did the trick. He learned three travelers with rifles had stopped by, but made no trades. Wadi's gang loaded into a large canoe where they found three paddles to help propel them downriver. They made good time and camped by the river that night.

At camp, Wadi suggested Uchungu and Kajeli conceal their brands with an over-brand. They agreed, and he went into Dr. Parke's kit and found in the money compartment a U.S. half dollar. Using some of the doctor's long tweezers, he first heated the coin in the fire. Next, he carefully placed the sizzling coin directly over the "T" on Uchungu. He was a huge man nicknamed Bull Neck by the white men on the expedition. Even so, he yelled in pain. Wadi put salve and a bandage over the burned spot. He knew healing would take a while. Kajeli looked terrified, so Wadi gave him a shot of morphine from the kit to help. When the hot coin was put in place, Kajeli moaned and passed out. Now, if they were caught, Tippu-Tib's men would not be able to identify them, since many slave traders used the same spot to brand their property. Once Wadi had everything needed for the group's existence, he could plan for a way back home.

In the morning, they woke up to sounds of gun fire and screaming deep in the jungle. With Kajeli still groggy from the morphine, Uchungu stayed back to look after him while the rest headed in the direction of the noise. After crashing through jungle foliage, they came to a wide circular clearing, an elephant bai, complete with a huge mud hole in the center. Forest elephants create these bais throughout the jungle for the salt they crave, which accumulates below the mud holes.

As the group entered the bai, they saw a herd of rainforest

elephants moving slowly into the jungle. Then, they noticed the source of the screams. Three men lay dead at the edge of the clearing, stomped and gored to death by the herd. The corpses had been pulverized and their skulls crushed. The victims' rifles lay scattered, pressed into the mud, but otherwise okay. Wadi Adam and his two men picked up the weapons, took knives and other useful items from the dead men, then trekked back to the river. Once there, the group of five cleaned, oiled and tested the rifles. Now, they had plenty of fire power, ammunition and a mode of transportation. Another canoe and rifle would be nice, but Wadi hoped to pick up those at one of the many villages they would encounter.

Two more days on the river got them close to the Ugarrowwa station, so they stopped for the night. Early the next morning they floated quietly by the sleeping settlement, hugging the far bank of the river. That night, they paddled steadily, making good time. Later, they carried the canoe past some big rapids. Before they put the canoe back in the water, they stopped along the Aruwimi River, which would soon flow into the much larger Congo River. They had to make some hard decisions.

If they followed the Congo downriver to the Atlantic Coast, the two slaves might be recognized and to make matters worse, a rear column of Stanley's expedition was plodding along somewhere in front of them. Wadi asked the other men if they had families to return to. Uchungu and Kajeli had been sold away from their parents when they were very young. They had no idea if their parents were still alive. They didn't want to go back to Zanzibar. Wadi, Swadi, and Salim all wanted to go east, Swadi and Salim to British controlled areas that no longer allowed slavery, and Wadi to Somalia where he had a wife and child. All five men agreed to go east above Lake Victoria to the British coast, and then Wadi would head north to join his family. They would travel the Congo River a short distance, go inland and north to Sudan, and across Africa to the east coast. Wadi had found a compass in Dr. Parke's luggage that would help, but they knew the villagers would trade for food and directions.

For the time being they were free, a good feeling, but traveling over a thousand miles through treacherous lands, being shot with poisoned arrows and attacked by wild animals left little margin for error. The five native Africans might know how to survive in the jungle, but carnivorous animals were always waiting to eat them for dinner.

Six months later, Wadi left his four friends in the area of what is now Kenya, and journeyed northeast into Somalia. Thirty more days of travel got him to Mogadishu, where he found his wife and son impoverished. They had to move in with her parents to survive. While Wadi had used much of the cash to buy food and provisions for his band of escapees, he still had money left to buy a small farm. He had his pistol and rifle, but no need for the baggage from Dr. Parke. Instead, he needed money for his family. In Mogadishu, a dealer in fine gifts and antiques was excited to purchase the kit from Dr. Thomas H. Parke and offered Wadi ten British pounds. Wadi countered with fifteen and they settled on twelve.

The antiques dealer sent out messages to his other shops in Mombasa, Kenya and Addis Ababa, Ethiopia. An elderly doctor in Addis Ababa wished to have his piece of history, so the kit was sent there, but the doctor died before buying the item. The luggage was placed on a high shelf and eventually was hidden from sight behind steamer trunks and valises. Dr. Parke's kit was listed by handwritten Arabic script in inventory as "doctor's bag." Eighty years later, in 1966, Emperor Haile Selassie needed a unique gift for the Haitian doctor, known as Papa Doc Duvalier, who was President for Life of his country. An aide to Selassie was delighted to come upon a fine leather satchel that had belonged to the now-famous Dr. Parke at the antiques store. The luggage was in excellent condition because of the dry desert climate and the many pieces of luggage rested on top of it for years. Nothing had been removed from it since the bag arrived at the store, and the outside had been cleaned and refurbished. Papa Doc loved the important piece of history. Once Emperor Selassie completed his state visit and returned to Ethiopia, Papa Doc began to explore the contents.

Chapter 4

August 1966- Port au Prince,
Haiti

Papa Doc carefully examined his gift from the Ethiopian ruler, excited to discover what was behind every zipper. Dr. François Duvalier understood that Dr. Thomas H. Parke, a white man, would have harbored a great deal of prejudice against a black man combing through his personal items. That thought made him smile and continue to explore. After finding the bottom pocket and pulling out the journal and three bags of ore, he opened the journal and read the last entries. Dr. Parke had marked the longitude and latitude near the old quarry, with detailed accounts of everything his tent boy, Binza, had told him.

The Haitian President had made deals with people outside of his country before, as Haiti was always cash strapped and in need of revenue from any profitable arrangement. Recently, he had given an American geologist a share of Haiti's sisal business in exchange for prospecting for minerals in the country. So, maybe the American would take the quarry description and run with it.

John Cole was not only a geologist, but a professor at the Colorado School of Mines. Upon his arrival in Haiti, he had been told to stay clear of the Norte gold mine in the mountains near Cap-Haitien. Something about a special contract, and John was smart enough not to quiz Duvalier's agent. The gold mine was one of the most secret projects in Haiti. Enough gold was shipped to Africa to pay for the operations back in Haiti. Bank accounts in the Ivory Coast dispersed the money without paperwork. Questioning activities at the mine would result in a visit by Papa Doc's Tonton Macoutes. People disappeared or ended up stacked with other bodies on the Presidential Palace lawn. The secret bank account was the ultimate slush fund for Duvalier.

John Cole was in Haiti for the summer at the request of the Haitian government and was staying at a small hotel in Port au Prince when he received a visit by Henrico Monet, Deputy Finance Minister for Duvalier. The man explained to John Cole the theft of Thomas Parke's luggage, ore samples, and journal. John felt as though he had been handed an eighty-year-old treasure map. He was intrigued, yet leery, of anything connected to the Haitian government.

"Cole, go to Africa and find this quarry. Claim it for Haiti if it has any value. Our bank in the Ivory Coast will arrange financing for the exploration. You will not be paid a salary, but you can have a twenty-five percent share of what you find," Henrico said.

"Mr. Monet, this is a fascinating story, but if you knew for sure something of value was there you guys would go on your own. I will not risk my ass in the jungles of the Congo unless I can have a true twenty-five percent permanent ownership of this mythical quarry," John said. He waited while Henrico spoke to someone on the phone.

"We don't normally give out ownership, but since we don't have anything in our hands, there is a good chance you will get twenty-five percent of a pile of monkey shit wrapped in banana leaves," Henrico quipped, as he corrected and initialed the contract. Henrico felt this was another of Papa Doc's crazy schemes and John Cole would never be heard from again. He handed John the contract, journal, and ore samples. John told Henrico he wanted to test the ore samples before signing the contract.

John smiled, knowing the man was probably right about the monkey shit.

An aide to Papa Doc gave John a letter of instructions for the banker in Africa. The agreement was to remain secret; however, John was free to hire whomever he wanted and communicate only with the bank. He would travel to Abidjan in the Ivory Coast and report to the International Bank of South Africa (BIAO). His mode of travel to Abidjan was a government contracted tramp freighter called

Afrik-Rev that Duvalier had exempted from normal paperwork, as the owner was Captain Plato, Papa Doc's favorite cousin. John felt sure the conditions would be somewhere south of comfortable.

He found a lab at the College de Port-au-Prince suitable for mineral testing. Since the local chemistry professor didn't complain, John didn't have to play the "Crazy dictator will get your ass" card. The professor let him have the run of the lab. Much of the equipment John had brought from Colorado, but some samples were strange enough to warrant special testing.

The green soil was a simple classification for John, who suspected from his first glance the famous kimberlite ore found in diamond-bearing areas of the world.

"*Well kiss my ass. I was right on target from the start,*" John bragged to himself. He had done his master's thesis on diamond-bearing ore, his first trip having been to Arkansas to study the green variety of kimberlite pipe.

John knew the green soil samples likely contained diamonds. Most geologists wouldn't have recognized the soil, since common forms usually present as "blue ground' or "yellow ground." Green kimberlite occurs when kimberlite is mixed with serpentinized olivine, which is uncommon. Diamond ore usually exhibits as a pipe brought to the surface by eruptions deep within the earth. John carefully explored and sorted all the soil, selecting two small diamonds and a larger one with a pinkish tint that was more than a karat. He figured the tent boy in the Stanley expedition had not stayed long in the quarry and therefore had quickly grabbed a few handfuls of soil. The area must be very rich, John thought.

The orange ore could have been a myriad of minerals, so to rule out common arsenic, John ran tests using both his and the chemistry lab's equipment. He checked his results, pulled out one last item from his field geology bag, and turned on the machine. The Geiger counter came to life and buzzed and clicked repeatedly as John waved the machine over the ore. Next he measured exactly 1000 grams of ore and tested the intensity for a given amount of material by cpm (counts per minute.) He had made his determination. The orange ore was uranosphaerite, commonly known as uranium.

"Holy shit!" John murmured. This ore was the strongest "Dan class" and emitted 1,033.58 MilliRem per hour on the hand. The maximum adult dose for the hand is 50,000 m/Rm per year and the lethal dose is 400,000 to 500,000 m/Rm.

John turned off the noisy Geiger counter and sat quietly, looking at his notes. So far, the first two minerals he had tested were worth a fortune, with one more mineral remaining. He speculated that the people who were digging before Binza came upon the mine had no use for uranium or appreciation of its value. They only understood diamonds and gold.

Testing the third sample, a silver-colored ore, was relatively simple. Scientists knew the ore as semi-rare "coltan," short for columbite and tantalite. Since coltan had no major use, John was relieved he would not have to devise yet another mining plan.

John signed and sent off the contract without mentioning the valuable ore he had found. He was aware that doing business with Haiti was very dangerous, even on a small concession contract. Haiti had been attacked repeatedly by factions wanting to kill Papa Doc. Stories abounded of large-scaled public executions and mass graves. No one doubted the tales. Papa Doc brought the head of one murdered enemy to his residence, put it in a bucket of ice, then tried to communicate with it.

John started thinking, *"Papa Doc. What a fucknut! I've got to get out of this country before this wacko puts my head in a bucket of ice and asks if I'm a Virgo or a Sagittarius."*

After a few days' planning, he notified his college in the U.S. that he wouldn't be teaching classes in the fall, but would give credits to senior level students for field study in Africa at their expense. He hoped one graduate student in particular would bite on the offer. She was Vikki Hanover, a Texas beauty who had a fortune waiting from her dad's oil and gas wells in three states. She was not the unkempt, unattractive female geology nerd who looked more masculine than most males. Vikki was a sexy, blonde, fashion model type who had wandered out of a photo shoot with a rock pick in her hand.

John was in his early thirties, divorced about five years and had no children from the marriage. He had taken Vikki out a few times, but nothing seemed to be happening between them, other than they had fun being together. The expense of an African adventure would amount to pocket change for her, so John invited her on this field trip with the knowledge that she could pay for herself. Her parents may not want her playing in the jungle with her geology professor, but he certainly wanted to take on the part of a great white hunter. Here, he thought, was a way to win her over, and if things worked out, he would have the wealth to compete for her while duly impressing her parents. Visions of having unlimited sex in every possible position in a tent in the jungle would occupy most of his fantasies.

John made contact with the freighter captain, Plato, who gave him a sailing date two weeks away. Vikki was not at all reluctant to go, but convincing her mother, Susan Hanover, was a challenge. John made a personal visit to Texas, outlined his meticulous arrangements, which included a portable short wave radio for the trip. Her mother paid for every kind of snakebite anti-venom available, even for serpents that didn't live in Africa. She hired individual safari guides in the Congo region to go along with them, while also checking the guides' inventory of guns. A doctor would now join what was becoming a duplication of Henry Stanley's expedition to find Livingstone. Satisfied her daughter would be in good hands, Susan wished them well. John expected to find her in the tent with them at some point. Susan was blonde, well put together, and very hot for a rich lady in her late forties, so John wouldn't have complained.

Her father, Mike Hanover, on the other hand, was more interested in the ore and value of the find. John told him he wasn't at liberty to discuss the find, but hinted that just about every known mineral in the world can be found in Africa and more specifically in the Congo. Their discussion centered on the engineering issues of establishing a mining operation deep in the jungle. He suggested if the geology was worthwhile, he might be interested in being a partner. Although Mike Hanover wasn't a geologist, he was a chemical engineer who helped build a dynasty in the oil and gas business. However, none of his wells were in the godforsaken middle of the African Congo.

Other graduate students wanted to go on the expedition, but since they could barely pay their bills, they declined his offer.

Vikki had the choice of flying to Africa and waiting for John, or soaking up the ambiance of a tramp steamer, rubbing up against sweaty men, eating meals in a dirty galley, and having very little privacy. She decided that she would do the freighter, since "it would be just like college life."

She flew into Port au Prince and they left on the *Afrik-Rev* the same night.

On board ship, John tried his best to slowly work his way into her heart, but Vikki recognized his tricks—and his motives. It was not that she didn't want to sleep with him—he was so handsome she wanted to attack him at times. Deep blue eyes and Robert Redford-type blonde hair made him hard to resist. She hesitated out of fear the relationship would take her to the edge. If her feelings were no longer kept at bay— they might easily be dangled over a ledge. Vikki had experienced that awful pain that lay at the bottom. She had really cared for men in the past who later dumped her after they got what they wanted. Vikki was beautiful, and had been the target of many slick guys. She had been there.

At this point, Vikki and John were like fencing partners using invisible swords.

"I'm going to the galley to get us dinner. Your choice of pork chops or pork chops. What will it be?" John asked.

"A big ole greasy pork chop. And my selection of wine tonight?"

"That would be a wonderful, full bodied red wine lacking a label and found aging under the sink next to the Comet cleaner."

"Sounds perfect. Should we let it aerate a bit?"

"Not necessary, my dear. My suggestion is drink fast followed by large slices of pork chops."

"Great! Hurry back, dear."

John returned a few minutes later with dinner and the suspect bottle of wine. They ate and finished off the bottle. Since Plato loved rum and the crew drank beer, fancy drinks were scarce and of dubious quality. After all, this was a freighter, not a cruise ship.

Several bottles of wine and three days and nights on the open ocean elapsed before Vikki let John stay in her cabin. She admitted she had always liked him. Since he was tall, athletic and handsome, keeping him away from cute college girls in his classes would be a problem. Did he only have fun and sex on his mind? His conquests of pretty young ladies had cost him his marriage. Vikki was well aware of these issues and tried to hold back her feelings, but each was falling for the other more every day.

"John, I really care about you. How do I know we will be together when we get back home? I see how all the girls flirt with you. Am I going to be another notch on your gun?" Vikki asked.

"Do you have my gun? I haven't seen it lately."

"Quit screwing with me, John. Talk to me. The divorce—all the girls? Having kids? A real family life? I want all the goddamn answers," she demanded.

He knew he better reach down deep in his gut, or she would rescind the invitation to her cabin.

"Vikki, I have been a royal jerk—not to you I hope, but in general. I married for all the wrong reasons. My ex didn't want kids— at least not with me anyway. I did, but I'm so glad I didn't have any then—I wasn't ready and would have been a lousy father. I wasn't a good husband—too tempted by young girls in class. I was weak, but I learned I wanted things other than a wild carnal adventure. Sex is exciting—fresh flesh—a conquest, yes, but fleeting and after a while, sort of sick—knowing it doesn't mean anything. It has to be part of a relationship. It has to be permanent, strong, lasting—a relationship has to develop stronger and stronger with children and family. It has to be real. I know that now, and that's all I want in life—to be part of a permanent family. Vikki, I hope you believe me," John said, his eyes watering.

"I do believe you, John. I hope it will always be exciting for you. That'll be my job. I'll have to seem like fresh flesh and all that." She laughed and sounded relieved by John's speech.

"I will force myself to get into it as best I can—maybe even with some enjoyment," John said, laughing.

John kissed Vikki, but hesitated before he let their lips touch and took in her breath for a while, then kissed her deeply and long. They made love that night and both were ready, the perfect time, the perfect place, and the perfect two people. John made her feel very comfortable, but unleashed every bit of passion he could and she responded. Their first sex was wild, sweaty, and athletic. All their pent up emotions flushed through their bodies, satisfying needs they couldn't define, yet acted upon without hesitation. Afterwards, their love making was slow, with much pillow talk, then touching softly, and intense eye contact. John was a potent lover for Vikki and she returned the intensity with great care. Her body was incredibly beautiful and John couldn't believe how lucky he was. They made love so often they lost track of time. Each one realized, given the adventure in front of them, they would need commitments–life changing commitments. This moment in their lives, on a tramp steamer in the middle of the Atlantic Ocean, on the way to an African safari in search of diamonds and uranium—was wonderful, exotic, mystical and sensual. They were falling deeply in love. This time would never exist again.

Chapter 5

Abidjan, Ivory Coast

John Cole and Vikki Hanover were physically sore from a week of around the clock love-making. When they stepped on the docks in the Ivory Coast, their legs barely worked. They were also paying the price for traveling on a small freighter that bounced around on the high seas. Both were smiling like drunken monkeys, convinced nothing mattered except their relationship. John was surprised Plato accompanied them to the BIOA bank to discuss the terms of the expedition. Plato was more than a tramp steamer Captain, John realized. As they left the docks, five small trucks pulled up, and a crew loaded several heavy wooden crates from the boat.

The three piled into a taxi up on the dock, Plato up front and John and Vikki in the back seat groaning and laughing. The city was huge and unlike what John had pictured for Africa. Abidjan was teeming and dirty like so many in third world countries, yet gleaming tall buildings cast shadows over festering slums and trash-filled streets.

"Where the hell is Tarzan?" Vikki said.

"He would play hell convincing Jane to shack up with him in this place," John said.

John and Vikki were impressed when the taxi pulled up to a modern, multi-storied building, with huge smoked glass windows reaching all the way to the top floor. A handsome man in a custom-tailored suit opened a large glass door with chrome handles. They were soon to learn the bank had several Haitian ex-pats working in managerial positions. As Plato introduced the pair to several employees, John and Vikki surmised why this bank kept the offshore assets of a country located several thousand miles away.

"Haiti has lost some of their finest and best educated French speaking citizens to this bank here in the Ivory Coast," Plato explained, while he shook the hand of a tall, distinguished black man with salt and pepper hair.

Romulus Jean-Baptiste watched over the holdings of the Haitian government, whether the money was in accounts or safety deposit boxes, or, as they were about to learn, in underground safety deposit vaults. About that time, five small trucks pulled up to the rear of the bank, escorted by the police. John crept to a window and spotted police and military types, standing in line, their guns drawn and ready. Workers hauled the crates to the rear of the bank, and down the steps leading to an underground storage area. Romulus excused himself. He went to supervise placement of the wooden crates, and possibly, even their contents.

"John, the bank officer can see us now," Plato said. He motioned the two Americans to a handsomely appointed office, decorated in African tribal motif. Masks, spears, arrows, and crude knives were displayed on the walls, along with a painting of Africans dancing madly and a line of natives banging on colorful drums.

"You must be John Cole." The senior bank officer sat behind a mahogany desk made of enough wood to have wiped out half a forest.

"Yes, I am, and I would like you to meet Vikki Hanover."

The gentleman rose, took Vikki's hand, and introduced himself as Cangé Petit-Frere, also a Haitian transplant.

Then, he got right down to business, except for laughing and smiling at inappropriate times.

"John, the letter you delivered to us on your arrival charges this bank to finance and oversee an exploratory trip to the Democratic Republic of the Congo and the upper Congo region, to determine if mining various ores are economically feasible. If it all pans out, so to speak." He chuckled at his own pun.

"Then, to contract with that country for long term mining leases, for which you will receive a 25% share in ownership and net production revenue." He laughed and picked up another file, which he explained had arrived from Haiti a few weeks before; instructions were to contact and engage certain individuals within the government of the Congo.

"Boy, getting in touch with those folks was fun, since they all seemed to be moving targets. But, we did find a few people in place who weren't afraid to make a decision," he said with a large smile.

Cangé looked up from the letter lying on his desk, and shook his head. "Are you sure that this is what you two want to do?" Before they could answer, he shook his head again and laughed out loud.

"The Ivory Coast went through a civil war a few years back, and we are not back to normal. Whatever normal is in Africa." He laughed at his own comment.

"The Congo just replaced their president through a coup. The new President is Joseph-Desiré Mobuto. A real piece of work." He smiled and sort of chuckled.

"In May of this year, he hung his former Prime Minister Evaristic Kimba, and three cabinet members in front of 50,000 people." He shrugged. "His idea of entertainment for his constituents. You know the history of Trujillo in the Dominican Republic, and, of course, Papa Doc in Haiti. This man, Mobutu, may well make them both look like members of the Mickey Mouse Club." He followed this statement with a deep laugh.

"You are going to a dangerous and unstable place. Over one thousand Haitians live there. Some are fleeing, as we speak. All are part of the brain drain from Haiti, where there is almost no opportunity for well-educated blacks. I think the only reason they come in the first place is 'French and Creole are spoken here.'" Smiling and amused, he continued. "Not nearly a good enough reason to get shot or hung."

"Under Papa Doc, talented people leave as soon as they get out of school. The medical school in Port-au-Prince has graduated about 280 doctors in the last ten years. Only three of them practice medicine in Haiti. On the other hand, if Papa Doc is an example of what the school produces, maybe they all should leave." He felt this observation deserved a long sustained laugh.

"Canada has more Haitian doctors than Haiti." He was either in the middle of a sermon or a stand-up comedy routine. John hoped it would be over soon.

"I do see from your earlier notes that you, or that is, Ms. Hanover's parents provided a doctor and some other personnel for the trip. That is a good idea. A full M.A.S.H. unit might be better. In fact, the 101st Airborne Division would also be useful." He smiled and laughed, but didn't look at them. "We have contacted our most trusted mining contractors in Kinshasa, along with native guides who know that area well. You do know that some of that region is basically unexplored, even in these modern times. You might find Bigfoot." He didn't wait for an answer before he gave what was now an expected laugh.

"We have contacted the Republic of the Congo's Department of Mines concerning a possible mining concession. They were not opposed to an upstart concession from Haiti since Mobutu respects Papa Doc and is aware that hundreds of Haitians live in his country. Be warned though, if mining there is successful, he just might take it over. If you were prospecting from Europe or the United States, the answer would have been a big 'Hell, no!' You are going to a remote area where employment would be welcome. There is talk that Mobutu will nationalize the Union Miniere du Haut Katanga mining company, which accounts for about 50% of their economy. A royalty of twenty percent of the net mining profit will have to be paid to the government of the Democratic Republic of the Congo in the beginning, but expect that amount to grow to 50% or even 100% if they take it over. You are going into a country that may nationalize everything of value until Mobutu is out of office, which doesn't appear likely for a while. Once you have proof of valuable ore, they will issue the Haitian government a standard ninety-nine year lease, that actually will be closer to a ninety-nine minute lease, if Mobutu so desires it." He gave a muffled chuckle at that statement.

"All sales of ore or minerals will go through us in the BIOA here in the Ivory Coast. We will pay you for your share. If minerals need to be sent to processing plants, then those plants will send their revenues here as well. Any questions?" He looked up at the two Americans and peered over some very narrow lens glasses. They could have belonged to Ben Franklin.

John and Vikki had several questions, and Mr. Petit-Frere answered them with great patience.

"Sir, if our mine produces at a very low volume, will it be less likely to be nationalized?" John asked.

"If you can hide the potential ore values from Congolese officials, they wouldn't be as likely to go in and run it themselves. The approximate location of your search is the middle of nowhere, so I don't think they will be poking around very often. There is no guarantee. This is a case where failure may pay off." After that statement, Cangé really cut loose with what was now irritating merriment.

"Just as an example, Cangé, what if we found some—let's say—some precious stones of some sort. Could the bank be counted on to sell these in the market slowly and pay all the interested parties without triggering an army march to kill us and take it all away?" John knew this question would alert as to what they might be after.

"Ha! Ha! This is Africa, my friend! Selling precious stones goes on every day. The Belgians were the best, but Mobutu will not trade with them. Believe me, this bank has the best contacts. We will take a tiny commission to act with great care, and make sure to pay all parties." He threw in a small laugh. "We can arrange couriers to transport to us what you might find, so Mobutu doesn't get his hands on it first," he said with a monstrous grin.

After a few logistical questions that Cangé answered, John asked if he would recommend a local restaurant. Cangé suggested one of the large hotels would be excellent and safe. Plato did not want to join them, so they left in separate taxis.

Over dinner, John smiled and looked into Vikki's eyes. "Who will cheat us first—Papa Doc or Motubu?" he said. They both laughed and tried to imitate Cangé.

A few days later, the *Afrik-Rev* left the Atlantic Ocean and churned up the muddy Congo River. The freighter docked at the port of Matadi, the farthest point ships can travel up river on the DRC side, due to cataracts.

Several anxious explorers waited at the docks in Matadi by the vehicles. The first to meet them was the expedition leader, Sony Bodha, who introduced himself first to Vikki and then to John. Next in line was Jan Leeghwater, a white South African doctor, who looked pleased that someone of his race was going along on this ride. Congolese geologist Marcelin Fofana greeted them and after that the native associates who would serve as porters or gun-bearers. They lined up, and John and Vikki walked the gauntlet as they were introduced to Joseph, Antoine, Jean-Pierre, Ike, Sani, Jomo, and Jaja. Off to the side, were a couple of military types with guns, who were Africans, but not from the Congo. They snapped to attention when the two employers walked up to them. The first to speak was Zuka Koffi. He was almost seven feet tall and admitted to a Zulu heritage. He held his AK-47 to his side while he shook hands with the two Americans. The second mercenary stood a little over six feet tall, was very stocky and appeared to be a weight lifter. He said his name was Earnest Balogun, and he was from Central Africa. John knew there were no shortages of ex-military on the continent, since some sort of insurrection was always going on in one of the fifty-four African countries. He hoped two trained killers would be sufficient.

"Ready to ride off into the sunset?" Sony asked.

John and Vikki were pleased he had a sense of humor. They figured some levity would come in handy on this trip. All the luggage and gear was loaded on the trucks and Land Rovers, and they set off on the first leg of their journey. Sony drove the Land Rover for Vikki and John, with Dr. Leeghwater riding shotgun.

"John, do you have your and Ms. Hanover's shot records and current meds for me to look over?" the doctor asked.

Vikki had her records in her backpack and handed them to the doctor. He opened the envelope and started reading the list of vaccinations, softly repeating the inoculations to himself.

"Yellow fever, hepatitis-A and B, malaria medicine, ummm, booster pills for that, ummm, where the encephalitis…oh yeah—there it is…." He was in his element.

"Familiar with itinerary?" Sony asked.

"Only partially," John answered.

"Decided to go by road. Ferries not dependable–trucks don't fit well. Roads are crap and full of fucking thieves and pseudo-military idiots. Spend the night in Kinshasa–take off early in the morning. Go to Kenge, then Llebo and north to Iketa–take the ferry across at Stanleyville. Once there, we go to Batialia and as far as our four-wheel drive will take us along the Aruwimi River—then we'll be hoofing it. Ok with you guys?" He seemed to abbreviate everything. John hoped he hadn't planned the trip the way he talked.

"Tetanus…where is the typhoid…there it is. Birth control pills— what the hell?" He glanced up for a minute. Vikki nodded her head in an affirmative manner. The doctor resumed mumbling to himself.

"MMR, DPT, and polio all in order. Wish there was a vaccine for African Trypanosomiasis," the doctor said.

"What is that shit?" John said.

"African sleeping sickness, caused by the tsetse fly. No shot for schistosomiasis either, which you shouldn't get unless you go swimming in the rivers. We need to watch out for rabies and dengue fever as well. Ebola is also found here. The Center for Disease Control should move here since the Congo has them all—including monkey pox."

"I'm not going to ask. I hope to avoid petting any monkeys or any other frigging animals," Vikki said.

"The natives sell the meat in local markets as bush meat. I doubt we will be shopping there," the doctor said.

"Staying at the Hotel Le Renaissance tonight. Be there less than an hour. Planning meeting after dinner—my room." Sony relayed in his usual choppy sentences.

A few minutes later the convoy of six vehicles pulled up in front of a tired looking hotel. Everyone headed for the lobby.

"Last chance to check gear. Anybody short on anything let me know. Have it for you before we leave. See you—my room eightish." Sony grabbed a pack with about a hundred loose straps hanging from it and walked over to the registration desk.

John and Vikki headed for the bar. "Need drink?" John said.

"Drink, sex, dinner, meet Sony," Vikki said.

Now, they had someone else to make fun of beside Cangé.

Chapter 6

Inland Congo

John and Vikki slung their backpacks in the rear of the Land Rover and slid into the back seat. Both were wearing cargo shorts, but knew they would need long pants for the jungle. They were still several hundred miles and at least a week away from worrying about clothing options. The meeting with Sony last night had gone well except that everything he said was an abbreviation of normal speech between humans. He spoke in a sort of linguistic shorthand where sentences started in the middle, were almost void of adjectives and ended where most people would just be getting cranked up. His speech patterns gave John and Vikki fodder for a new style of short humorous sentences.

"John, got water—snack—need sex—maybe later—hand job then—bug spray—condoms—nice day—might rain," said Vikki quickly before Sony got to the vehicle.

"Wait for real sex—no snack—rain for sure—got pills—hate condoms—hope rains—hot here," John said as he worked hard on the imitation.

The couple reverted back to normal speech as they saw Sony approaching the car. This time the shotgun position was being occupied by the geologist and mine engineer, Marcelin Fofana.

"Good morning to you two. I hope you realize the comfortable bed you were in last night was your last for a long time. Hotels are primitive until we get to Stanleyville. Our tents with cots and mosquito nets will do just fine though." He seemed cheery enough and actually spoke in full sentences which they knew would clash with his seat mate.

"Off to Kenge—rain may slow us—next stop for petrol—three maybe four hours—need to pee—just yell and I'll pull over." John Wayne had to be smiling somewhere.

"Marcelin, tell us, what type of mine work have you done in the past." asked Vikki.

"All kinds, but call me Marc," he said. "I worked for a while in the big Haut Katanga copper mine, and then I worked gold, diamonds, and even on a little small uranium oxide surface mine. You know the Congo has trillions of dollars of mineral resources that are untapped. From what I have been told about the quarry we are looking for, there is a good chance it was never mined properly," he said with a big smile across his face.

John and Vikki knew about the giant mountains of mine tailings that were piled up by the world famous Katanga operation and hoped that wasn't the fate of their little quarry.

"Sony?" Vikki was trying to get his attention.

"Yes, darlin." He tried to be cute.

"Did I hear you right last night at the meeting that the trip just to Stanleyville is 2622 kilometers or about 1600 American miles?" She knew the answer but couldn't wrap her mind around it.

"Try to do about 300 to 500 'merican miles a day. Gas up when we can. Some towns have small guest houses—other places we'll camp. Should be to Stanleyville five…six days. Is a shorter route but roads piss poor. 2622 kilometers not bad for Africa—big fucking country," he said, laughing.

John and Vikki were getting to where they liked the amount of information Sony would give them in such a short amount of time, but nonetheless they looked at each other and smiled like crazy every time he spoke.

John whispered, "Sony could have written War and Peace in two chapters." Vikki couldn't hold back the laughter.

Marc turned around. "You two kids are having way too much fun."

"Well, this trip would be long and boring if we can't have a few laughs," John said while trying to compose himself.

"Marc, you have seen the write up on the old quarry from Stanley's expedition, and you've seen the lab reports on the sample ores. What do you think we'll find there?" John asked.

"The fact that there were four diamonds in a small ore sample speaks volumes. All the diamonds were excellent specimens although three of them were small. The large pink one made up for flaws in color and clarity. For pink ones to exist in the ore is something to be excited about. What has happened there in the last eighty years? We will just have to find out if it has been mined during that time," Marc said.

"Is there any record of mines in the Ituri region?" asked Vikki.

"There is no record that a claim was ever formally introduced through the Minister of Mines, the Mining Registry or the Directorate of Mines. But, smaller mines usually don't get registered and operate until someone in the government finds them. It's unlikely they would ever find this place. Since much of the area around this location is unexplored, it's not on anyone's mining hot spot list," Marc explained.

John asked, "Do we have clearance for exploration from the DRC?"

"Yes. We have a permit which is subject to an environmental impact study and the rights of indigenous or aboriginal people. Both of these issues may come into play since the area is next to a river and according to Stanley there were native villages in the vicinity."

"And the uranium ore?" John inquired.

"Rich…very rich. Since trees were stunted inside the enclosure, it makes me wonder if there might be 'pitchblende' which is black in color as opposed to the orange colored ore in your sample. There has never been ore as rich as the sixty to seventy percent pure uranium that was used for the first American atomic bomb. The Manhattan Project got that ore from the Shinkolobwe Mine located right here in the Democratic Republic of the Congo," Marc said.

"Where is this mine?" John asked.

"Near Katanga. I worked at the Haut Katanga copper mine for a while, and we mined a little uranium as a by-product of the copper. The Shinkolobwe, however, is just a shadow of its former self, and I think it shut down in 1960. Mines shut down and then new techniques come out and they reopen. Vikki, kind of like your dad does with the fracking on the old oil wells," he said, looking back at her and smiling in the hope he said something of interest.

Conversations about various mines and their history would continue for much of the long trip. Sony stopped in Kenge for gas and a meal break, and then on to Kikwit for an overnight stay at a small motel which looked like someone's private home. They would spend the night in Kananga, Kabinda, and Hindu before arriving in Stanleyville. They pulled up late at night in front of a real hotel for the first time since Kinshasa.

"Wow! It is so nice to be in a town that doesn't start with a 'K,'" John said.

"Hate to bust your bubble—natives call it Kisangani," Sony laughed as he spoke. "Planning meeting—morning at seven—private dining room. Gets rough from here."

Vikki entered their hotel room and smiled when she saw a queen size bed. John explored the bathroom and found a huge shower lined in colorful tile featuring African animals. No search for snakes and insects were needed in this room. Being bounced around in the back of a Land Rover would soon be forgotten after a hot shower. They stripped and tossed the dirty clothes all over the room.

As they adjusted the water to a heat level that was a few degrees below what would remove skin and boil body parts, they stared in each other's eyes. Vikki elected herself as the one in charge of soap. She applied it to herself and then rubbed her body against John. Steam fogged the glass doors of the shower. John reached over and wrote "save me" on the glass with his finger. Vikki worked up a great deal of suds on John's groin which resulted in a full erection. She smiled as she explored it with her fingers. John could wait no longer and picked Vikki up and pressed her against the back of the shower. She eagerly wrapped her legs around him and helped him enter her. Warm water ran over their bodies as they made love. Afterwards they stayed in the shower kissing each other until the water started to cool.

The whole crew was up at around six for breakfast, at which Sony would give the abbreviated version of whatever fate would befall them on this day.

Sony was shoveling down eggs and following up with gulps of orange juice and coffee. He buttered an oversized biscuit and worked it into his mouth on top of the eggs. He ate in a modified wood chipper style much like he talked. He was a big muscular man who looked as if he could take care of himself in a bar fight. A scar above his right eye was a souvenir from his time in the Congolese Army. Sony had attended a community college in New York. There he likely learned to talk fast and appreciate John Wayne movies. Once John and Vikki learned about the Duke factor, they would quote lines from John Wayne movies to see if he could name them. He appeared to be another strong, black Congo native, but there was much more to Sony than one saw on the surface. He spoke both English and French, but his choice of language was the John Wayne version of combat-cowboy talk because it was comfortable for him. Sony, however, was the real deal.

Once everyone was seated and Sony had failed to choke himself to death on breakfast, he began his talk.

"Best I can tell our island is 185 miles back from the Ituri's meeting the Aruwimi River. Stats given on longitude-latitude places it dead center between Bafwasende and Bunia on the river. Topo maps show pig trails for a few miles near the river, but we'll have about seventy miles of wild-ass jungle. Some native villages—'bout the same ones Stanley found. Things don't change in the jungle. Zuka—take point— Ernie the rear. Hand guns for all. Wear your big boy pants. Gonna be rough. Not up for it—stay in the hotel. Pick you up on the way back," he said looking directly at Vikki.

No one blinked. After breakfast everyone headed to the vehicles and a strange quietness settled over the group. As they headed out of town towards Bafwasende, the road started turning into an enlarged rut between the trees. It wasn't a road as much as a large drainage ditch. The Land Rovers were in four wheel drive constantly as they slid from one side of the road to the other. The drivers hit big mud holes hard and fast so the Land Rovers wouldn't realize they were actually submerged. To relieve the horrible conditions the road would turn to gravel for a few miles lulling the crew into thinking the bad road was behind them. No sooner had everyone relaxed, the roadbed would turn to quicksand and the whining of the engines and transmissions could be heard fighting against sinking below the surface. Occasionally a Land Rover would get hopelessly buried, and either a winch had to be used, or another Land Rover with a cable had to pull them out. After six hours of this on and off travel and mud crawling, the expedition pulled into Bafwasende.

They ate a meal described as pork, but most felt it was of a dubious origin. The gas tanks and five gallon spares were filled, and they were off again in an attempt to get to the jumping off place and set up camp. Two hours of bad road later, Sony found the pig trail that ran along the Aruwimi. The trail had a solid rock bottom for the most part and the group made good time. In about three hours the road ended at a large rocky cliff going skyward about one hundred feet next to the Aruwimi River.

The group had passed a couple of villages along the way and except for some t-shirts with American movie heroes and European soccer stars, the villages had not changed since time began. One such village was located where the group set up camp for the night. Ernie found he could speak their language and said they wanted to trade with them. Trading had been done for thousands of years so the travelers expected it would be the custom in this village.

Five native women for John's blonde woman was the first offer. He made a motion to Vikki as though he was seriously considering it but backed off. The villagers had contraband such as ivory and leopard hides to trade. They had a hard time understanding the group couldn't accept them. Then they brought out a small beautifully decorated basket that had a top piece with a handle. The chief, who was the principal business man in the group, removed the top and reached in the basket. He held his hand in front of the group until everyone was gathered around. As his hand opened, a huge rough diamond the size of a hen's egg appeared. Marc, John and Vikki passed it among themselves and marveled at its size.

John spoke, "Vikki, if they want you for this diamond—it's been nice knowing you."

Vikki hit him hard on the shoulder, and hoped she wouldn't be sleeping with the old native chief that night.

Ernie began addressing the chief in a kind, slow manner, bowing all the time. "I told him we didn't have anything to trade that would match the object he had shown them. I told him to keep it because it was very valuable."

The chief reached back into the basket and pulled out a smaller but still very nice diamond, and said to Ernie he really wanted to trade since the group had been very honest.

Sony brought out beautiful blankets and cloth. Then he displayed sacks of costume jewelry and cooking utensils. They made a trade and the natives seemed deliriously happy. The villagers helped to set up camp and talked with Ernie and Sony about the route they were going to take. Both groups shared food for the night. Vikki and John went to their tent after dark and lay on their cots.

"Vikki, I overheard them telling Sony there were still native villages along the river that used poisoned arrows. We need to stick together like glue and watch every movement in the jungle for anything that is out of place. Are you sure you want to do this?" John feared for her safety.

"John, I knew this was going to be dangerous from the start. I'm in no more danger than you, or Sony, or Marc. You know the natives wouldn't kill me since I'm too big a prize for any chief who wants another wife. You on the other hand would find your head on a stick in a New York minute," she said, laughing, but John knew she was probably right.

They kissed each other good night and suddenly realized there would be no cots after this night. Just small tents and thin sleeping pads which they would be carrying on their backs as they walked through the steaming jungle dodging poisoned arrows. Sleep did not come easily.

Chapter 7

The Jungle

Breakfast had an eerie feel to it—like possibly it would be the last for some, and there was no small talk about the trek ahead. After everyone put their packs on and lined up for the trail, they gave gifts to the natives to watch over the parked Land Rovers. Pistols were loaded and shells were pumped into the chambers of the .45 automatics. All the pistols were identical updated versions of the military Browning 1911s allowing for shared rounds. Everyone had taken target practice while the group camped along the way to this area. Vikki owned a 9mm so she had more recoil to deal with on the .45 but adjusted just fine. Most of the men had done some military service, and the two who hadn't shot well enough after great instruction from Zuka and Ernie. Of course, the two mercenaries did their thing with AK-47s and new prototype .40 caliber Glock automatics. One would be a point man and the other would take rear guard.

The expedition slipped their way up the steep incline of the hill in front of them. On the other side they did the same, finding at the bottom a well-traveled jungle trail almost parallel to the river. The morning coolness was burning away, and sweat was pouring off of everyone. Only a half mile in, everyone stopped for water and started shedding clothes. It wasn't raining but everything was wet including the ground and every piece of foliage dripped water. Their boots were making a sloshing sound and water dripped off packs, clothing, hair, and skin. Insects abounded and appeared to enjoy the repellent everyone had generously applied to their bodies and clothing.

"John, do you think it would be okay to put on the insect net under my hat? Vikki asked while she took off her Texas Longhorn ball cap and dug around in her pack for the netting.

"Try it, but the air is so heavy and wet, you might find it hard to breathe."

"Hell, I'm breathing in insects now. Wet air can't be that much worse," Vikki said with an ample amount of sarcasm in her voice.

"Insects do contain a little protein, dear."

"Screw you, John."

Vikki placed the ball cap back on her head over the insect netting. At first she stumbled along with her hand on John's shoulder because her visibility was impaired. He could hear her breathing hard and cursing after a few miles.

"Can't stand this shit anymore!" Vikki ripped the netting off her head and stuffed it in a pocket of her pack. "Can't breathe—can't see! Believe I'll eat some insects for a while."

John didn't say anything, since he knew she was irritable and didn't want to add to her frustration. He did notice she was now walking faster and not gasping for air. It began to rain, and the pained look on her face didn't seem to welcome chit-chat.

At one point the trail crossed an elephant path which looked well used. When the trail occasionally took them near the edge of the Aruwimi River, they could see slide marks where crocodiles had been sunning on the shore. Although they heard monkeys and chimpanzees they rarely saw them because the jungle was so thick.

Sony was determined to do ten miles before camp, but saw the fatigue and inexperience of carrying loaded packs in the heat were wearing on the group, so he halted them at eight miles and found a small clearing to set up camp. Once dinner had been prepared, consumed, and everything was cleaned and packed, he assigned guard duty for two men at a time in two hours shifts. John had the first watch with Jan, the doctor, who recounted all the insects that would make their home in your body. He explained the gruesome outcome of their hatching into worms or larvae, eating you from the inside out. John cringed and thought being attacked by a large carnivore might be a welcome relief. During John's stint as protector of the sleeping, Vikki woke up and needed to relieve herself. John walked with her a short distance and looked all around with his hand on his pistol. Her mission completed, she gave him a quick kiss and headed back to her sleeping bag. Soon it was Sony and Marc's turn, and John headed to his tent, where he collapsed into a sleep so intense it bumped up close to death.

As they woke in the morning one of the mercenaries, Ernie, said he spotted a leopard at the edge of the clearing last night, that walked by and disappeared into the forest. A fire had been left burning to ward off most creatures, or at least to give the group a mental sense of safety.

The sun came up to meet a foggy mist, which rose from the ground and hung over the river, rising as high as the trees. Letting the tents and sleeping bags dry out before rolling them up was impossible because of the oppressive humidity. To make matters worse, the water logged gear added weight to an already almost unbearable load.

The travelers got their second wind and made twelve miles on a narrow path, where they had to use machetes regularly and endure intermittent rain. They set up camp, prepared food and cleaned up hastily for the rewards of tent time and much-needed sleep. Less experienced men had the early guard shifts, while the para-military types had the later ones. Chimpanzees were especially loud that night, but the natives could tell by the sounds they made whether the simians sensed danger close by and interpreted their sounds as benign.

The absence of rain allowed the expedition to make great time the next day. It had rained every day, off and on, since they began. They were slowed when the trail wandered inland into a large clearing. The natives recognized an elephant 'bai.' These areas are created by elephants so they can roll in the mud and reach down deep into the pools of water to extract salt from the earth. Ancient elephants, untold generations removed from the present, had made this clearing. The unmistakable bellowing of elephants could be heard not far away. Hurriedly the group crossed over toward a path some two hundred yards away, when two bull forest elephants rushed out and charged directly at the group. Sony waited for the bluffing charge that many elephants make, but quickly raised his weapon when he realized they were not stopping. Ernie and Zuka opened up with automatic fire striking the big animals primarily in their skulls. One fell and struggled to gain his footing, but a second blast of AK-47 rounds finished him off. The other bull slowed but regained his composure and charged again.

"Vikki raise your pistol and fire!" John yelled at her as he saw her freeze when the huge bull raced directly toward them.

"Shit—it's goddamn huge! Vikki said as she moved close to John and started firing her .45 at the huge creature.

This charge was met by everyone who had a weapon, and .45s opened up along with the two AKs. Dust, skin, and blood blew off and out of the enormous creature's body, and he crashed to the ground directly to the right of were Vikki was standing. The barrel of her pistol was smoking and she held another clip in her hand, but she would not have been able to reload in time. No one knew who fired the bullet that killed the beast, and no one cared. The men wanted some of the meat for dinner, but Sony would only allow them a few minutes to cut some loose and then everyone ran across to the bai to the trail. They realized the path was an elephant trail that had been used for centuries, wide and well-packed, but offering the specter of running headlong into a herd of elephants. Hopefully the rest of the herd were behind them mourning the death of their dominant bulls. The expedition skipped their normal lunch stop and made fourteen miles before camp. At about mile eleven the elephant trail had split with a smaller trail and although they had to do some trimming along the way, they were glad to be off the pachyderm roadway and on a human trail. The evening meal featured elephant meat that had hurriedly been cut from the rear hindquarter of the beast.

"Vikki, does it taste like chicken?" John asked, laughing.

"It taste like elephant, and I might have been the one who killed it," She said with a huge smile and took a bite, twisting her mouth like a wolf eating a fresh kill.

"Damn, I've created a monster!"

Each day the group made over ten miles, and on the eighth day serious trouble began. While they stopped for a prepackaged lunch near an abandoned village, two small natives walked out of the jungle about twenty yards away, took arrows from a pouch, pulled back their bows, and let two arrows fly directly at the assembly. The first arrow barely missed Marc's head, but the second one struck Jomo in his hand and went completely through between his thumb and finger. Zuka and Ernie dropped them both with short bursts. Everyone fell to the ground or found cover behind village huts and fallen logs. At the same time, ten pygmy natives ran at incredible speed out of the forest and started shooting arrows in the direction of the group; pistol and automatic AK-47 fire stopped the small natives. John had taken off his pack and had taken a position lying behind it, when an arrow struck his sleeping bag and bounced off. Vikki watched an arrow as it arced and struck the ground next to her as did another. Twelve dead natives were lying in front of them. Although they had to protect themselves, none were happy about the killings. Jan asked the men to retrieve the native's arrows and quivers. When he inspected the arrows in the quivers he noticed they were wrapped in leaves and smelled very bad. Afterwards, the pygmies' arrows were thrown in the nearby river so they wouldn't be reused.

"Ummm…not a good sign. It means these arrows were poisoned." Jan sniffed the arrows and detected a strong human feces odor. "Well, they have poisoned them and then shat on them for good measure," said the doctor.

"Tell Jomo I need to give him a shot." Jan started digging in his medical kit for a heavy dose of antibiotic to counteract fecal bacteria on the arrow.

He cleaned the wound with alcohol and a surface antibiotic and bandaged it. He then had Jomo drop his pants for an injection. Jomo made sure Vikki wasn't looking, and she politely turned her head away.

"I need to get on the short wave radio," Jan said.

Sony summoned the men who had been carrying the radio.

"Doc, we need to get the fuck out of here!" Sony yelled.

"Do you want this man to die on you?" Jan said and didn't expect an answer.

The doctor fired up the battery-powered unit and put out an open call to anyone within range. After adjusting his set several times he finally touched base with someone in Kinshasa. He gave them a landline number to call in Johannesburg and patched the number though. He had reached the poison control center at the biggest hospital in that city. Shortly he had the chief resident on line, an old friend of Jan's.

"Jan, this is Peter Hoovell. Where in the hell are you to have to call on a shortwave hook up?"

"North Congo, next to the Aruwimi River in pygmy country. One of our men took an arrow through his hand. The arrow was wrapped in a leaf that looks like tropical night shade, but I can't be sure. Also there were human feces on the point. I gave him a big shot and will follow up with Cipro, but I need some help on counteracting the poison. Can you help us?" Jan knew this man was his best hope.

"Describe the leaf, Jan," Peter requested.

Jan went over the size, shape, color and detail of the plant. "It's not nightshade, but it's in the same family— but they use the roots to make their poison," Peter said. "Write this down." Jan produced a pencil and paper as the doctor in South Africa put together a plan of treatment that would save Jomo's life.

"Also, I want you to take a blood smear of the native who shot him. I'm guessing since you are alive you guys have neutralized the enemy. Later, we will check for other diseases that the Cipro might miss," Peter said.

"Peter, thank you so much, and I'll give you a call when I get back. Lunch on me," Jan said.

"Jan, we need to move out before you get an arrow in your ass!" Sony said.

"Sony, this will only take a minute," Jan said calmly.

Jan opened a kit that included slides for microscope examination and asked for Marc to take samples of the native that had gotten off a lucky shot.

Using several compounds of chemicals and a mortar and pestle, he began crushing and mixing until he had the mixture he wanted. He added water and filled a bottle with the liquid, using a funnel. He did it quickly, as he saw Sony pointing at his watch.

"Ok, let's get ready to move out—we're wasting daylight." Sony wanted to leave the area as soon as Jan finished.

"Jomo, would you come here please? Take a regular spoonful of this every two hours until the bottle is empty, starting right now," Jan said as he gave him the first dose. Jomo made a face but did as he was told. He also had to take a couple of cipro pills a day. The doctor told him he would die if he didn't take the medicine, so Jomo got the message. Marc had assisted Jan and helped write down the formula in case anything happened to the doctor. Now they were both in a hurry to get the medical supplies packed up and take off behind the others.

"Sony, I'm going to have Jomo walk with me so I can keep an eye on him," Jan said.

"Fine. Guns in your hands! Eyes peeled! Let's make good time." Sony ordered.

The group picked up and moved on, as far away from the scene of the attack as they could in the remaining daylight. One good thing about the day was that Sony told them they were very close to the quarry.

As they camped that night, several miles from the attack, John found Vikki walking to the edge of the jungle looking at the green glow of fungus on the jungle floor. She had a note pad in her hand.

"In the U.S. they call that foxfire," John said.

"I know. I think the natives here call it chimpanzee fire because they thought maybe the monkeys caused it. Beautiful, isn't it?"

"You know some of this fungus is so bright that you can read by it."

"I wrote a children poem about this stuff. It's silly. Do you want to hear it?"

"Yes, Emily Dickinson, go for it."

"The floor of the Congo shines green and blue at night

They call it chimpanzee fire, but that's not right

Some fungus and mushroom and stuff glowing in the dark

They eat what falls on the ground gobbling like a shark

It's pretty to see, like jewels all aglow on the jungle floor

Don't lie down after sunset cause they'll eat everything and a little more

The chimps and monkeys are not to blame
It that damn jungle, it's impossible to tame."

"Really clever poem. Do kids say damn?" John asked.

"Most of the kids I know back in Texas learn 'shit' right after they master 'mama' and 'dada.'"

'Fuck' works its way in somewhere between the third and fourth grade," Vikki said.

"Are you okay after today?" John asked.

"I was scared to death, and I still am."

She hesitated, and her voice cracked, and tears swelled in her eyes. "I've never seen anyone killed before. I hate that they died. They belong here—we don't."

John took her in his arms and hugged her while she cried. He kissed her and blotted the moisture below her eyes with his red bandana.

"Vikki, I love you and your tender heart. None of us wanted to shoot the pygmies. We didn't have a choice."

"John, I love you so much. I didn't know this trip was going to be this hard. I want us to be back home in a bed—making love—in our house—married. I want to have a baby with you." She kissed him long and hard.

"Dear, we'll do all those things. I love you, too—probably even more." He kissed her again.

"John, why does it always have to be a competition?" She laughed and kissed him softly.

John and Vikki stayed and admired the glowing fungi for a short while and then walked back
to their tent.

Late morning of the next day, the island became visible, huge with towering cliffs at the center. They hiked almost a half-hour to the river bank directly across from the east end of the island where the land was level with the water. Sony had purchased a few inflatable four-man rafts and foot pumps for getting across to the island. John took turns on pumping duty and was glad he didn't have to carry the rafts during the expedition. There was a good chance they might use them to go back down stream instead of hiking. Small plastic paddles were furnished with the boats, but they wouldn't help much in a strong current.

With most of the gear left on the bank of the river, the first boatloads of the group crossed the fast moving stream. Although they didn't land exactly where they had planned, the crossing was easier than expected. The rubber rafts then returned to the river bank opposite the island, picked up the gear and the rest of the expedition and made it back across. After securing the rafts they started up the steep cliffs. At times they would have to take off their backpacks and pull them up afterwards with ropes. Once everyone was assembled on the top of the bluff, they climbed another, less steep bluff to reach to the forested area.

John and Vikki agreed with the old journal that the trees were so close together, most likely they had been planted many years ago. Some of the men scouted around to see if there was a trail through the jungle, but no one could find an opening. Therefore, the expedition members started cutting and squeezing through any opening they could find. This process went slowly, sometimes requiring backpacks to be taken off and pulled through an opening in the trees. Deeper into the forest, the trees were not as thick, since sparse sunlight retarded the growth quite a bit. Using compass readings, they pushed on for nearly an hour.

Suddenly, everything was murky as though darkness had fallen in front of them yet daylight remained behind them. They could see a ring of tall, wild date palms surrounding a black lava stone wall that was excellently crafted. John knew the gate would be nearby. The group walked several hundred yards and came to an open set of ironwood doors about twenty feet tall. The doors appeared to be in good condition. All the expedition members stood at the entrance of the quarry, staring in amazement.

Chapter 8

The Quarry

The group of explorers gazed all around the enclosure, focusing on the beautiful blue hole situated almost dead center. A deep blue color surrounded by green soil almost hurt the eyes with such a burst of bright hues. Beyond the loud blues and greens were piles of orange and silver colored soil. One area was entirely black with no vegetation growing on it—yet bones were scattered over the surface.

A peculiar stone structure sat at the northern shore of the blue hole. It was made of stone blocks and had originally had doors and windows, but now they were sealed with the same type stones. The roof sloped down towards the water and formed a porch where three stone columns supported it. Steps led down into the water from a sealed door.

Everyone moved into the enclosure and walked towards the stone cottage. It was then they noticed the snakes. A low hissing sound caused everyone to freeze and check the proximity to the serpents. It seemed they were everywhere and most were venomous types such as forest cobras, boomslangs, twig snakes, Gabon vipers, and a few green mambas. So many small animals came to the watering hole it was a feasting table for the snakes. Machetes were quickly employed to cut up the snakes, but the burrowing asps dug in before they could be killed. The natives dug them up and chopped them apart.

After machetes put an end to the snakes, John, Vikki, and Marc set out to survey the mineral deposits. A black spot among the orange soil towards the north part of the quarry alarmed them. Maybe twenty feet across, the black spot had no vegetation, and bones lay both on and near the surface. Marc and John looked at each other and in unison said, "Pitchblende."

High grade uranium that was sixty to seventy percent pure had been found only once in the world. That ore, from the Congo, was used in the first atomic bomb dropped on Hiroshima at the end of World War II. Proximity to the black surface sent John's Geiger counter to the maximum. Immediately they marked off the area with sticks so no one would accidently take a damaging dose of radiation. The orange ore was a good grade of ore as well, but not really toxic.

Besides the kimberlite and coltan ores, another section of the compound had quartz outcroppings containing small veins of gold. The three geologists took and tested many samples. Additional findings included copper, iron, bauxite, and several other ores. Most were not rich enough to pay for the cost of mining them.

"This place is a freak of nature to have such a collection of minerals. There is a town in Arkansas called Magnet Cove that has dozens of minerals in one small location, but none of them are minable ores like the kimberlite and uranium here," John said not able to contain his excitement.

"John...Marc...do you see the masks and stuff on the walls?" asked Vikki.

"What in the hell are they doing there?" asked John

Closer inspection also revealed shields attached to the walls and handmade dolls not unlike voodoo dolls John had seen in Haiti.

"I do believe this place may be sacred to the natives, and if they catch us here, we will be in trouble," Marc explained.

"If I am correct, those are pygmy markings on the shields and masks, and judging by the amount of them a very large tribe may be nearby. I wonder if the pygmies are the ones who planted trees so close together to protect this spot," said Marc, a native of the Congo, who had some knowledge about native customs.

Sony directed the setting up of camp, after conferring with Marc about the possibility of a pygmy attack from atop the walls or through the front doors. Marc recommended the tents be placed some distance from the uranium ore and as far away from the walls as possible. They took shields from the walls and propped them up on the sides of the tents for protection from arrows and snakes that might strike at warm bodies inside of the tents.

Once the tents were pitched and meals prepared, John, Vikki and Marc, along with a couple of native porters started removing the stones that sealed the front door to the cottage. A material similar to mortar or concrete sealed the doorway. After an hour of whacking away with rock picks and folding shovels, they cleared the doorway of rubble. Vikki was allowed to use the 'ladies first' rule and flicked on her flashlight to enter.

"Wow...Jesus!...Look at this place!" she exclaimed.

John, Marc, and Sony walked in behind her, and Jan stood at the entrance peering in as well. Stacked to the ceiling in one corner was a steam-powered compressor, a motorized shaker along with all kinds of mining equipment dating from the early 1800s. A circular metal entryway was in place in the center of the floor. A few feet away metal hoses led through the floor to the area below and appeared to be set up to pump in air. As much as the two porters tried to unscrew the sealed area the wheel would not budge; however they were able to slowly move the circular wheel a few inches with a metal rod Sony handed them. Sony stuck his head out the door and asked for his pack to be brought to him. He dug around in his pack and found a can of gun oil and applied a generous amount to the edges of the metal gangway.

With some stopping and re-oiling the round door was freed. Four members of the crew pulled. Hissing air and foul smells met them in the face as the hinges opened. Vikki explored first using her flashlight and then her body as she found her footing on the metal ladder that led down to the next level. John followed and Marc was next. Sony stayed topside and had the crew cleaning and oiling the seals on the airtight door.

The door was a design first used on reefer ships that carried ice all over the world for ice houses so frozen water could be used in the summer months, a luxury commodity enjoyed by those who could afford the high price of ice. The airtight door was designed to make the ice storage area totally insulated, and early submarines and warships used the same basic design. A large round rubber or leather 'o' ring and a center wheel, when tightened, pushed four metal bars towards the outside ring to seal the door. The door didn't provide a very large opening, just enough for people to squeeze through. It was heavy and left the whole group wondering how it and the other equipment were carried to this location.

Vikki, John and Marc explored the lower room first with their flashlights. They carefully picked up items and examined them with the beams of light. Soon they found oil lamps with wicks.

"Lift up the glass so I can get to the wick with my lighter," John said to Vikki. Eventually, after turning it over and letting the oil flow into the wick, it fired up, illuminating the room with a ghostly flickering flame. They found other lamps and lit them. Now the items in the room were taking shape. There were a couple of wooden chairs and sturdy tables perfect for holding the lanterns. Marc was walking across the room when he tripped over something—another airtight bulkhead door. The three geologists summoned Sony, along with the doctor to join in a heated discussion. *Why was there an airtight compartment under the ground next to a blue hole in the middle of the Congo?* , they mused. Jan said the compartment appeared to have been set up as a chamber to equalize pressure, so water would be kept out of the lower regions of the tunnel to make diving or mining possible. Everyone voiced an opinion on the purpose of the airlock, but all agreed the integrity of the seal should be kept intact. The group explored the room in search of journals or logs, but noted the room had been cleaned out when the previous occupants had abandoned the quarry.

Sony instructed some of his men to start oiling the lower bulkhead door and gave strict orders to not attempt to open it just yet. The group went topside while the men worked oiling and cleaning both airtight doors. As they walked out into the fading sunlight they noticed the men had pulled the steam powered engines out of the cottage. A manufacture's plate on the steam engine stated it was built by the Medhurst Company in London, England. The date of the patent was 1830 but didn't nail down the date the engine was purchased and brought to the deepest reaches of Africa. Everyone believed it was carried in pieces and reassembled inside the enclosure. Speculation was several safaris and hundreds or even thousands of porters carried the equipment to the site. Jan recalled that Stanley lost 511 people on his expedition to rescue the Emin Pasha in 1887-88, and although he carried a steel boat and a Maxi gun, he would have lost many more men carrying this mining equipment. After checking patent stamps and plates on all the equipment, the latest date found was 1833. This would have been one of the earliest full scale expeditions to the Congo in history and apparently the most secretive, since there was no known record of the expedition anywhere. The only logical explanation shared by the group was no one survived to tell of the adventure.

Vikki and John held hands and walked over to the front gates to marvel at the huge doors. A couple of the men were banging on the bronze hinges to free them of at least a hundred years of corrosion.

"I wonder if the walls and doors were built before the expedition in the 1830s?" asked John.

"I don't think the expedition had the capacity to build this compound. It was built by an ancient civilization where hundreds of people worked for many years," explained Vikki who minored in archeology and spent her summers on digs in Egypt.

"I believe you are right, dear."

"I'm always right, my love," she said, being cocky. They kissed for a minute then walked just outside the gate to look around. The distance between the line of palms and the wall was about fifteen feet and provided a good killing field for anyone trying to breach the wall from the tree line. Sony was building ladders to reach the top of the wall so he could post guards on both sides of the gate.

"Excuse me a moment," John said, pulling out his machete and cutting a forest cobra in half as it moved behind Vikki.

"Could I interest you in a lovely pair of snake skin shoes?" He walked to the edge of the forest and pitched the dead snake into the underbrush.

"Thanks, anyway. I usually wear them for brunch at my dad's club. Hate for you to tote them all the way back to Texas." She grabbed John and huddled next to him after he disposed of the big serpent.

"Probably use rattlesnakes for shoes in Texas?"

"Mainly cowboy boots. We eat 'em too. Mighty good." She was laughing as she took John's hand as they walked towards the cottage.

"Taste like chicken?"

"Sort of fishy chicken. Maybe a cross between frog legs and alligator."

John realized that she had eaten several critters that he had never found on his plate.

"Is there a restaurant in Texas where I can try all that stuff?"

"We may have to go to two different ones, but I promise I will find all of them for you." She smiled and kissed him slowly for a long time.

Outside the cottage, the men were tinkering with the steam compressor. They primed it and pulled a rope that turned the crankshaft. It sputtered but refused to come back to life. More adjustments were made and more fire was used to heat the steam. Vikki sat down on a rock near the compressor so she could watch the men work and began a conversation with Jan and Marc, who were seated nearby.

"I think that the stone wall could be 500 to 1000 years old," she said nonchalantly.

Both men agreed with her, but had she invited them to bathe naked in acid with her the horny guys would have agreed to that as well.

"You realize that there are similar walls in Namibia which, many believe, was the city of a black king. It also dates back several hundred years," Marc said.

"I've seen pictures of it, and it's really interesting. Didn't some people think it was one of King Solomon's temples?" Vikki inquired.

"Yes, but according to most biblical scholars, King Solomon was way up in North Africa and never had any mines. You know if he was ever in West Africa this quarry could have been his," Marc said.

Vikki laughed. "It makes for a good story, but I prefer the movie version with Stewart Granger."

They talked a while, and Vikki left to go to her tent.

When darkness fell, night guard duty consisted of two men on the wall and one on the ground at the gates, to kill snakes as they came out of the jungle toward the camp. Tomorrow they would break the seal on the lower part of the tunnel below the second airlock. Vikki had trouble sleeping amidst the thoughts of what was hidden there and other things such as the smell in the tent. John had been on top of her and pumped hard but he had kept very quiet. Moans would project through to all the tent occupants around them. She felt he had tried to catch up on the lack of sex in the jungle. He was now snoring and apparently a happy man. Her issue was not with the sex, as she enjoyed it as much as John, but the raw smell of John and her own body was beyond a passable stench even for a Texas girl who ate frog legs, alligators, and rattlesnakes. Vikki thought about the beautiful blue hole. Tomorrow she would take a bath if she had to strip naked and jump in the blue hole in front of the whole crew.

Chapter 9

The Blue Hole

In the early morning darkness, Vikki shook John. "Get up," she whispered. "I want to take a bath in the blue hole."

"Are you kidding me? In front of all these horny men?" John desperately tried to wake up.

Vikki dug around in her pack and found a small camp towel and a light weight blanket. She grabbed her change of clothes and unzipped the front of the tent. Since she and John slept commando style, they were naked as they exited the tent, but John stumbled into a pair of shorts that included his utility belt. Vikki wrapped the blanket around as much of her body as she could. As they walked toward the blue hole, few people were stirring. The guards on the wall were changing shifts on the wall, and the two men climbing down the new ladders were expected to go to their tents for some sleep. The main fire was burning a distance from the cottage and blue hole. John noticed one of the men putting branches on the burning pile of wood.

Vikki walked to the front of the cottage and placed her change of clothes near the steps that led into the water. Quickly she pulled off the blanket, slowly walked down, and put her feet in the water. The light from the distant fire flickered across the compound, and revealed a lovely silhouette of her perfect body. Her long slender legs disappeared under the water, followed by curvaceous hips that melted into a slim waist. He could barely see the outline of her firm breasts.

"John, would you hand me the camp soap?" she asked, as she came back up the steps to take it from him. "Are you coming in?"

"I am standing guard so a bunch of hard dicks don't jump in and screw you to death."

"Well, you have already tried that with little success."

"I felt it was a noble effort on my part," he said, laughing.

Through the water, Vikki noticed a dark object coming towards her and yelled, "John there is something in the water!"

"Get out! Get out!" John pulled his machete from his belt, and dove into the water behind Vikki.

The object preferred Vikki, and angled for the attack. Suddenly a giant snake raised his head a couple of yards from Vikki, and exposed a mouth full of curved teeth. She realized she couldn't get up the steps before it struck, so she grabbed the huge snake directly behind its head. The snake instantly started to move his enormous coils around her. Before the snake could complete the first phase of constriction, John had his hand next to Vikki's on the giant snake's throat, and made his first full strike with his machete on the spine of the creature. The snake reacted by quietly wrapping death coils around John. He could feel the breath leaving his body, and knew that once he breathed out the snake would compress more and more until he died. To make the situation worse, he was being pulled into deep water. He might drown before all the bones in his body were crushed.

The explosion of a bullet fired through the skull of the huge snake was a sweet noise for both John and Vikki. A second, and then a third shot caused the snake to go limp.

"John…Miss Vikki? Me hopes you okay. Did snake bite you?" Zuka said. The tall Zulu warrior was genuinely concerned.

"No Zuka. We are fine," Vikki said.

"Speak for yourself—my ribs will never be the same," John said, uncoiling the snake. Several people had joined them in the water with hands on the snake, pulling it to shore. John and Vikki both thanked Zuka profusely, who had just climbed down from the wall when he heard Vikki scream.

Jan checked for injuries. Vikki got examined first and it appeared to John for way too long. A naked blonde lady really needs to have everything checked out. Several members of the expedition looked at her with a perverted concern for her injuries. Vikki began to protest, so Jan turned his attention to John's ribs. Some may have been cracked or at least bruised, so Jan wrapped them and told him to take it easy for a few days.

Vikki pulled the blanket around her and began the walk back to her tent. Laid out next to the cottage was the snake. Marc declared the creature was a twenty-one foot long African rock python *sebae*. Its den must have been close by the cottage, and after further investigation Marc said it was a very old female that had not laid eggs in a while.

Vikki and John went back to the tent. After both were dressed, Vikki looked at John and with tears in her eyes she said, "John, thanks for saving my life. You were almost killed, and I don't know what I would do without you." She started crying and pulled John close to her. John felt it was a release of emotions from the terror that she had just gone through, and let her cry. He felt that the sex later would be really intense.

Once she had her composure, they both headed for the stone building to see about opening the second airlock. Jan met them there and explained they had to be extremely careful once they were sealed off below.

"John, I believe that you and Vikki are certified scuba divers—is that correct?" he asked.

"Yes we are, but we have not been diving together," John said.

"I don't know how deep this tunnel might be, but we must treat it like a dive. We believe that air has been forced into the lower parts of the tunnel not only to keep the water out, but also to provide the air for you to breathe as though you had on a scuba tank, since the air has been pumped in at pressure. I will bring a tape measure and you guys will have to remember your no-decompression dive limits as we go down," Jan said.

Vikki had been certified a year ago with a PADI instructor. "I don't have the tables memorized, but I do recall that anything over one hundred feet deep would only allow for a 5 to 15 minute dive without decompression."

"That's correct plus, you must consider our altitude and compute that figure in with the table readings," John added, not really knowing much but wanting to sound smart.

"As I recall, you would need to make an adjustment from an eighteen meter dive to that of a twenty one meter dive at 5000 feet. We may be 1000 feet above sea level so it wouldn't require much of an adjustment—maybe a slight one for diving in fresh water instead of sea water," Vikki said, giving more information than John wanted.

"We ain't diving anyway," John said.

"John, we don't have to be diving if that damn tunnel is pressurized. We will have to follow the same rules as if we had tanks on our back," she reminded him.

"We'll have to get that antique to…what the hell!" As he spoke, he heard the hit and miss of the steam air compressor come to life.

"These old things are simple as hell. Don't take much to fix," Sony said, who had a huge grin on his face. "Hope it's powerful enough to pump some good air."

Hoses were attached and air began flowing into the airlock and the lower tunnel. The airlock wasn't keeping the air pumped in since the hatch was open, but the lower tunnel was doing fine. The gauges were crude with no pressure per square inch markings. The crew decided to let the pump run for an hour, put six people into the airlock, and run air for thirty minutes. Next, they would open the hatch into the lower tunnel and four would go in, two staying at the top near the hatch. John and Vikki had elected to hurry to the bottom of the tunnel, scout around and come back to the hatch where they would perform a safety stop. They would wait about ten minutes to release any stored up nitrogen in their system. After that, they would go into the airlock for a few minutes, sealing the lower tunnel below them. They would measure the distance with a long tape Jan had. Everyone knew there wasn't a decompression chamber in the Congo and very few in South Africa. Any mistake and they could color themselves dead.

Six of the crew went into the airlock. After thirty minutes, the group placed a metal rod through the screw mechanism and four strong men started turning the wheel of the hatch cover. The oiled cover opened more easily than the airlock hatch. Hissing air and a really foul smell caused Vikki to cover her mouth and almost vomit.

John wanted to go first. He used a ladder attached just below the hatch. As he climbed down on the tunnel floor and shined his flash light around, he saw two skeletons lying next to each other, partially clothed.

"Vikki, don't be alarmed by the skeletons in the tunnel," he said, dreading her reaction.

"What the hell are you saying…oh my god!" She had seen them.

"Jan, will you check to see if you can find a cause of death," John said.

"Unless there is a knife stuck in the bones that will be damn hard to determine," Jan said.

"We are headed down and won't stay long," Jon said. He and Vikki followed a winding path that included steps and gouged out areas where mining had taken place. They fed out the tape and hurried as fast as the passageway would allow. The air was dank, smelled horrible, but was breathable. After about fifteen minutes they spotted a pool of water they assumed would join up eventually with the blue hole. Lying next to the pool were two full diving suits with helmets. Two skulls stared into the glass port holes. Vikki screamed but didn't back away.

"Vikki, we have about three minutes to take these off and start back."

John removed one helmet with the skull inside. He helped Vikki unscrew the one from her unfortunate diver.

"We are at 127 feet from the bottom of the lower hatch and about 137 to the ground level. We are going to be cooked if we don't move fast." John studied Jan's tape as he spoke.

They arrived at the hatch exhausted from carrying the heavy brass diving helmets. Jan's eyes opened wide when he saw the skulls. Ernie, the other member of the crew, let out a yell when it was his turn to examine the helmets. They looked at the clothing left on the other skeletons, and created wild theories about what happened to the people in the tunnel. An easy theory stated that something happened to the men topside who were running the compressor, that in turn caused the divers to die first and the others later. Maybe someone jammed the hatch so they couldn't get out. Maybe a methane gas leak or the whole expedition may have been attacked by natives and all were killed, with those below left to die.

"If any of those theories were true, then who stacked the equipment so neatly, and sealed the stone building so securely? And why didn't they go get the people below and bury them?" John asked.

"Survivors may have come back after a few days just to seal the place out of respect and had no time to recover the dead. Probably got killed later, left no records—no survivors," Jan said.

"Whatever occurred, they never got the chance to come back down here. I'll tell you why," Vikki said. She held up an old leather sack. "Wait till you see what's inside."

Chapter 10

Diamonds and Snakes

Vikki opened the sack and flashlight beams caused an explosion of sparkling reflections, illuminating thousands of uncut diamonds. Around the skeletons and on the other side of the tunnel were dozens of leather sacks all full of diamonds in different shades of color.

"Holy shit!" John said.

After a short stay in the airlock the subterranean crew walked out of the stone building carrying leather sacks of diamonds and two diving helmets with skulls inside.

It was raining so hard their tent was taking on water in a few places. John and Vikki ate lunch in the tent alone in the company of four bags of diamonds. They celebrated the discovery of the diamond cache and their narrow escape, with passionate lovemaking. They both knew this time in their lives would end someday. Their intense passion was as rare and delicious as their new found diamonds. Vikki took a position on top of John, taking care not to further damage his ribs, and directed their love making, moving up and down slowly and sensuously, creating an act of such pleasure that John explained to her later as 'wonderful sexual torture.' At this moment in time, they both felt that life could not get any better, even if they had all the diamonds and money in the world.

After they rested, they decided to sort the bags of precious stones. Most were white, but a few were pink, light blue, yellow and some were brown. About half the gem stones were three karats or less, quite a few were between five and ten karats and a small number were huge rocks that looked like large hunks of glass. They placed the stones back in the bags and listened to the torrential rain.

After an hour or so, Sony yelled for everyone to meet in the stone cottage. The rain had slowed, so everyone made a dash for the building. Except for the guards on the walls and the gate, all the expedition members were present.

"Found a load of diamonds. Need special diving gear to do more mining. So, we need to get out of Dodge quick. Our guards have been spotting pygmies in the trees—a whole herd of them. Attack is coming soon. We ship out tomorrow. Take the shields and protect the rubber boats from arrows. Some of you men, carry the equipment back in here. Use those sacks of mortar we found to seal this baby again. We have three new boats. Protect the hell out of them. Check our old boats that we brought up the hill for holes. Keep patches ready. We'll make a new trail in the morning—old one booby trapped. Stay on east side of river. Arrows can't go that far. Hippos and crocs on east—be careful. All diamond bags in something that will float. You die—we'll catch the diamonds down river. Mostly be floating—rapids we'll go inland. Eat big in morning—won't stop much till we get to vehicles. Should go fast. Good luck." Sony wasn't much on speeches, but the whole crew got the message. Unless they were careful, they would have poisoned arrows stuck in their asses, their rubber boats would sink, and all the while they would be fought over by hippos and twenty-foot-long crocodiles.

John and Vikki sought the sanctuary of their leaking tent. The pair placed the diamonds into plastic bags filled with air. Vikki wrapped her journal in plastic after she made her last entry. Her writings were more like a diary that included a scientific log and contained her intense feelings for John. Jan, Marc and Sony all kept a type of journal. Jan had many medical references, and Marc concentrated on the geological findings. Sony's was an account of the men, the work and the equipment. Most of his sentences were less than five words long and absent of adjectives or adverbs. John just made notes when something interested him.

Everyone in camp found it difficult to sleep that night, because of the rain and the impending doom that would most likely occur the next day. Vikki lay on John's shoulder and told him she was really scared about going back on the river.

"If anyone can make it back, I believe it will be us, since we have so much to live for," John said.

"John, thanks—but you are full of shit." She laughed and kissed him on the cheek.

Suddenly, there was a 'thunk' sound near their tent—and then another and another.

"Vikki, those are arrows hitting our shields!" John yelled.

Both of them moved to the center of the tent to obtain the maximum shelter given by the four large wooden shields propped next to the tent. Within minutes, arrows began to tear through both ends of the tent, which were not protected. Now they could hear automatic gunfire and pistol shots. More arrows stuck up in the shields, and very heavy gunfire could be heard all over camp. As quickly as the attack started, it came to an abrupt stop.

Sony came over to the tent to say, "Stay in your tent. Antoine and Ike killed. Arrows to the skull. We killed bunches of those bastards. We have two wounded—not bad. Doc will give the medicine."

Later, they would learn that Sani and Joseph were the two who had minor arrow wounds. Minor, except for the little problem of poison and human feces on the arrows.

There were no more attacks that night, but no one got much sleep. At first light everything was packed up. Everyone walked out in continuing rain, and they noticed the great doors were functional again. Not far from the front gate, were two more graves plus the four that contained some of the skeletal remains of the old expedition.

With Zuka and Ernie leading the way, the group cut a new path through the dense jungle and tropical forest and finally reached the edge of the cliff. Gunners were posted at the edge of the drop-off to protect the climbers as they descended from the top. Vikki was in a trance-like state since the death of the two men. She now knew she or John could die at any minute and realized the expedition was likely to get more dangerous once they got on the river. John had a determined look on his face and watched every movement down below as he climbed off the high ridge. The climb down was made even more difficult because everyone was carrying a shield, with ropes lowering down extra ones. Once everyone was down from the cliff, several members of the crew stood in a semi-circle holding up the shields to protect those airing up the boats and repairing any that had holes in them.

Two pygmies who shot arrows from the top of the cliff were killed with a short burst from Ernie's AK-47. The projectiles hit shields before they could do any damage. With the boats inflated, the expedition made a launch from the east part of the island. This was the first test of the shields while floating downstream. Five bright yellow inflatable rafts caught the current and moved nicely between the large island and the eastern shoreline. As the little flotilla approached the southern part of the island, pygmies let fly dozens of arrows from the top of the cliff. Their aim was surprisingly accurate. Had it not been for the shields, no expedition member would have survived without at least a wound from a foul smelling, sharp metal point. Zuka and Ernie blasted several pygmies off the cliff, and the rest took shelter in the trees. Two boats took hits and had to be quickly patched and air added. Sony calculated the eight day trip on foot would be shortened to a couple of days if they also traveled at night. He reminded the group there were two bad sections of rapids they would have to walk around, meaning there would be times they would have to choose between territorial hippos and pygmy poison arrows.

The Aruwimi River had been three or four hundred yards across most of the first day. As they rounded a bend and headed almost due west, the river narrowed to about a hundred yards and became very shallow. This wouldn't have been a problem, except for a large herd of forest elephants enjoying a bath in the shallows. They bellowed when they saw the crew and made menacing charges towards the group from a great distance. As the boats drew closer, Sony asked everyone to fire their weapons in the air. The elephants took off–all but one. The elephant that remained was the dominant bull. He stood his ground at the edge of the river.

"That bastard ain't afraid of shit!" John said.

Almost immediately, all the little boats moved next to the opposite shore line and trained their guns on the big bull. He headed directly toward Sony's boat, where Jan and Marc were passengers. Zuka and Ernie opened up with automatic fire and struck the skull of the big beast several times. None of these hits from large caliber weapons stopped the determined patriarch. As all the men bailed out of the craft, the elephant slid his trunk under the rubber boat and tossed it over his head. The two men with automatic assault weapons were closer now and filled his brain with steel jacketed bullets. The monster fell in the middle of the stream.

Quickly the survivors of the tiny ship wreck swam after the boat and made quick repairs. After everyone was moving again, the crew frantically set about fixing damage not noticed on the first repairs. Sony yelled to the rest of the crew if the repairs didn't hold they would be abandoning their boat for one that didn't resemble a sponge.

Later in the day all the rafts pulled up to a clearing to the east so a meal could be prepared and repairs made. Sony's boat was determined to be not safe enough to risk staying in at night. The rips had been patched but air continued to leak out and a hand pump had to be used at all times. Of the twelve members of the expedition still alive, three were receiving treatment for poisoning. Jan's antidote seemed to be working, but the side effects were nausea, diarrhea, loss of appetite, and general weakness. That meant these wounded warriors were pretty much just along for the ride now. Sony had calculated that some boats would be lost and felt confident they could get by with three if necessary. If he had calculated their time on the river correctly, they would have deep water and few interruptions during the night. Tomorrow they would encounter the first series of rapids, requiring a portage through the jungle until they found good floating water again.

Vikki had to relieve herself, so she asked John to go with her and stand guard. John told her to inspect the area before stripping down. She found a spot that had quite a bit of ground foliage, and looked for any movement. Nothing stood out to her, so she pulled down her cargo shorts and began to pee.

Seconds later, John heard Vikki's blood curdling scream. "A snake just bit me!"

Chapter 11

Hippos and Arrows

John grabbed his machete and cut the snake in half as it tried to slip back into the undergrowth. He examined the right cheek of Vikki's bottom and found one fang mark. She lay on the ground screaming and crying.

Jan ran up and looked at the green and yellow snake. "Boomslang—got one fang in you—I can treat it—you will be okay—need to calm down—makes it worse," Jan said in Sony type sentences as he patted her back. In his medical kit, he found his supply of freeze dried anti-venom vials.

Vikki stopped crying. She knew that Dr. Leeghwater was mixing a cocktail that would save her life. Suddenly, she realized that there were twelve fellow travelers surrounding her exposed bottom, showing great concern over a small snake bite. Sony would later say it was likely the prettiest rear end ever exposed in the Congo to date.

"Okay, let's give Vikki some privacy," John said, while he covered her bottom with his shirt. The disappointed onlookers backed away.

Jan gave her several shots, cleaned the wound area and placed a bandage on the fang mark.

"The boomslang has a neurotoxin that is very slow to act, but when it does, it's not pleasant. The anti-venom is very effective, however, and you should show minimal effects of the actual bite. Boomslangs have rear fangs. Lucky for you that means they don't get good penetration when striking objects such as a large bottom section. Not that you have a large bottom..." Jan sputtered and his face turned red. "It is difficult to tell how much you were invenominated, but I would guess it was enough to make you very ill, yet probably not enough to kill you," Vikki already felt much better. Jan wasn't going to tell her that boomslangs are on the list of the top ten most deadly snakes in the world, and they make people bleed from every orifice in their body. He just hoped the bleeding didn't happen to her. Complete blood transfusions are a common treatment for this snake bite, but that was not going to happen on a riverbank in the Congo.

"The anti-venom does make you a little sick to your stomach, and may affect your digestive track. It will keep you alive, and there is a good chance I will need to give you shots each day. You will be sleepy and John will have to help you with daily tasks," Jan said. He and John helped her on her feet. Jan had given her injections around the area where she was bitten, along with a strong antibiotic.

Sony directed the loading of the four boats. He made sure there were plenty of shields in each boat, and enough fire power to give good coverage for attacks from the shore. The plan for traveling at night was risky, but Sony wanted all of this expedition back in the vehicles as quickly as possible.

Vikki slept most of the way. So did the three men who were taking Jan's poison antidote. They passed some hippos which were, thankfully, on the west part of the river. Otherwise, the trip went fast with no more attacks. As the sun came up, a large bluff could be seen on the right and even at a distance Sony could see dozens of natives positioned on top with bows drawn.

"Ernie and Zuka—start blasting away—soon as you are in range. Everyone—under your shields—pistols ready. This could be bad—give them hell!" Sony screamed at the top of his voice.

At two hundred yards, the two AKs came to life and raked several natives off the cliff. The rest scattered out of sight and would wait until they were right under them to fire off their arrows. Sony directed the boat to the far shore which put them almost out of range but not completely. Suddenly, it seemed as though a hundred arrows were in the air at one time. Almost everyone was under shields waiting for the initial onslaught. The sound was an awesome combination of arrows striking wooden shields at different places, creating an almost musical drum tone.

Jean-Pierre, a quiet and hardworking man from Kinshasa, stood up and came out from the protection of the shield to fire his pistol at the pygmies. An arrow pieced his skull and killed him instantly. He slumped over the edge of the rubber boat into the river and floated down the river almost even with the boats. Since the first wave of projectiles had stopped, the AK-47s started taking out dozens of natives. Zuka and Ernie were running low on ammunition, but Sony told them to use most of it. Sony figured they would be beyond their range of arrows for the major balance of the journey. Some of the pygmies ran back to the edge to shoot the rest of their arrows as the expedition cleared the cliff and headed for open water. Everyone except the sick and wounded opened on the natives and laid waste to all who were in view. Their numbers were severely depleted, and no one considered them much of a threat anymore.

All the boats had arrows in them and the travelers patched frantically. The boats seemed to be okay, but the whole group knew further repairs would be needed. Hugging the east shore, they now passed thick jungle with little room for landing boats. Ahead were the hippos that Sony was concerned would present a big danger. The hippos were along the east shore, with some of their numbers extending to the center of the river. The rubber rafts kept to the west shore and they watched as a couple of hippos moved from center to almost in the path of the boats. One of the hippos moved back to center, but one eyed the boats and blew water in the air. The expedition paddled as fast as they could to make it by the lone hippo. Apparently, he was waiting for the last boat and submerged just as it passed him.

For a little while everyone felt they were past any danger. An explosion of water interrupted the calm and the boat with Sani, Jomo, and Jaja was thrown in the air at least ten feet. Sani and Jaja were good swimmers and headed fast for the other boats. Jomo was weak from the poison in his system and the effect of the antidote. The hippo had him in his monstrous mouth. One horrifying bite crushed most of the bones in Jomo's body including his skull. The hippo slung him around for a while like a doll, then discarded him and swam back to the other hippos. The boat was damaged but patched and continued to be a part of the flotilla.

Vikki had been asleep, but now she was sitting in the boat, crying. As she looked around at her friends in the boats, she noticed that most had a stoic, emotionless and lifeless combat stare. No one else was crying because they were honed in on survival. She tried to stop weeping, but found she was barely able to do so. In a few hours they approached the first set of rapids, and this time they pulled the boats over on the west side of the shore, since most felt the threat of the natives was eliminated.

The ancient elephant trail greeted them like an old friend. They made good time after stopping for a quick meal and continuing to perform maintenance on the rubber rafts. The walk in the jungle seemed strange after being in the boats for so long. Traveling downriver had cut six or seven days off their travel time, but none of the group except maybe for Sony, had expected the level of danger they encountered. It was growing dark, so they set up camp in an area near the river that was up river from the cataracts. The group would launch in the morning and have one set of rapids before reaching the vehicles and the native village.

It seemed as though everyone had something wrong with them. John, Jan, and Marc only had blisters on their hands from paddling the boats with small plastic oars. The rest of the expedition except for Vikki, who had her own problems, had been at least nicked by the poison arrows. Jan had given them all antibiotics but because little of the antidote was left, the rest had only a few sips.

Since all the sacks of diamonds were packed to be buoyant, the expedition had only lost one sack of diamonds, a tent, and a few cooking supplies. Most suspected that the hippo swallowed the jewels and probably crapped it out on shore some place. No one was volunteering to dig through hippo dung while being attacked by a herd of two-ton beasts. Lightning struck a tree not far up river, and a huge limb fell, into the river causing a several crocodiles to slap the water with their tails and submerge. A clap of thunder sounded as night fell on the expedition. They all hoped that tomorrow would be an easier day, but most knew the river to be unforgiving.

Chapter 12

Cataracts

The rain in the Congo was relentless and averaged almost a hundred inches a year. The next day would have been better spent staying in the tent and reading a book. It was a steady hard rain with lightning and thunder. Sony nixed the staying in the tent part and had everyone up preparing to leave. One of the rafts had deflated during the night, so they decided to leave it and pack everything into three boats.

Most of the next day was uneventful which was good since moaning was the favorite method of communication among the crew. They passed by forest elephants drinking at the water's edge and later a troop of chimpanzees in frenzy at the edge of the jungle. From a distance the jungle was beautiful since there were tropical flowers and lush green plants, trees, and palms for mile after mile along the Aruwimi. The rain stopped and steaming heat took its place.

The group stopped for a quick lunch and break on a low bank along the river. A couple of huge crocodiles spotted what they believed to be their next lunch and moved from the opposite side of the river toward the group. No one in the expedition was in the mood for any more drama. As if summoned by a higher power, pistols and assault rifles fired at the crocs as they surfaced close to them. Even Vikki fired her weapon at the surprised animals. The big reptiles could be seen rolling in the water in a death dance that would be theirs this time.

Everyone was back in the boat and energized by the thought that later today they would be riding in Land Rovers. The current was picking up, signaling that rapids were ahead. Sony was looking at the shore line on both sides for a spot to pull the boats to safety. As the river turned and gained velocity, the crew noticed high rock cliffs on each side. There wasn't a place to pull out, and the rapids had grasped the small flotilla of yellow rubber rafts without warning. They were being pushed towards the sounds of churning and torrential white water that was beyond a kayaker's classification.

To the right and left the rapids were blasting through a series of rock-strewn death traps. A series of water tunnels fell through the center of the river at unbelievable speed. Rock walls on each side of the river had off chutes that led down to a hellish death. Sony's boat hit the water tunnel first and found the center well enough. The mighty river grasped his boat and thrust it through a series of waterfalls that slammed the little boat into rocks as it dropped to the bottom of each waterfall. The last fall went straight down into a washboard of churning white water. Sony's boat popped out upright even though it had no riders. Sony, Zuka, Ernie and Joseph swam after the boat and the supplies.

Next through the water tunnel were John, Vikki, Jan, and Marc, who also hit the center of the raging channel, however; the rubber craft started spinning before it slammed into the bottom of the last steep cascade, Mark was ejected and fell on his side into the boiling water. The boat suffered the same fate as did Sony's boat with the entire party being thrown out. Vikki was not swimming well because of her weak condition, so John slid his arm under her and swam towards their now empty boat. Jan had found Marc floating unconscious, and with Sony's help they pulled him to shore.

Jan started chest compression, which quickly caused Marc to throw up water and then, screaming with pain, he reached for his right arm which had the fibula protruding from the skin. Jan administrated morphine and waited for it to take effect so that he could set the fracture.

Meanwhile, one more boat was being directed by the great river to the tunnel of evil. Joseph, Sani and Jaja were yelling at the top of their lungs as their boat spun out of control and slammed into the wall of the water passageway. Then the unthinkable occurred, and the boat flipped, ejecting all the passengers before the big drop over the falls. Joseph and Jaja could be seen being spit out by the rush of water. Zuka and Ernie swam out to help them. Both had broken ribs, and cuts and bruises but were alive. Jan didn't have time to help them until he had set Marc's compound fracture.

Everyone waited for Sani to be thrown out of the rapids. After several minutes it became clear he was not coming. He was probably knocked unconscious and jammed beneath one of the side chutes under rocks. They had lost the fifth member of the expedition and hoped he would be the last one to give up his life on this mission.

The exhausted team lay on the shore using their own first aid kits to bandage cuts and lacerations. Jan promised to take care of stitches once he had Marc's arm set. Sony and John helped him set the fracture and place the splint. Marc's puncture wound where the bone protruded was stitched and the morphine had calmed him and eased the pain. Jan was bleeding from a cut on his head. John and Sony cleaned and placed gauze on the wound. The doctor then began to stitch and clean all the wounds suffered during the encounter with the rapids. Jan didn't stop to think how many lives he had saved on this trip but his efforts didn't go unnoticed by everyone else.

"Jan, I just wanted to thank you for saving my life—everyone else too!" Vikki said.

"You can thank me when we fucking get out of here," he said with considerable tiredness in his voice.

Once everyone was patched up, the boats were loaded again. Some of the team had been swimming around picking up supplies as Jan was doing his job. With bandages displayed on almost every expedition member, they appeared to have all just descended from a wartime Pork Chop Hill.

A couple hours later as they rounded a lazy bend on an increasingly widening river they spotted canoes coming fast toward them.

"Boss, I'm out of ammo," said Ernie.

"Me too—I got nothing," yelled Zuka to Sony who was in a boat with the doctor and Marc.

"It's okay—we're safe!" remarked Sony who had realized that the canoes were from the village where they had left their vehicles.

Chapter 13

Safe

Shortly afterwards, the Land Rovers came into view and cheering broke out among the remaining nine member of the expedition.

After they were ashore, the natives asked questions through the translators in the group. Two of the rafts had shields still in them and one was given to the chief along with about twenty arrows sticking in it. Sony gave them a few diamonds for keeping the vehicles safe. The chief was very pleased and actually liked the shield better than the diamonds.

Everything was loaded into the five Land Rovers and the less crippled were assigned as drivers. As soon as they started moving, Sony was calling in on his built-in short wave in the lead vehicle. He wanted helicopters for the wounded and poisoned, which included just about everyone. He found a large clearing off the main road that would serve as a heliport and called in the coordinates. The copters would come from Stanleyville and fly directly to their airport. Then private aircraft would take the poison and snake bite victims to Johannesburg's largest hospital. Marc was okay to fly to Kinshasa and go to the hospital there. Jan chose to go to South Africa with his patients, plus he needed medical attention as well. John had not been nicked by a poison arrow and had only suffered some cracked ribs, cuts and bruises. He would fly to the Ivory Coast with the diamonds which were now three bags short. A division for payment to the crew would give packets of diamonds to all crew members, including the ones who lost their lives. Sony would make sure the families of the deceased men would get a fair share. Every person on the expedition received over a million dollars in diamonds, and the royalty agreement for John Cole's family would most likely generate payments for a hundred years or more.

As they approached the clearing, two large military helicopters were waiting. The Land Rover and supplies were left to be retrieved at a later time. Once in Stanleyville, John kissed Vikki goodbye and said he would join her in Johannesburg in a couple of days.

She whispered in his ear, "John, require that our part of the diamonds be placed in the 'Cole Family Trust.' That way our kids can get it after we're gone."

John knew that no such trust existed but would very soon. Vikki's words were her way of saying they would be married, and she wanted to have a family with him. He was all smiles but concerned about a little blood that was dripping from one of her ears. Jan gave her another dose of anti-venom.

"Vikki, I've been giving you freeze dried meds, but in South Africa you will be given a much stronger liquid product so you will be well much sooner." Jan had called in all the medical conditions and expected a quick recovery for everyone.

John hung around the Stanleyville Airport until Vikki was safely on her way. He then took a flight to Kinshasa and then to the Ivory Coast. There, Cangé met him at the airport where John presented the diamonds and three journals, to be copied and returned to Sony, Jan and Marc. John spent a good deal of time at the bank suggesting that about a million dollars a year of the diamonds be sold and then divided, twenty-five percent going to his trust and then twenty percent to the Democratic Republic of the Congo. The rest would go to Haiti but would be held by the bank.

A call was put in to Plato, who agreed to what was already contracted except for the yearly payments. He suggested the amount be increased a little each year. Cangé still laughed as he spoke but really felt bad about the expedition members who died on the mission. John presented him with one of the shields with dozens of pygmy arrows sticking in it. Cangé was thrilled and hung it immediately. Jan had taken a quiver of leaf wrapped arrows to South Africa so that the poison center could provide a more exacting antidote.

John caught a flight to South Africa the next day and met up with Vikki in the hospital. The couple was married a few months after returning to the states. All the members of the expedition were invited but only Sony, Marc, and Jan were able to attend. Zuka came to visit later that year as he was in Texas to try out for a semi-pro basketball team. Most of the expedition members stayed lifelong friends.

John and Vikki worked in various capacities for her dad. They didn't need the income so much, since money rolled in every year from the bank in the Ivory Coast, but it was good to have grandparents close by to help with the kids who came along in rapid succession. He and Vikki never returned to the Congo, as they were too busy raising a family.

Their kids, however, couldn't wait to follow in their parent's footsteps as they had heard all the stories about Africa since they were small children. John and Vikki had beautiful, tall twin daughters named Jan and Zuka after members of the expedition. They also had a son named after Vikki's dad, Mike. He was given a middle name of Sony and was told many times how the expedition leader would shorten sentences in a John Wayne combat method. Young Mike practiced this until he was irritatingly good at it. So many people called him Sony that it stuck as a nickname. A time in the very near future would find young Sony repeating the same dangerous expedition that almost killed his parents

Chapter 14

London 2010

Getting this trip planned and executed took much longer than the group had hoped. The word 'executed' also described what happened to Chris Zacharius, when his wife Lu discovered the real plans for this trip. The men in the group convinced the ladies to go on an African Safari booked through Holland and Holland of London. All of them would ride in on elephants and stay at a lodge so plush most self-respecting wild animals would considered it unfit. They would take pictures, relax and generally be on vacation.

The devious part of their plan was going to be difficult to pull off. If it worked, the girls would not find out until they got back home, or at least on the plane ride back, since air marshals would be on the plane to protect the guys from being murdered. Mit Kruger, Modesto Tejeda, and Chris Zacharius had booked a side trip out of the lodge for three nights to go on a lion hunt to kill those deemed as "man eaters" in a Tanzanian village. They would fly in from an airstrip at the lodge and camp in the area where the lions were last seen (and had last eaten some tasty villagers.) Each of them would have a gun bearer, and a game warden would supervise. At least, that was the story told to the girls, Lucero Zacharius, Modesto's wife Gretchen, and Mit's longtime girlfriend, Angel Dominguez. The lion hunt would be something the men would look forward to, if they survived the task.

The girls wanted no part of this macho "kill-or-be-killed adventure" and made sure all the life insurance policies were handy, just in case. Their plans were to have drinks on the veranda and watch the leopards chase down monkeys. Afterwards, they would beat a path to various spas, go on photo jeep tours, and elephant rides. What the guys were really going to do was much more dangerous.

This scheme originated in the Dominican Republic, about three years before. After chasing down a tremendous treasure hidden by the tyrannical dictator Rafael Trujillo, they also found that his arch rival dictator from Haiti, Papa Doc Duvalier, had been sending huge shipments of gold from his northern Haitian mine, which he briefly owned with Trujillo, to Africa. The log from his ship recorded sixty-seven trips before Papa Doc's death in 1971, and none after, suggesting that Baby Doc was not aware of his dad's African connection. The secret gold shipments to Africa were uncovered when the three friends translated the log of the *Afrik-Rev* given to Chris by her captain, Plato Duvalier. Plato was a first cousin to Papa Doc and also a cousin to Baby Doc. Chris' cousin in Memphis, Tennessee, who studied family trees, told him. Plato would be a first cousin once removed. She, however, also told him she traced Chris' background to a rare tree ape in Borneo.

Since they had the money to spend, Chris and his pals hired private investigators who spoke both French and the local African dialects to poke around using the leads that were provided them from the log. They had been sniffing out clues and interviewing anyone in the vicinity of the Ivory Coast who was still alive, where Papa Doc's gold ship docked every month or so. To ward off suspicion, they posed as historians and anthropologists studying African influence on Haitian society. It took almost three years of work to finally hit the jackpot—or as any sane person would say, it was a sure way to die. The bizarre discovery of the investigators was not what anyone expected. A trip deep in the jungles of the Congo would be required in an area that might be classified as unexplored.

Mit, Modesto, Chris and their companions flew to London for the connecting flight to Nairobi, but couldn't talk the girls out of a brief layover in London to shop at Harrods. They just had to have the very best safari wear in the world, or at least the most expensive. Lu picked out a khaki short culotte skirt and a khaki long sleeved hunting shirt, with a matching vest with slots for large cartridge shells. She wouldn't need bullets or a gun on her camera safari, but the outfit would look cute when she showed up at the spa for her hot rock massage. Modesto's wife, Gretchen, and Mit's longtime girlfriend, Angel, emerged from the dressing room with slacks and authentic bush jackets. If Vogue photographers had been there, all three ladies would compete for the cover.

While the girls were loading their credit cards with purchases for the trip, the three non-Vogue contenders headed to the gun shop. The men had made their purchases some time back and had the guns shipped to the lodge, but they wanted to see what was new. All three had their orders in for the 100th anniversary Holland and Holland .375 which was coming out in 2012, but for now, Mit and Modesto were going to use .458's. Chris was going to stick with an older model .375 which many hunters declared to be the most versatile caliber for big game. Chris had watched videos of people shooting the new .577 T-Rex cartridge and decided that having his face smashed to pieces after the recoil of the first shot wouldn't leave much enthusiasm for a second shot. Of course if he hit his target on the first shot, there would be no need to repeat. Holland and Holland made that cartridge model several years before. While they were looking at their guns, they saw a couple of the old relics.

Modesto, an avid reader of everything, pointed out something the others didn't know.

"Did you guys know that Henry Stanley and two others in his party put five rounds of the old .577 in an elephant on one of his safaris in 1887? The elephant didn't even slow down! They were not pleased, and one in the party, a Dr. Parke, actually traded his rifle for food during a bad time on the expedition. Stanley was used to shooting 8 and 10 bore guns which he said never failed. The old rounds may not have had the more powerful loads that are used today."

"Where do you come up with this shit?" Mit said

"I read *In Darkest Africa* for this trip. Mit you should put down the *Sports Illustrated* swimsuit issue and read a real ass book," Modesto said.

The appeal of Holland and Holland had to be the quality of workmanship and engravings. It certainly wasn't the prices which seemed to start at over a hundred thousand pounds and go up from there.

They left Harrods carrying the girls' new duds and headed up to Knightsbridge Road and over by Wilton Row. Someone had suggested dining on Beef Wellington at the Grenadier Pub. The group learned the pub was now a part of a chain and no longer served Beef Wellington. It was supposed to have a ghost. Maybe the ghost was someone waiting for one good English meal before they transcended to heaven. Although the guy drinking a beer wasn't exactly a ghost, Chris noticed the young black man sitting at the bar watching the three couples in a casual sort of way as he sipped on a Guinness. He appeared to be strangely familiar, so Chris jabbed Modesto in the ribs and told him to sneak a look at the guy. Chris's wife, Lu, glanced at the man at about the same time Modesto did. Both Lu and Modesto froze, turned back and stared at Chris. The color drained from their faces. He bore an unmistakable resemblance to the drug lord Lu killed on the night they were recovering the biggest gold stash in history, off the shores of the Dominican Republic.

"Chris, this guy has to be kin to Jon Jon Vieux!" Lu blasted in his ear. She meant to whisper, but in her excitement, she forgot the volume control.

Before they could look again, he was gone. Modesto rushed out the door of the pub and saw him some distance away in the parking lot aiming a pistol with a silencer attached. The gun made muffled sounds as three rounds struck the pub sign over Modesto's left shoulder. The holes were spaced within an inch of each other and were meant only to detain, rather than kill him. It worked, and Modesto calmed himself. He walked back into the pub smiling, with no intention of telling the girls what just happened. A man with a firearm in London, where they were outlawed, spoke of a well-connected criminal. Modesto just said he couldn't catch the man. Apparently, they were being followed by someone who didn't believe in the safari ruse.

After drinks and burgers, they headed back to the airport for their flight. All of them had first class fares on British Airlines that left at 7:00 pm and got them to Africa in about six hours. They would arrive in the middle of the night, stay at a local hotel, then catch a flight to the pick-up area for their safari. Now everyone was keeping their eyes out for others who might not believe the group was on vacation. Their movements were always watched by those who waited like buzzards to cash in on anything the group of treasure hunters found.

Modesto broke out his computer and started to use his contacts to find all the living relatives of Jon Jon Vieux. Before his computer warmed up, a name came back from Interpol. Apparently, Jon Jon had a younger brother Barbos Marcel Vieux, cooling his heels in a Florida prison while the three couples were dancing around dodging bullets from his older brother. Barbos was released on parole a year ago. He hadn't been seen since.

"Lot of warrants out for him now," Modesto said.

The six friends felt certain there would be other interested parties waiting on them when the group arrived in Africa, but at least the three couples had the name of one of their admirers.

A few years back, Barbos Vieux's brother, Jon Jon Vieux, had kidnapped Chris's then girlfriend Lu, and attempted to rape her in front of a large crowd. She was rescued before he finished his crime, but he hounded the entire search and recovery of a fortune in gold uncovered in the Dominican Republic. While a final battle with the drug lord's army raged on the ship *Afrik-Rev,* Jon Jon slipped on board and held a knife to Lu's throat. She had a gun hidden on her and shot him several times, killing him before he took her head off with his knife. Now that she had seen Barbos at the Pub, she knew instantly this guy was a relative. Her instinctive fear was that she would meet the brother of the evil person she had shot to death. It would occur somehow, sometime, someplace and she would have to deal with him. Lu hoped she would be ready when it happened.

Chapter 15

Abu Camp, Okavango Delta, Botswana,
Africa

The jungle drums were powerful, sensuous and so fitting for this large piece of African paradise. Chris and Lu were experiencing their first night in the Abu Lodge. A nearby native village had furnished the drum and dance demonstrations. The small crowd clinked together stylish glasses filled with after-dinner drinks in celebration of what was most surely a large checkmark on their respective bucket-lists of accomplishments. They all watched the sun go down over the wet delta, but most of the guests could not take their eyes off the furnishings in the beautiful lodges. The floors were polished teak as was much of the furniture. As difficult as it was to believe, every lodge was actually a tent. The huge beams and framing made them arguably some the most beautiful tents in the world. Most of the bedrooms had real zebra skin rugs and zip up full length doors to the outside deck. Most of the rooms had outside bath tubs and if you were really brave there were 'star beds' that allowed for a romantic evening completely in the open above the elephant enclosure. Everything opened up to the wild—even bedrooms had that option. Parts of the conversations could be heard, including such phrases as, "Don't these people know there are wild animals out there that can eat our faces off?"

While the drums sounded out a traditional dance melody, Lu and Chris had devious smiles on their faces as they sat at a small mahogany table with a designer lantern placed in the middle. The smiling couple was sharing the table and the extraordinary view with their best friends, Mit Kruger, Angel Dominguez, and Gretchen and Modesto Tejeda.

Mit spoke first. "Are you goofballs still going to go out on an elephant tonight?" He was also smiling like a monkey.

"Hell yes!" Chris and Lu spoke in unison.

"Did you guys tell the elephant driver what you guys are going to do in the backseat of that elephant rack thingy?" asked Angel who was suppressing the urge to laugh.

"Yes, I believe he got the picture, and the driver is called a mahout. We think there will be room in that padded thingy to…get the job done," Chris answered.

In a few moments a native wearing an Abu Camp shirt stopped by their table and introduced himself as Jambi. He asked Lu if they were ready for the night elephant adventure. They were most likely part of a long line of tourists who had requested this little mile high club on the back of an elephant.

"Jambi, do you mind if I take my pistol along for protection?" Chris asked.

"If it makes you happy Mr. Chris, but you can no shoot it here since this no a hunting camp," Jambi answered with some apprehension in his voice.

Chris and Lu headed to their rooms and asked Jambi to wait for a couple minutes while they dressed for the ride.

Lu and Chris had stripped down to total nakedness, wrapping themselves in bathrobes that sported large Abu Camp monograms for the great safari lodge. They made a concession to put something on their feet, so both were wearing huge hiking boots. Although the clunky boots were unlaced, they looked ridiculous with the robes. To make matters more absurd, Chris strapped a pistol on his waist, but not just any pistol—a .50 caliber Desert Eagle which arguably was the most powerful handgun commonly in mass production.

As their elephant mahout, Jambi met them on the deck of the lodge. He was poorly suppressing an urge to laugh out loud. He led the two, who were stumbling around in the dark, to the side of a huge female elephant named Cathy. She was down on her belly making the loading process less of a chore, yet still a nice climb up a portable step ladder. The basket seat they had awkwardly fallen into had a padded bottom, two seats and side rails. There was a raised seat on the back side of the contraption, and Chris and Lu were now plotting their next move.

Jambi was not new to the safari business. He was accustomed to rich couples wanting to live out fantasies, yet just being on the Okavango Delta on the back of an elephant might be enough for most people. Not rich people. They always wanted something bizarre, and for a couple to have sex on the back of an elephant sloshing through swampy water in the heart of Africa was more common than people would expect. Chris and Lu had paid dearly to have Jambi put together this little adventure. If you're paying a few thousand a day for the safari then what's another thousand for a little nighttime fooling around? Thus another reason Jambi was smiling.

The elephant was causing a rolling and up and down motion. Chris took off his robe, placed it into the storage bag behind the back seat, and strapped his pistol belt around the side rail. Lu looked around to see if Jambi was facing ahead, then she slowly dropped her robe and exposed her beautiful body that was illuminated only by an African moon. Chris was pleased Lu had kept her gorgeous up-turned breasts and her flat stomach after giving birth to their son Reid three years before. She knew Chris was turned on by the completely shaved look, so she complied without complaining. If anyone knew Lu, getting her to do anything without causing a temper tantrum was difficult. She was to be feared when she was mad, and that was often.

Lu kneeled down and used her mouth to get Chris erect, and then she slid into his lap facing him and gently put him inside her. For a while they just let the movement of the elephant do all the work. They smiled at each other, kissed, and whispered short conversations to each other. It was magical and brought back memories of making love on Chris's speed boat, the *Blazing Lu,* after putting it on cruise control. At the time they had just verified the location of three billion dollars of gold that had been hidden by the Dominican dictator Rafael Trujillo. The vibrations of the boat had made that love making session an epic event. This time it was Africa. They could hear drums in the back ground and couldn't tell if the sounds were coming from their lodge or from a native village. Now Lu was moving faster trying to keep up with the beat of the drums.

Jambi had directed Cathy out of the marshy waters onto land and was sending her in the direction of a group of acacia trees. Lu would look Chris in the eyes and tell him she loved him, then look up at the millions of stars, then back at him. She was moving faster now and it was obvious she was moving into her orgasm, which was usually a loud affair. Because Jambi was only a few feet away, Chris was hoping this one wouldn't involve screaming since the elephant might stampede. Lu's moaning was softer now and apparently Chris was spent as well. Shortly after the two lovers had finished, Lu spoke quietly.

"Chris, darling, thank you so much for taking me on this safari. We really needed to take a break away from Reid and…what was that?"

No sooner had Lu gotten the last word out of her mouth than Chris saw a flash of yellow run across an out stretched limb of the acacia tree and landed right behind Lu on the edge of the front seat of the double elephant saddle. His tail brushed against Jambi's back. The leopard opened his mouth, snarled and flashed his enormous teeth.

"Don't move!" Chris commanded.

As the leopard laid his ears flat and growled, he also lowered his body in position to spring. Chris found the safety on the .50 caliber pistol, clicked it off, and pulled Lu closer to him. He held the pistol behind her bare back with a bead on the big cat. The dilemma was firing at the leopard without killing Jambi in the process.

"Lu, cover your ears!" As soon as she did, Chris fired a round well above the cat and woke up the entire country of Botswana in the process. The big leopard flew off the elephant and disappeared into the brush. Animals all over the area sounded off, but Chris and Lu could barely hear anything as they were temporally deafened by the explosion of the mighty weapon.

Their troubles were not over. Cathy was scared shitless and was on a dead run back towards the marsh. Jambi slid off his perch behind the giant ears of the elephant and hung on to one of the tusks for dear life. The two lovers grabbed the sides of the basket and did their best to hold on. Two naked people being bounced in and out of the basket and their mahout hanging on to a tusk would have made a great video. However, if Jambi fell off and was trampled by the huge beast he might rather have the .50 caliber slug in him instead. As the elephant hit the water it was obvious she was going to the elephant enclosure at Abu Camp. She wanted to go it alone though, and once in the water she shook off the riders and headed for home.

Completely naked, wearing hiking boots, and dripping swamp water and weeds, Chris and Lu walked onto the back deck of the beautiful Abu Camp Lodge while the other guests were sipping drinks and eating hor d'oeuvres'. Chris had his pistol in hand and threatened to shoot anyone that laughed at them. Regardless, they all laughed. Jambi could be seen running after his elephant. Chris and Lu knew their robes would be delivered to them the next day washed, ironed, and ready for a new adventure.

Chapter 16

Elephant Rides

An elephant safari filled the next two days and nights for the guests. By day, they traveled on the backs of elephants. At night, they enjoyed first-class food and beverage service in luxury tents. On the first night, Chris and Modesto sipped bourbon and African creek water near the campfire in the bush. Some members of the group went on a guided hike.

Chris was on the satellite phone to Bruny Jean-Baptise, the head of the Haitian expedition to Africa. He was a graduate of France's military academy and had served five years as an officer in the French Foreign Legion. Now, he was Haiti's Military Liaison Chief, a strange title, since Haiti no longer had an official army.

"Chris, we are now in Kinshasa putting together our convoy. Most of our supplies are here, including the scuba gear and the compressor you guys wanted. Our estimate is we will be able to get our truck within twenty miles of our target. We'll have to walk the rest of the way in. We do have a couple of copters to ferry some of the supplies to the site though. Will you guys be ready in about three or four days to meet the advance party at the airport in Kisangani?"

"Should be, Bruny, since we told the ladies we were going on our big lion hunt about that time," Chris said.

"Good deal. We will call you about twenty four hours before we reach the target. You guys have fun on the safari."

Modesto looked at Chris and frowned. "My sources tell me Kony's LRA forces might be active in that part of the jungle. Don't you think they'll get wind of what the Haitians are up to?" Modesto shook his head. "Truckloads of mercenaries with guns strapped to their backs guided by some of the Democratic Republic of the Congo's best soldiers. Guess what? That stuff will be communicated to everyone using everything from jungle drums to e-mail."

"Maybe we should have made an announcement on the African five o'clock news." Chris smiled, but he realized this was not the secret mission everyone had hoped for.

"Nothing we can do now, but I'll put those Haitian mercenaries up against anything the Lord's Resistance Army can throw at them. Don't forget our friends, Jackie and Devil Man, are with our group," Chris explained.

Jean-Jacques Boyer was called "Jackie," and his life-long friend Heraux Dartiquenave answered only to "Devil Man." Both of these Haitians had been rejected from hell. Jackie had an indentation on both sides of his cheek where a round had penetrated. It also knocked out teeth and jawbone. Devil Man was much worse. He had a hideous scar at the top of his right scalp that traveled down to his glazed, white eye. From the eye the scar branched off, one branch leading to an ear with a large chunk missing. The other ran down to his deformed lip. He stood over six feet six inches and weighed in at about two hundred and eighty pounds. Both of these men had proven themselves to Chris, Modesto, and Mit in battle in Haiti and the Dominican Republic. As monstrous and fearless as they were in battle, they were faithful friends. Lu loved them and had invited both to her wedding.

Loud talking and laughing signaled the return of the guests from the nature hike. Lu ran over, sat in Chris' lap, and kissed him.

"We had fun while you boozers stayed safe by the campfire." Lu said. She kissed him again. Gretchen went over and whispered something in Chris' ear. Angel followed and did the same thing.

"No! They're not going to let you go out at night on elephants after what we did." Chris was in disbelief after getting the message from the two girls.

"Oh, yes! My man, we can go, but you and Lu are banned for life from humping on elephants. If you haven't noticed, Cathy snorts any time you guys get near her." Mit said.

"From now on, what you two did is going to be a "Rite of Passage" for this camp—required of all Abu Camp guests who can still get it up," Gretchen said, laughing

Chris looked at Lu. "Well, dear, maybe we can climb a tree, and do it up there while they're gone."

"If the leopard will move over for us, then I'm game." Lu sounded serious, but Chris hoped she wasn't.

The Okavango Delta shifts from savanna flat lands with trees and bush to wet marsh lands that are green with vegetation. Chris planned this trip for the season when those contrasting environments existed. They were in the time period, after the wet season, before everything dried up and the animals migrated to areas where they might find more abundant food. The trip happened several months after the devastating earthquake in Haiti in January the same year. This earthquake gave dire importance to the alternate part of this safari vacation for the country of Haiti.

Chris had met with the captain of the old ship, the *Afrik-Rev*, in an attempt to learn what was going on with the gold shipments to the Ivory Coast. The old captain, Plato, was helpful, but there were still too many unsolved mysteries. After reading the original ship logs, Chris realized Papa Doc never made a single trip to Africa—not on the *Afrik-Rev* nor on any other ship, airplane or other mode of transportation. Research showed no record of Papa Doc ever making such a trip. His only connection to the continent was a brief visit in 1966 from Emperor Haile Selassie of Ethiopia to Haiti. The two men exchanged some sort of made up medals. Ethiopia became the only country to make an official state visit to Haiti during Papa Doc's reign. The two rulers also exchanged gifts, and Selassie hit the road, never to return.

On every journey to the Ivory Coast, the *Afrik-Rev* docked outside the major city of Abidjan. Trucks met the boat and departed to places unknown with that month's load of gold. Records indicated the trucks always numbered five. It wasn't clear if there was enough gold to require more than one truck, but five always made an appearance. One or two Haitian government officials would tag along, and they would disappear for several days. Presumably, they traveled hundreds of miles inland. Since none of the officials who came back on board ship ever disclosed where they went, no one really knew. These government representatives would never discuss the purpose of the trip while traveling to Africa or on the voyage back to Haiti.

The wooden crates were never opened on board. Usually, there were only ten or twelve, but when the crew came to unload them, they appeared to be heavy. Plato's crew was not allowed to touch the crates, either in the loading or unloading process. "Property of the Haitian Government," stenciled in French, was the only marking on the crates.

After 1966, a different sort of personnel began to make the trek with Haitian officials. Geologists took the passage along with their support personnel. They packed gear for the bush and didn't always come back with the crew when the ship departed. At times, some of them never were seen again. These changes started happening after the Selassie and Papa Doc meeting, so in some way, the state visit to Haiti had to be connected.

Only after Chris told Plato of his planned trip to Africa, did the real truth emerge. Plato revealed he now felt confident that a real expedition was going to take place, so he gave his most secret and coveted journals to Chris. The journals far surpassed what had been written in the ship's crusty old log and validated some of the information Chris received from his private investigators. Included were copies of Sony, Marc, and Jan's account of the trip to the quarry. Later he would obtain John and Vikki's handwritten journals with personal relationship passages deleted from Vikki's entries. They told the real story of all the trips to Africa and presented an accounting of every asset that belonged to Haiti. The truth was astonishing and incredible—and could possibly help an entire country recover from a horrible earthquake. Plato had been the officer in charge of millions of dollars of assets from the very beginning. Papa Doc would trust no one else.

Angel and Mit were the first to return from the elephant ride. If huge smiles could be interpreted as "the sex was great," then their faces said it all. Both of them just wore shorts and tee-shirts so that little time would be wasted.

"Did you guys see the leopard?" Lu asked.

"It could have been in the basket with us and we wouldn't have noticed," Mit said.

"He came to visit us because he was attracted to all the passion," Chris said, laughing.

"It was Lu's fake orgasm! He just had to see for himself," Angel said.

Angel and Mit had been together for three years but had yet to tie the knot. Angel had been married to a rocker who wouldn't get off of drugs; Mit's wife was killed in a car accident back in Germany a few years back. From the time they first met there was a special connection. Maybe it was the shared pain of failed first marriages, or maybe they liked the freedom of a partnership without paperwork. In either case, they hadn't picked a date, or discussed marriage, except when Chris, Lu, Modesto, and Gretchen pestered them.

The next elephant to lumber into camp had Modesto and Gretchen hanging over the side rails laughing and hanging their tongues out to show their exhausted pleasure. Chris and Lu were really glad those two workaholics were having a good time. Modesto had completed law school a year back and was the Dominican Republic's assistant Attorney General with his sights on even higher public office. Gretchen had finished her residency requirement at a large teaching hospital in Santo Domingo. She joined the staff as a vascular surgeon and was in charge of every German tourist who walked through the door. Modesto stepped down as head of the D.R.'s military intelligence to go to law school. Both were at the top of their class in everything they did, and none of their other friends felt they played or had nearly enough fun. On this safari, however, they were off to a good start.

The camp staff invited everyone to sit at an elegant long table replete with candles. The glassware sparkled and the gorgeous china and silverware were in place, as it would be in the Dorchester in London or any fine hotel. In the distance, monkeys, hyenas, and an occasional far off lion would sound off for their benefit. Behind the table on both sides were magnificent tents decorated with lanterns. The setting was more than magical. Everyone just looked at each other like they were in a dream taking place in the bush in Africa.

They didn't care to wake up.

Chapter 17

The Lion Hunt

The lion hunt would be tricky. Besides the deception they were putting over on their wives and girlfriend, the men had only three days to bag a few rogue lions and then meet up with an expedition to explore a deep blue hole in the middle of the Congo. All this in the general region where the Lord's Resistance Army killed people for sport. Rational tourists would have stayed in camp and continued to have sex on the back of elephants.

The adventure following a three day safari had been planned for the next morning after returning to camp. After lunch the three men would be flown to an airstrip, transfer to a private jet, and fly for several hours to the airport in Kisangani, formerly known as Stanleyville. A jet helicopter would take them deep into the Congo to rendezvous with other crazy people like themselves.

A few nights previously, the phone conversation had changed everything. Chris learned the expedition they were to meet might not be on site for two or three more days. The lion hunt would have to come first.

Rogue lions and elephants have lost their habitat in so many areas of Africa that sometimes they come into villages and kill livestock and humans. Once they become man-eaters, a cycle begins that requires them to be removed by lethal means. Rangers hunt them and issue game licenses and permits for hunters or guides for a sanctioned kill. Permits are not free, but cheaper than the thirty or forty thousand dollar lion hunts that take place in some African countries. Man-eaters present a special problem. Since the lions normally attack at night or at dusk and have no fear of humans, the hunts are particularly dangerous. Such was the case in the village of Mlogulu, south of the town of Tabora in the country of Tanzania. Game wardens did not often frequent the area because it was not part of a protected game reserve. A special expedition would be called in to protect the village. Chris, Mit, and Modesto paid for the hunting permits and two guides to go with them, and the local game warden.

Their small plane landed on a dirt strip north of the village. The game warden met them and introduced himself as Frank Stiner. Behind his thick German accent was a very friendly gentleman. Frank was reaching retirement age, maybe he already had, and was just hanging in there. He was short and slightly built, and his face was wrinkled beyond his years from the African sun.

They loaded all the equipment into the Rover and waited on another Range Rover that held the experienced big game hunters the group had hired. The second car fell in behind Frank's vehicle for the hour-long drive to the village. Most of the hilly and dry terrain looked too poor for farming or cattle raising. The land appeared desert-like except for some areas around rivers and streams that had vegetation. Maybe a goat would be happy here.

"Frank, what's this I hear about Tanzania's lion population being in such good shape?" asked Chris.

The game warden had given his speech so many times that the words were second nature, and would fill the time needed to reach the village.

"Tanzania has the best record for maintaining their lion population of any country in Africa, and they do it by killing lions." He looked at the three men to see if they were shocked, but they were composed. "You duck hunters in the U.S. understand this somewhat twisted logic, since 'Ducks Unlimited' uses a similar conservation method. Duck hunters provide the money and direction to insure that the ducks are allowed to maintain their flyways and nesting sites. The hunters vigorously coordinate limits on types of ducks and quantities harvested with state and federal wildlife officials.

Tanzania operates a similar program with laws that only allow killing of mature male lions. The country fiercely protects females, cubs, and young male lions. Their lion population is the largest in Africa and fairly stable. Poaching is still a problem everywhere in Africa. Income from hunting supports the economy and funds conservation of the lions. Proposed laws in the U.S. are putting this income in jeopardy. If the United States passes a law restricting the import of lion pelts because they see lions as endangered, which they are in other countries, then Tanzania would lose sixty percent of their hunting related income." Looking at all the men he continued. "You Americans would not come to hunt a species that you couldn't mount on your wall back home especially after spending thousands of dollars on travel and hunting fees. This strange dilemma is something we Tanzanians understand, but the rest of the world is left scratching their collective heads." He smiled with pride, for being so well informed.

"Uh, Frank, my man. I am not an American—German." Mit explained.

"Frank—dude…I only went to college in the U.S. I'm Dominican." Modesto added.

"Sorry, I guess I should have made my speech with an international flavor," he said sarcastically.

"Arkansas is almost a third world country," Chris said, laughing.

The two Land Rovers slowed down before they reached the village, so the red dust wouldn't blow from under the vehicles and turn Mlogulu into another Pompei. Both vehicles came to a stop outside the thornbush barricades that surrounded the village. The scene looked like a thousand others in Africa.

This village rested in an area of Tanzania which hadn't been converted to Christianity. Mormons, however, were active nearby so the locals needed to stay on their toes. The people of the village have clung to a strict Muslim faith, so they don't eat wild bush pigs. Since the swine were never thinned out, the bush pigs often raid the vegetable crops grown in Muslim villages. Lions followed to prey on the pigs. Being opportunistic animals, lions had been killing and eating the villagers who were slow and catchable rather than pursuing the speedy wild pigs. Now that the big cats had developed a taste for the local natives, they had placed the villagers high on their menu of delicious and easy prey. Although the village had built bush pig fences around the crops, it was too late to stop the lions from attacking.

Chris, Mit and Modesto were told the theories behind the attacks on the village of Mlogulu. Entire prides of lions had killed at least a dozen natives in the last two months. Because of their hunting permits the three friends would be allowed to kill any lions near the village regardless of the lions' sex or age. Mit had a game warden friend in Kenya who had alerted him to the problem. They had been in contact with the Tanzanian warden by phone. The latest phone call to Mit was urgent, since another attack had occurred three days before. Lions need about eleven pounds of meat a day to survive but can eat as much as seventy or eighty pounds at a time. The overall assessment was the lions were about to head back to the dinner table.

In some places in South Africa, lions are raised in captivity and then released into the wild a few days before a hunt. This type of hunting is often called "canned lion hunts." These hunts have caused uproar from conservationists and the general public. On the other hand, surely the lions these men would face would have no fear of humans. The men might be a canned hunt for the lions.

The three men from Abu Camp introduced themselves to the hired guns and learned their names. Mickey Hanson and Will Carpenter worked for a safari firm in Northern Tanzania. They looked the part and according to their resumes, were the real thing. Both were about six feet two inches tall with sun bleached hair and skin that was burned brown.

Will requested a quick strategy meeting. He asked the village chief where the lions normally came in. They walked the area, a low naturally wide path between two ridges. Some trees dotted the otherwise arid land.

"Here is what I suggest, and I will defer to Frank since he is the local warden. We don't need to be out in the open to face up to ten to fifteen lions at night. A hunt in the daylight would be a challenge since their nature is to attack once they see you. You just wound them— they come right at you. Fast, deadly...perfect killers. So, I suggest two tree stands and two Range Rover roof stands. Put the stands in those two trees." He pointed at two of the tallest acacia trees, and then he indicated where he wanted the trucks stationed.

"I will ask the chief to surround the trucks and the base of the trees with thorn bushes and to help with building the stands. Frank, what are your thoughts?" He turned his gaze towards the warden, who had been silently nodding in the affirmative.

"I agree with you, Will, but we need one hunter to be in the village to take out lions that get through or go around the other hunters. The lone hunter will be pretty exposed—maybe around a circle of thorn bushes, but he must be able to pick off the beasts quickly," the warden said, suddenly aware of the frigging danger of this hunt.

"For those of you in tree stands—lions climb trees in a split second. Those on a Rover roof—they can jump over the thorn barriers in a millisecond. Kill spots will be hard to judge at night. Keep extra rifles, handguns, and ammo close by. Once you hit a lion and he goes down—shoot him again. They have a bad habit of coming back to life. Watch your buddy's back," Mickey spat this out as if he was about to take an unnamed suicide hill in Korea. No one said much—just a few "holy shits" and a "fuck me—we're toast," from the group of non-professional hunters.

In addition to the rifles brought by the three amateurs, Will and Mickey issued back up weapons to everyone. They were bolt action Weathersby .460s, and could stop a dump truck at a thousand yards. However, one needed to be a good shot, since it only held three cartridges—two in the receiver and one in the chamber. One special weapon to be used by the person stationed at the village was a Barrett 82A1 .50 caliber semi-automatic rifle with several ten round clips. When Will pulled the Barrett out of the back of his Range Rover, the group gasped audibly. This weapon had been used by combat soldiers in Iraq and Afghanistan to take out targets at some distance. The rifle was so powerful and accurate it was deemed—"one shot, one kill."

Will asked the group if anyone had ever fired that weapon.

"I own one and the conversion kit for taking it to a .416 caliber."

Chris said. Modesto and Mit were not surprised, as they felt certain Chris owned an Abrams tank. He was a gun nut beyond reason.

"You will guard the village then. What other gun did you bring?" Will asked.

"My Holland and Holland .375 and my Desert Eagle .50 caliber pistol." Chris stated proudly.

"Fancy crap! If it gets down to you pulling out that pistol, you might just shoot yourself rather than being eaten alive." Mickey said. Though he smiled as he spoke, he meant every word. He gave the impression of being battle tested, rugged, and a loyal partner in a foxhole.

Will and Frank were deciding where to place people according to each person's experience. Mit had spent the least time with large caliber weapons, but he was a damn good shot. He had seen action where people actually shot back at him. Modesto had trained with all kinds of weapons including a few rounds through a Barrett .50 cal. He and Chris had fought and survived a small war in Haiti a few years back. That kind of fighting was not anything either of them wanted to repeat. The three friends from Abu camp wondered what the hell they had signed up for. At first, they had been led to believe there were two lions at the most. Now it was a pride—or maybe two prides—that just might out-number the guns pointed at them. This was scary, but it was too late to back out. The villagers' lives were at stake.

Mit and Mickey teamed up in a tree stand built with scrap lumber from the village. Modesto was stationed on the top of a Land Rover. Frank took the other vehicle, while Will got in the second tree stand and pulled up his rifles and ammo by a rope. Chris found his way to the little fort made of African boxthorn and climbed up using two ladders. Inside the fort were thirty gallon barrels, so he could stand above the bushes to shoot. A huge ceremonial drum was even taller than the barrels. Chris asked for blankets to drape across the top of the thorn bushes, so he could place the big Barrett on them for support. He also received thick rugs, promised to be more useful, since it would be difficult for the three-inch thorns to penetrate them. The hunters were enjoying a meal of vegetables prepared by the villagers.

Everyone hoped the attack would come before dark, but in case they were unlucky, each man had spotlights to seek out the lions.

Since the circle of thorns was set up in a large clearing next to the dirt road leading into the village, Chris had great views. He was about 200 yards to the rear of the Land Rovers. The tree stands were farther still. If a lion escaped the other five hunters, Chris would be able to kill the lion before the pride reached the front of the village. Directly to the rear of Chris's position, was a hillside infested with a thick growth of thorn bushes. Chris realized that beyond poisonous snakes, crocodiles, and man-eating lions, thorns were the next worst threat in Africa. So many varieties of thorns peppered the land— there were even thorn trees.

The sun colored the sky with pastel orange streaks, and the light became much softer. All the men were on high alert, hoping the big cats might come in before dark. A runner from the tribe came up the trail at a fast clip and told Frank he had seen movement from the pride, several miles away. The villagers had tracked the lions and found where they usually bedded down. The pride was up and walking around. No one knew if the lions were headed in the direction of the village, as the natives didn't hang around to see. One of the natives said he had never seen so many lions. Frank passed around this information on two way radios, and said something few of the hunters could comprehend. "Could be a super pride—couple prides combined," Frank said. His voice sounded tense.

In the heat, insects thrived on stationary targets. In Africa at dinner time, every living being appeared to feed off the next lower animal on the food chain. Night would be upon them, and in the darkness, bellies were filled at the expense of others. Africa can be terrifying at night, but for now, twilight still reigned.

Chris thought he heard something on the brushy hill behind him. He turned to look, but didn't see anything. Just to be sure, he swung the Barrett around and adjusted the scope. He guessed the edge of the thicket was between one hundred and two hundred yards away. As the scope was focused it gave a read-out of 163 yards—elevation 27 feet. Chris worked the scope in grids, seeing only dense grass and bushes. No movement.

Then, he realized that a thorn had pierced his hunting jacket and was trying to poke a hole in his arm. He placed a thick rug on the thorn bushes, and stood on the big drum. He took another look through the scope moving to 189 yards—elevation—46 feet. A blur of yellow fur flashed behind a bush—then another and another. Chris felt his heart pounding as loudly as the drum he stood on could be played.

He pulled a cartridge out of his vest. Sliding the lever on the .50 cal. back, he inserted the extra bullet, leaving a full ten in the magazine. He sent the bullet into the chamber, clicked off the safety, and adjusted the tripod on the front of the barrel. The big cats had decided to flank everyone and attack from the rear, avoiding the mass of hunters on the lion's much used trail. All the lions were running—how could he get a shot?

A male lion, still for a second, popped his head out around a thicket. Chris took the shot. The recoil almost knocked him off the drum. The lion fell immediately, but Chris scrambled to get back in position to fire again. Unlike firing from the ground, there was nothing to absorb the recoil but Chris's own body—he would just have to adapt. The thorn bushes were no help. Back behind the scope, he tried to find a stationary target, but couldn't. Near the bottom of the thicket, he spotted two yellow objects, soon to be in the clear. He focused on them. His walkie-talkie in his vest crackled, but there was no time to answer.

The first lion emerged. In an instant, Chris made part of his head explode. The second lion never slowed—charged straight for Chris, with his eyes on him like a missile locked on target. Chris fired and hit the hindquarter, causing the lion to flip over. To Chris's disbelief, the lion came up and locked on target again, aiming for him. This time, Chris's shot found the head and spine. The male lion turned his head and magnificent mane, just before he collapsed and slid into the maroon colored dirt.

The first two had been males—bigger and slower than females. At this instant, three immature lionesses hit the level ground at lightning speed toward Chris's little fort. Chris decided to take a quick shot on each to slow them and come back for the kill. His semi-automatic allowed him to accomplish the initial shots with three taps of his finger. Amazingly, all three lions got back up to charge. *What are these animals made of?* Chris thought. He tapped three more times. Only one got up again—another tap from Chris.

The two way radio was going nuts, but four lionesses and a young male had just broken free of the bushes and headed his way. Chris slapped another magazine in the Barrett, even though he wasn't sure of the count. He found each of the speeding lions and sent a round into each one. Four of the lions got up like ghosts from the red African dust and came at him again. Chris had never seen a more persistent beast of any kind. Chris found all of them again in his scope and popped them with head shots.

On the heels of the four he had just killed were three more—all mature lionesses—and closing in fast. He found one and brought her down. He moved the scope. He pulled the trigger and heard a click— out of ammo with no time to reload—he grabbed the H&H .375 and fired at one of the lions. She flipped over a couple of times, but kept moving. The other lioness had reached jumping distance of the fort. She took the leap and cleared the thorn bushes. Chris fired while the cat was in the air and hit her underneath. The wounded cat fell into the fort. Though she was bleeding profusely from her gut, she remained hunkered, ready to pounce from the opposite end of the enclosure beside the metal barrels.

Chris found the handle of his pistol and brought it up to fire. Before he could shoot, the other wounded lion pounced on the rug where the Barrett was lying and was preparing to launch herself. In a second, a pink mist blew out of her head, and then the sound of a gunshot could be heard from behind Chris. Without hesitation Chris started sending .50 caliber pistol slugs into the lion who had invited herself into his fort. By the time he spent his last shell, there was no more movement in her carcass.

The men packed up and readied themselves to head to return to the airstrip, but not until the village chief gave Chris a ceremonial spear, shield, headdress, and a small bag made of an animal skin. Chris peered into the bag. Ten large uncut blue tanzanite stones, found only in Northern Tanzania, astonished him. How the chief came to possess these rare and valuable gems, Chris had no clue, but he was thrilled and divided them with Modesto and Mit.

Later, Chris learned that Mickey had taken that shot from 300 yards. Soon, all the men gathered at his compound, amazed at the carnage. Fourteen lions lay dead, and Chris had taken all of them but one. If Mickey hadn't made that shot, the last lion probably would have killed Chris. Facing both of those wounded lions would be the subject of some sweaty nightmares for years to come.

Hopefully, thought Chris, the natives would now be safe from the lions. The Mormons, however, moved closer to the village gates every day.

Chapter 18

Spies

Since they left the Dominican Republic a few days before, Chris and Lu Zacharius had been under constant surveillance. Even though the team assembled for the secret expedition to the Congo was small, they had security leaks. Of course, the information highway runs more smoothly when money is allocated. Barbos Vieux had a keen interest in anything Chris Zacharius did, since in most cases Chris' efforts involved a treasure hunt, no matter how cleverly he might disguise them. Barbos didn't buy the story of the safari and felt quite sure the three amigos would make some excuse to leave the girls at the lodge and head out on their own. He arranged for a young couple at Abu Camp to call him with daily reports on the comings and goings of the group from the Dominican Republic.

Roland and Zoe Dishongh were white Haitians who had lost a great deal of money in a venture in Port au Prince. They accepted the spying job from a private detective agency for assistants offered through a newspaper ad. Their mission would be to report on a group of travelers at a safari camp in Africa. They would be paid handsomely and get a free trip to Africa. Dead broke, they bit on the offer and made few inquiries about their new employer. They had worked very hard to build a resort in Haiti. All their savings and borrowed money from their parents was literally wiped out on January 12th when the earthquake hit. Insurance only paid a small amount of their mortgage after the huge deductible for earthquakes. They didn't have nearly enough money to rebuild. Who would be so crazy as to put up a new resort in such a broken country? The couple longed for a new start, and no pair on earth deserved a vacation more than Roland and Zoe Dishongh.

So far Roland and Zoe had left Barbos the information on his cell phone concerning the three couples, including nighttime elephant rides where sexual activities took place on the backs of unsuspecting pachyderms. Barbos laughed and said "kinky." However, the couple left out the part where they themselves did the same thing on a different night. During cocktails one evening, the two spies had drinks with the group and learned the boys were planning a lion hunt. Mr. Vieux received that information more enthusiastically than details about elephant sex.

The two attractive, young, well dressed people made friends easily and mixed well in a crowd. Both were college educated in Miami and came from very good families. Had either set of parents known their kids were working for a famous drug trafficker, they would have flipped out and given them all the money they needed. But this couple didn't want any more handouts from parents. Also, if a yuppie class existed in Port au Prince, these two would be charter members. They liked being around educated and well-heeled people, even though Roland and Zoe had no idea where their lives would take them after this African gig. Also, they had no idea how the information they were giving Barbos would be used. People planning to make investments in Africa needed the information. Barbos assured them nothing illegal was involved.

The truth was, Barbos Marcel Vieux had done little in his life that could be classified as remotely legal. He was released from jail in Florida because of an overcrowded prison system. Deportation was a free trip back to Haiti to piece together the crumbling drug empire of his brother, Jon Jon Vieux. Barbos found he had to eliminate some excess personnel who had slivered into management slots in the organization. All in all, 2008 was a rebuilding year for Barbos. At times, blood ran freely. Solidly back at the helm of Haiti's vast and profitable narcotics trade, Mr. Vieux was flying high.

Then came the earthquake. Planes couldn't take off, ships couldn't get in the harbors, and worst of all the roads that allowed ground transportation to the sites where drugs leave the country were destroyed. Haiti was often called the drug parking lot of the Caribbean, but this time the drugs were truly parked. Barbos worked desperately to repair the roads, with many in the country praising his efforts as a humanitarian. He accepted the accolades in stride, but had his own devious reasons to patch up the potholes and cavernous gaps in huge sections of the highway.

Stealing all or part of Chris Zacharius' treasure would surely recoup some of Mr. Vieux's losses. He had his own twin engine plane and would shadow Chris and his two friends all over Africa if needed, which is exactly what he did. After the lion hunt Chris, Mit and Modesto left the village of Mloguhu, Tanzania and traveled to the nearby airstrip to be shuttled to a larger airport where Chris's aircraft was waiting. When they arrived on a small plane at Tabora to board their private jet, Barbos' private Gulf Stream was sitting in the dark awaiting take-off. The surfaced, treated, gravel airstrip was better for the jet and the Gulf Stream than dirt, but still was not a real runway. Barbos had paid local airport officials to find the jet's flight plan. However, no one aboard the Gulf Stream had a visa for the Democratic Republic of the Congo, where Chris and his friends were going. This problem could be fixed, but would require time and dealing with some of the most wretched people on earth. There was one particular person Barbos had done business with before and had sworn he wouldn't make that mistake again. The man's name was Joseph Kony.

~~~~~

Zoe was most likely going to be a problem for Barbos as well. She was too perfect for the part—pretty, well dressed and hip. Before long, Lu, Gretchen, and Angel latched on to her and took her everywhere they went—photo safaris to take pictures of cheetahs, a trip to town for shopping, but mainly to the spas. Not only the spas at their resort, but any within reach of the private helicopter at their disposal. Zoe's husband Roland either played pool with the men or went trap shooting and seemed fine that Zoe was having a good time.

As they sat in a nail salon getting pedicures, Zoe shared with the group what had happened to her resort. She and Roland had built a large shed from the rubble and provided jobs for Haitians at ten dollars a day to rescue mattresses and furniture, to be stored in the shed. Anything that could be saved—such as lamps, toilets, mirrors, shower curtains—anything salvageable was brought to the shed. Serviceable lumber was stacked under tarps next to the shed, along with concrete blocks and bricks. Guards watched over the items twenty-four hours a day. Their earthquake insurance had a deductible of ten percent of the value of the resort, which was about one million US dollars. After that, insurance only covered less than half of their mortgage, paid directly to the bank. They would be required to make the monthly payments again, starting the first of the year. So far, the bank had not agreed to give them money to rebuild, and they had no desire to do business with anyone in Haiti.

"Tell me about your parents, Zoe." Lu said.

"My father is a cardiologist who works between Port au Prince and Santo Domingo, and my mom owned a jewelry store in town that was destroyed by the quake. All the inventory was in a safe and survived. My dad's clinic was flattened, but he can work in the hospital, which has been partly repaired."

"What is your dad's name?" Gretchen said. She had told Zoe that she was a doctor in Santo Domingo.

"Dr. Stefrey Brouard."

"I know your dad!" Gretchen blurted. "I have actually assisted him on a stent placement during my rotation. He is one hell of a doctor and a damn nice guy."

"Thank you Gretchen. He and mom helped us so much, I just couldn't go back to them again, especially since I have a brother and sister who always have their hands out."

"What about Roland's parents? And by the way, he looks like a French race car driver. One frigging hot catch for you," Angel said. She couldn't help but notice Zoe's hunk of a husband.

"Well, they have helped as well. Roland's dad is an attorney and well placed in the government in the Department of Justice. His mom inherited some money from her dad so she doesn't work. He has four brothers and three sisters, and most of them have kids. He is the baby of the family and at the bottom of the food chain, so to speak."

"We owe both families money, and I hate it." Zoe's eyes were filling with tears. "We were doing well, and with all the relief workers there we knew we could make our mortgage payments for a while. Long term, I just don't know if it's worth rebuilding," she said.

"Please, let's talk about something fun. I don't want to mess up your vacation. Did I tell you that Roland and I went on the night elephant ride? How cool was that? And yes, we did it too!" She managed to smile and wipe her wet eyes with a Kleenex.

Zoe had no idea about the three girls' background. She got a sense they had money, because of their use of a helicopter and some of the jewelry they wore. She had worked in her mother's store and learned quickly. She guessed if the rose diamonds the girls wore were real, the combined value topped her mom's entire inventory.

What she didn't know was Lu alone could probably write a check for downtown Port au Prince with her share of the royalties on the gold found in the D.R. Then there was the hundred million inheritance from her dad's deceased wife in Boston. Gretchen and Angel also had equal shares from the DR gold. None of the ladies were worth less than a hundred million dollars. Actually, the value was much more, since everyone took shares in gold bullion, which had almost doubled in the last few years. The wheels were turning in their head, but nobody said a word.

Lu decided to lighten the conversation. "Look, Zoe. Our guys are off on some macho lion hunt in another damn country—so what is the chance that you loan us Roland while they are gone? We will take turns and return him to you in good shape….tired but in good shape."

"Me first," Angel said.

"Hey, I've seen him look at you guys. He always wants us to sit next to you or have a drink with you. He would be all for it, but then I might not get him back. Do you have any frigging idea how hard it was to land that guy? Don't make me go to that trouble again." She laughed, but down in her gut, she was in agony about spying on these people she truly liked.

Once their nails were dry, it was time for massages, but only after the four drank a nice white wine, which relaxed everyone. Zoe and Lu were the first to the massage room, where two tables were set up. Both therapists were native Africans who had been trained in South Africa. From the reports of other guests they were excellent. Zoe and Lu started face down in a heart shaped hole in the table, and the therapists worked first through the sheet, massaging lightly, and then moved the sheets down above the buttocks. They did nice long relaxing strokes with thin lavender scented oil.

Zoe's emotions affected by the wonderful massage, and the guilt raging through her body caused her to erupt in uncontrollable crying. The therapist stopped and asked if she was okay. Clients sometimes cry during the emotional release of a massage. This was not that kind of crying, but rather a gut wrenching bawling of the first order. Lu sat up on the side of her table, and called Zoe's name. Zoe didn't want to get up. Finally Lu went over, put her arm around her. Zoe sat up and started to apologize to Lu.

"Lu, I'm so sorry. I'm an awful person. I can't live with this anymore. Please forgive me," she said, while she sat on the table, sobbing. Her tears fell on her olive skin and all the way down to her exposed breasts. Lu looked at her. Here was a gorgeous young woman in distress, and Lu had no clue why.

"Roland and I were broke, working day and night for months, in what looked like an impossible situation. A friend alerted us to a newspaper ad from a private detective in need of a married couple for a few weeks. The requirement would be to go to Africa on a safari—all expenses paid, and cash—a lot of cash. The detective said it was all legal, and he just needed to know about possible investment opportunities that some people on the safari were looking into." Lu's jaw hung open. "I think all of you are great people, and I can't do this anymore," Zoe said. She got up and started putting her clothes on.

"Who hired you, Zoe?" Lu asked sternly.

"We never met him—just talked on the phone. He sent us the tickets and money by courier. But he told us his name was Barbos something—Vu or Vieux—I think. We didn't investigate much because we wanted to get away so badly."

Lu walked out in the waiting room completely naked, and addressed the other women.

"Girls, we got trouble! Let's get our asses back to the lodge. Does anyone have a sat phone with them?"

"I do," Zoe said.

🐘

Chapter 19

Sony and Carol

The expedition from Haiti arrived in Kisangani following a grueling journey from the capital, Kinshasa. They made good time—if three days could be considered good—for traveling almost a thousand miles. Kisangani was known as Stanleyville until the sixties, when Mobutu decided to rid the country of western influence. The airport was the assembly area, with some of the expedition flying out in helicopters and the main forces going overland.

Trucks and Jeeps took the same general path that John and Vikki Cole took in 1966. Some of the roads were paved now, and a few new logging trails would allow them to get within fifteen to twenty miles of the island in the middle of the Aruwimi River.

An overall expedition plan had been put together by Bruny Jean-Baptiste, who was in charge of the entire operation. Haiti had brought a few troops, the term used loosely, since Haiti no longer had an official army. Bruny's personnel from Haiti consisted of ten mercenaries and himself, along with two personnel helicopters and one large supply helicopter, two trucks, and two Humvees, donated to Haiti by the U.S. Along for the ride for protection and to solidify the government's interest in the mining concession were ten members of the DRC's military. This particular concession had been extremely profitable for the Democratic Republic of the Congo in the last forty-four years. As far as anyone knew, the government had never inspected the mine, yet they received a huge check every month for mining royalties. An Ivory Coast bank mailed the monthly check based on diamonds being sold off at certain times of the year from the large collection brought in by John Cole. John and Vikki had also received checks for their twenty-five percent ownership.

To represent the family, John and Vikki's son, Michael Sony Cole, joined the expedition. He was in his early forties, and a mechanical engineer who worked at his dad's oil company. His twin sisters, Jan and Zuka, wanted desperately to go, but everyone warned them about the dangers for women in this part of Africa. Kidnapping and rape occurred on a scale off the charts. Their brother, Sony, promised to fly them in later when the country settled down. No one expected that to happen until the next Ice Age. The twin girls were a few years younger and both had children.

Sony was recently divorced and hadn't done much dating. He wanted kids. His former wife couldn't have any, and she had no desire to adopt. Neither had really messed around, but the flame just went out, and they thought they would be happier going their separate ways. Sony needed an adventure.

The advance crew going by helicopter consisted of Sony, Chris, Mit, Modesto, and an assortment of geologists, mine engineers, military officers, a doctor, and a couple of cultural experts. Devil Man and Jackie would also go as security for the advance party. Each helicopter held six people and a lot of gear, but according to the logs kept by Vikki Cole, the dimensions of the enclosure would accommodate them.

Bruny had contacted John and Vikki by phone and in person in Texas before taking on his expedition leader job. He found them in good health. John, in his seventies, and Vikki in her late sixties, were retired and enjoyed being grandparents. Several of the original expedition members had kept journals, but Vikki's was by far the most precise. She gave Bruny a copy and added notes she thought might be helpful. Of course, her private notes referring to her relationship with John were removed. Since she had used the expedition as part of her requirements for her Master's degree in geology, she had written an outstanding paper that later became her dissertation. Bruny had also read the dissertation. The final work was also shared with the expedition leader. Most of the other prominent members of the 1966 trip had died or had not been located. Jan, Marc, and Sony had all passed away. Michael "Sony" Cole was fortunate enough to have met the real Sony when he came to visit the Coles in Texas about twenty years ago. The Coles had paid for a reunion of the expedition at their place, including travel expenses for the survivors who were willing to come.

John had taken the reins of Hanover Oil from Vikki's dad, Mike. Now Sony was in line to do the same. He had prepared for this expedition as though he were a NASA official planning a trip to Mars. He knew the types of snakes indigenous to the area, along with a full inventory of wild life. In his mind, the biggest risk was not disease, snakes, elephants, poison arrows, or any piece of the landscape's flora or fauna. Rather, the big peril awaiting them was rebel forces that had plagued the Congo for years. A downsized but still lethal remnant of Kony's Lord's Resistance Army was reported to be moving between the Central African Republic, Uganda, Somalia, and occasionally into the Democratic Republic of the Congo. No, the peril was dozens of so called rebel factions—most of them without names.

Sony may have planned his butt off for this trip, but he was not prepared for a young anthropologist who stood next to the large helicopter he was about to board.

She extended her hand "Hi! I'm Carol Barbot."

Sony was in shock. Here stood a woman brushing back long blonde-streaked brown hair from her face—a runway model face. Beautiful white teeth glistened behind a smile wrapped with gorgeous full lips. She flashed lovely green eyes. He also noticed her dark olive complexion. As her soft feminine hand shook his, Sony sized up her body quickly and efficiently. All was in perfect harmony. Even her breasts were in motion while she and Sony shook hands. He had to act cool, since this most likely was the most beautiful woman he had ever touched, even in the form of a mere handshake.

"Carol, very nice to meet you. I'm Michael Sony Cole. You can call me Sony," he said, as calmly as possible for a man who hadn't been laid in a year. Now he was holding the hand of a first degree sex goddess.

"Did your parents name you after their television set?" She said. Her lips curled in a quirky smile.

"After the clock-radio next to their bed. Seemed like the thing to do after conception," Sony said with a straight face. He had been down the Sony name road too many times.

Carol laughed out loud. She had met her match at smart-ass conversation. She might possibly have just met someone as handsome as she was beautiful. Sony was six foot three, slim, athletic, with a combination of his mother's and dad's good looks taken up a notch and capped off with a head of thick blond hair and piercing blue eyes.

"Did they hire you to be our expedition comedian, or do you have a real job here?" she quipped.

"My parents own part of the mining concession, and I'm not sure why I'm here. And you were sent here to keep our minds off of the perils of the jungle?" Sony said, a little sarcastically.

"Absofuckinglutely! Once I strip down to bathe in the river, the pygmies will line the banks, and you guys just shoot them all," she said, also with sarcasm.

Sony laughed, and realized this woman was a lot of fun. "Just in case—since I would be lining the bank to watch as well—would you mind telling them not to shoot me?"

"You're golden, Sony. I will save you from pygmies and friendly fire every time."

"Carol, now really, tell me about yourself with the least amount of fabrication possible."

"You make things hard for me, Sony. I was thinking about liking you—but now it's over." She was clearly having fun with him. "I am a certified first class cultural anthropologist. With three degrees, for which I am also—like a doctor. Not a real doctor who would ask you to drop your drawers—not that I might not ask that of you sometime, but the Ph.D. kind where you don't get to see people naked."

"So, Carol, we hired you for this expedition so that you can put tags on the toes of the natives we shoot? Or—maybe you are one of those bleeding hearts who will tell us not to shoot natives? I knew it! This expedition is not going to be any fun, and I want to go home." Sony delved deeper into dark humor, knowing she would probably protect natives with her life.

"Sony, any natives you shoot have to be cleaned and stuffed for our museum. So don't think you are just going to leave them in the jungle. The first thing you learn at anthropologist school is to not waste a dead pygmy. Very important to conserve the bounty nature gives us." She laughed at how far she had carried the dead pygmy humor.

"Carol, I can't wait any longer, since I'm beginning to think we could go on tour together. Are you married?" Sony realized all this banter could end quickly.

"No. Not this week. And you?"

"Not in the last year. Would you like to pretend we are married for the trip, and see if we would like it?"

"Sony—the man named after a clock-radio, I take you as my phony-ass husband as long as we are in the jungle together. Once we hit pavement again –it may be over."

"Carol, I take these vows of marriage as just a stupid excuse to have sex together in the jungle, and will treat them and keep them, use them, for my own selfish satisfaction. So help me."

"I pronounce us jungle married, and you may kiss the bride," Carol said, as she pulled Sony close to her and kissed him. Actually, it was a very good deep kiss. They kissed again, and Sony said, "I had a ring picked out, but didn't know your size."

"Uh—I don't know your size either. Maybe I should have waited to marry you until we had spent a little time together?"

"Oh, no! You are stuck with whatever size I am. Jungle divorces are almost impossible to get. Pygmies hate divorces and usually kill those who come before them with that request," Sony said.

"Yes. I remember that from anthropology school. But as I recall the man is killed, and the chief takes the woman as a wife or… slave maybe."

"Carol, you pull these anthropological assessments right out of your ass don't you?"

"You'll have to check later, sweetie, since it's all yours in the jungle."

"I like being married to you, Carol. You are so abnormal," Sony said.

"Ah, yes, a most charming trait. You seem to possess abnormality at a deeper, psychological level—a level that someday may require medication."

"Carol, I'll loan you my meds anytime."

While these two married each other and worked on a comedy routine, the jet carrying Mit, Chris and Modesto landed at the airport. The expedition would be headed out soon.

Chapter 20

Barbos and Kony

Barbos had wedged himself into a desperate position. In order to follow the group from the Dominican Republic, he was going to have to cut a deal with one of the most evil men on Planet Earth or risk going into the Democratic Republic of the Congo without documentation. The DRC lacks a sense of humor and has a military that isn't much different from Kony's Lord's Resistance Army. After he considered shooting himself, Barbos made the call.

"Joseph, this is Barbos Vieux. Can you clear an airstrip for me? Good. Hopefully, we can do some business."

Barbos got the instructions to a secluded airstrip in the Central African Republic, close to the border with the DRC. His men were not happy with the prospect of flying into a LRA encampment. One thing in Barbos's favor, however, was Kony's diminished army, as well as his lack of supplies and money. At one time, Joseph Kony led a force feared by the armies of at least four African countries. Many people in the free world embarked on a campaign to eradicate him, including a special unit from the U.S. So far none had been successful. Kony, always one step ahead of his pursuers, had mastered the jungle like Geronimo had mastered southwestern America.

Kony wondered why Barbos was so anxious to risk a vacation to the Congo. Kony's forces had shrunk and weakened. They were strapped for supplies from constant running and hiding. His exhausted group of raiders and rapists would welcome an infusion of money.

The answer must be related to the group at the Kisangani airport.

Kony's agents had kept him well informed, as they were-placed in the country. Two army trucks, two Humvees, and a couple of helicopters had traveled overland from Kinshasa. Hell, Kony sensed half of Africa knew about the Haitian's Congo excursion. No one knew where they were going, since the expedition organizers kept that detail a closely guarded secret. Bruny had flatly refused to tell the DRC military officials or anyone else that inquired who loaned out soldiers for the mission. He didn't want to have rebels waiting on him. Once on site, Bruny expected that one or more of the traveling circuses of militant factions might attack to see what they could steal.

Kony's landing strip was a pressing problem for Barbos. The pilot had pored over an aviation map, and nothing was there. A savanna appeared on a topo map, but no airstrip was indicated. Barbos's twin turbo prop Gulfstream needed 3000 feet of runway for landing and take-off, better than the 5000 feet Chris's Learjet 70 required. They had left Tanzania in darkness, but in daylight, they were ready to land. The pilot had keyed in the coordinates and was lining up his plane with an imaginary airfield. As they descended to a thousand feet, a dirt airstrip, cut out of the brush for a small single engine plane, became visible. Barbos's pilot set the plane down amid a torrent of dust and debris blowing from the back and sides of the big aircraft. Small bushes slapped at the wings as they went by. At the end of the airstrip, the Gulfstream bumped to a stop on a grassy area. The pilot rushed out to assess damage to the plane. He had landed without killing anyone, but taking off would be a different animal. He put most of Barbos's crew to work cutting brush and smoothing out the runway, which he judged to be one thousand yards shy of acceptable.

Five uniformed LRA waited near the end of the runway. Kony wasn't with them, and Barbos wasn't expecting him to be a part of the welcoming party. Joseph Kony had survived by staying away from his main forces and moving around to new camps almost daily. He rarely used communication devices. He only answered Barbos's satellite call because he recognized the number, and he actually needed Barbos's services. Since the bush didn't always provide enough game to keep his force of about two hundred soldiers fed, food was in short supply.

Anticipating Kony's needs, Barbos's crew began to unload crates of canned food, flour, rice, coffee and other essentials.

The five LRA loaded the crates on a jeep and took off after taking close up pictures of each one of Barbos' crew members. Their only instructions were to wait by the plane. While they waited, Barbos helped his crew rebuild an airstrip that might actually allow them to take off. Several hours later a jeep emerged from the nearby forest. Three uniformed officers got out and requested that Barbos accompany them back to their camp. Barbos grabbed a backpack and handed it to a coal-black colonel with several scars on his face. The colonel tossed the backpack in the back seat and invited Barbos to sit next to him in the front. Once seated, a blindfold was placed over Barbos's eyes.

They blasted over the savanna and drove down a narrow path into the forest. The little Jeep dodged trees, rocks, and large drop-offs, until finally; they came to a small clearing beside a stream deep in the jungle. The colonel removed the blindfold and ushered Barbos to a shelter made from canvas and camouflage netting. Sitting in a folding director's chair, smoking a cigarette, was Joseph Kony.

"Barbos, it is good to see you. Thanks for the food and coffee. I will share a cup with you, if you like." He smiled, and motioned for two young children to pour some coffee for his guest. Though the children looked to be both under twelve years of age, both were equipped with automatic weapons.

"Thanks. I trust you have some documents for us?" Barbos asked.

"Yes. They will cost you two thousand apiece. Did you bring U.S. dollars?" he said, and pointed to the backpack beside Barbos.

"Yes. Can I see the documents?" An aide to Kony handed Barbos a stack of visas designed to affix inside passports. They looked official, as well they should. After all, they were actual visas stolen from the government. Most visas don't require a picture, but these did. Each visa featured a picture of a gorilla in the jungle, with the visa holder's photograph placed on the upper right hand corner. All that was required was to take the gummed label on the back of the visa, and put it on a blank page of a passport. They were perfect.

Barbos opened his backpack and paid him. Kony looked up and said, "And there is another five thousand for the use of our airstrip."

Barbos did not blink, though he was beginning to realize he probably wouldn't leave there alive unless he emptied his backpack.

"Two thousand apiece for using our armed guards getting to the camp."

Barbos dug deeper into his backpack.

"Ten thousand for the pleasure of a personal interview with the world famous Joseph Kony. I am famous, you know. The Invisible Children's organization wears T-shirts with my picture on it." Barbos was about out of cash and relieved to not receive more cash demands from Kony.

"Now tell me, Barbos, about this expedition into the Congo. What's it really about?"

"Not sure. At first I felt it had to do with Papa Doc's gold he shipped to Africa many years ago. But I doubt he hid gold in the Congo. My guess is a mine of some sort, discovered by an expedition that took place in 1966. Pretty secret stuff, and something tells me the mine is in the middle of the goddamn Congo, where you are likely to find a pygmy's arrow in your ass," Barbos said with total honesty.

"Pygmies have shotguns now, to supplement their arrows with shit on them. Here's what I want you to do. You will take two of my men. They will dress as civilians, but will have weapons. I want a fifty percent cut of anything you get. When you bring my men back, I want a plane load of food as well. Do all that and you can live your life without fear," he said with a quirky smile.

Barbos knew full well what "living your life without fear" meant. He would be slaughtered as soon as the plane landed. Better to kill his two men when the time came, and never show up in Africa again.

Barbos was loaded back in the jeep, blindfolded, and driven back to his aircraft with two of Kony's most loyal men. He cursed himself for having being put in this 'no win' situation. The last time he dealt with Kony, he was to return with money for a drug deal on a desolate helicopter landing site in the Sudan. He knew he was going to be shot as soon as he stepped out of the 'copter. Instead he dropped the money from about three thousand feet, with a note saying the aircraft was losing oil pressure and needed to fly back for repairs. Even then they shot at him. Yet, if he wanted to follow Chris's trail he must have documents to land in Kisangani.

The big plane bounced around on the runway and took off just before crashing into an African thorn tree. Now heading to the same airport where Chris, Mit, and Modesto had just lifted off in helicopters, Barbos hoped he could rent or charter one. He was on the phone to the terminal and noticed every word he said was being monitored by Kony's goons. They also shared a satellite phone for reporting to their boss. Barbos realized that although these guys might have proper paperwork, they had to be on every watch list from Interpol to the local sheriff's office in Greenwood, Mississippi. Barbos signaled to one of his men directly behind Kony's nosy soldiers. They were listening intently to his conversation. Barbos' man was Henry Dumoune, former Tonton Macoutes, a man who never hesitated to kill. The Tonton placed two rounds into their skulls from a .22 caliber pistol, and pitched the two Kony employees out of the plane many miles from the airstrip. Most likely they landed atop a tree in the heavily forested jungle where a hungry leopard might find them for an easy meal.

In a few hours Barbos landed at Kisangani, clearing customs without incident. One helicopter and a small single-engine plane were available for rent. Barbos took both and transferred his weapons hidden on the Gulfstream. The only information he could get from the airport was the others had gone in a northeast direction. Barbos felt that by this time, Kony realized the report from his two guys was not coming. If he had assets on the ground in that region, they would swing into action.

When Barbos took off from the airport and turned north, he spotted a white vehicle. It pulled out of the woods and stopped. Two passengers got out. One fired what appeared to be a rocket-propelled grenade at the helicopter. The pilot took quick evasive action and avoided the missile, which exploded in a nearby field. The men on the ground opened with automatic fire, scoring a few hits on non-critical parts of the aircraft. The single-engine plane dropped a wing, made a pass, and fired on the small pickup truck with the two AK-47s. Both occupants were hit multiple times, and the truck was riddled with bullet holes. Barbos's two plane air force moved out of range. After an hour of searching, the helicopter spied a small caravan on a road leading to the north. Barbos decided to land both aircraft in a large clearing and wait. Later, the caravan would be closer to their target. Armed with eight men and automatic weapons, he would be able to grab at least part of whatever was found. He just didn't yet know how he would do it—or when.

Chapter 21

Lu Flies

Lu dialed her phone as fast as she could while getting dressed. She was yelling orders at everyone around her—spa employees were not exempt. Everyone was jumping and scurrying, either complying or moving quickly to avoid her completely. She was in full combat mode and noticed Angel, Gretchen, and Zoe stood with mouths open and ready to move at her command. Finally she connected with one of their pilots. Lu hoped she didn't ruin his day but knew it would be greatly altered.

"Listen, Bill, this is Lu. No, I'm not fucking okay! Chris and the boys are being followed by this drug lord skunkfuck Barbos Vieux. You talked to the other pilot, and they were going to a place in Tanzania on a lion hunt. Can you find the airfield where his jet landed? Call me as soon as you find out, and have the plane fired up for us when we get back to Botswana."

She had tried Chris, but knew if he was hunting lions he would have the phone turned off. They had taken Lu's jet to South Africa and rented a van for the drive to the Spa. As true jet setters, Chris and Lu had their own airplanes. Even though they flew commercial airlines from London to Africa, they both had their pilots fly their planes over for side trips. Chris brought his plane for the lion and for the side trip to the Congo. Lu brought her jet to go wherever for spas, shopping and sightseeing. Although Chris's Lear Jet was very fast, it only had a 2000 mile range which meant extra refueling stops in the super-sized world of Africa. Lu had opted for a Challenger 605 which had fourteen seats and a 4000 mile range. The top speed was close to the Lear and was made by the same company.

Lu dialed the lodge and talked to the main desk to request they pack bags for each of the women. Zoe got on and told them to round up her husband, Roland, for him to pack her things and meet them at the airport. Angel and Gretchen explained what they wanted packed. They ran towards the van and piled in, with Zoe's satellite phone in constant use. They had to drive to Durbin, where Lu's pilot was frantically filing multiple flight plans. First he would fly to Gaborne, Botswana, where they would meet Roland and pick up their luggage for the trip. They were hoping the helicopter was not in use so it could fly the luggage over. Then they would fly to Mbeya, Tanzania to warn Chris, Mit, and Modesto.

"If they have shot a lion, I hope they don't drag that damn thing home to nail on the wall. I will not put up with that shit," said Angel.

"I don't know. What if it's a lion rug and placed on the floor in front of the fireplace. Pretty sexy, huh?" Gretchen said.

Lu reminded her that she lived in Santo Domingo and didn't have a fireplace.

"Maybe I would have one put in just for the lion rug."

"If they shot a bear that would be perfect for our place in Austria," said Angel.

Lu was refusing to get in on the rug conversation. Besides, she was simultaneously driving and talking on the phone. In the thirty-minute travel time between the airport and the spa, Lu had talked to most of the population of southern Africa. On board the jet the calls kept going out from Lu, but she was using the phone she had left onboard. She became more and more confused. After landing in Botswana and everything was loaded, she announced there was no need to go to Tanzania.

"Our boys have left Tanzania and are headed to the Democratic Republic of the Congo. So are we. There is a secret delegation or expedition from Haiti going there, too. All I know is we are on our way to Kisangani. I have contacted a friend from Haiti who works in the State Department in the DRC. He will have visas and a couple of para-military types waiting for us at the airport along with a large helicopter fitted with a pilot. We need everyone's picture and a copy of your passport, and I'll have it faxed before we leave," Lu said through gritted teeth. She was pissed and had thoughts of shooting Chris herself since he left out a very important piece of information about the post-lion hunt trip. She was also scared that Barbos might get there first.

Lu walked up to everyone and took their picture on her cell phone. She handed the phone to an aide who ran at full speed toward the terminal. No one spoke to her, being fully aware of her temper. Zoe, however, was not enlightened, and made the mistake of asking what Barbos had to do with any of this. With fire spurting from her mouth, Lu gave an answer.

"He wants to kill us all—remove our heads—and fuck our skulls!! How do I know what he wants—he's your best buddy!" Lu went to the front of the plane and sat in the pilot's cabin, slamming the door behind her.

Zoe started to cry, and her husband and the other girls consoled her.

"We have learned not to speak to her when she's mad. Psycho! She will kill anything that breathes," said Angel.

"She and all of us have a reason to be mad. Our husbands knew we didn't want them on that expedition. They tricked us with that lion hunt shit. Did they really even go on a hunt?" asked Gretchen.

"Yes, I heard Lu talking to them in Tanzania. Chris shot thirteen lions and the rest only got one. Of course the one they got was about to eat Chris's head. He had a .50 caliber semi-automatic and they placed him in an area where no lions had ever come in before. Chris is damn lucky to be alive and Lu knows it—another reason she is so upset," said Angel.

With the documents faxed, the big jet lifted off, and Lu came back into the main cabin. She apologized to Zoe for being a raging bitch. Zoe apologized for being a really shitty spy.

"If I had been better trained and ruthless, you guys would be getting your butts rubbed by some muscle bound native spa employee about now," Zoe said with a smile. Even Lu laughed.

Lu reported to the group they would get to Kisangani by late afternoon and might have time before dark to fly into the area where Chris, Mit, and Modesto had landed in the helicopter. She would have to ask the pilot if that was possible.

"Whoa! Do you mean you know where they are? asked Angel.

"Pretty much. I got hold of Plato and browbeat him. He gave me the coordinates from the old journal of a Dr. Parke who was on the Henry Stanley expedition of 1887. From what I could find out, there was an ancient quarry on top of a bluff in the middle of the Aruwimi River. The last expedition there was put together by John Cole. Five people were killed on that small safari in 1966. The mine is jointly owned by the Haitian government and John Cole's family. Reports say his son is with the group going there now. My guess is half of frigging Africa knows something's up in the Congo. They won't know exactly where until they follow everyone headed in that direction. I have a feeling it will look like Woodstock before it all over," said Lu with a resolve that trouble was brewing.

Lu suggested everyone recline their seats, have a drink, and get some rest. It would be a long flight, as most are in Africa.

Henri Miot had not lived in the Democratic Republic of the Congo long. Two years before, he had taken a position working in the DRC State Department on the recommendation of Modesto Tejeda, who became the Assistant Attorney General of the Dominican Republic. Modesto had known Henri while working cases jointly with Haiti and was impressed with his knowledge of the law and his superior language skills. The DRC had a bad habit of stealing Haiti's brightest stars and paying them at least twice what they could get back home. Henri was offered three times his salary, and his wife was offered a job as the principal of a local high school in Kinshasa. The classes were taught in French, but both could speak English with a southern accent if needed. Henri knew Lu through Modesto and Gretchen and was glad to rush the visas over, along with a large helicopter. He had to scout several airports to find one, but assured airport officials there was no shortage of money from Lu and her friends.

The two body guards or para-military guys were a little more difficult. Henri's friends in the DRC Army warned him to be very careful. The military couldn't trust their own troops with rebel forces infiltrating the DRC army at all levels. Henri obtained the names of two brothers who worked well together and had moved to the DRC from Haiti. Like most fighters from Haiti they did have a connection to Papa Doc's old Ton Ton Macoutes, called FRAP in the 1980s and 1990s. People persisted in using the old title which was officially out in the 1970s. No one could tell the difference—still brutal, bloody and final.

The brothers were Jean-Jean and Osse Belcourt. They were about five foot ten inches, stocky, plenty of gold teeth, and looked very much alike except for Osse having more scars on his face. Both looked battle tested, but not as much as Devil Man and Jackie. They flew to the Kisangani airport on the helicopter Henri had arranged. They wore camo, with no military insignias, patches, or identifying markings on their clothes. Neither spoke English—Creole and French only.

Lu's jet landed about an hour after the helicopter arrived with the chopper pilot, Bonte Ballo, greeting the group on the tarmac. He explained in French about the two mean looking military men, whom he didn't much care for, who were seated in the helicopter. Roland was elected interpreter and could hold his own in a Creole conversation. Lu and her friends received their visas and went smoothly through customs aided by a well-placed call from Henri. Soon they were loading on the helicopter, a five million dollar Bell 412 beauty that could seat fifteen people in comfort. Bonte explained that one of the many mining companies in the Congo owned it and rented the craft out to reduce the cost of maintenance.

Sitting in the last two seats were the two trained killers. Assuming they spoke French or Creole, Roland went back and introduced himself and the others on board. He found out that Creole was preferred, and although they were polite, neither Osse nor Jean-Jean stood up when the ladies came back to greet them. There was a reason. Osse held a M16 in his lap, a large knapsack filled with ammunition and what looked like grenades. Jean-Jean had two weapons; one was on his lap and the other in the floor next to him. The one he held was a HK416 assault rifle, and near him on the floor was a Barrett .50 caliber semi-automatic. Both had pistols and knives, and Roland thought the two brothers might be able to overthrow a small country.

Roland had not had a chance to talk to Lu when she was not in a mood to injure someone, so he felt the time had come.

"Lu, we have only talked over cocktails, and since the revelation that we were hired by Barbos, I have not had a time to personally apologize to you. Please accept my regret for not finding out more about our employer and what he was up to. In the back of my mind I knew something had to be bad for someone to spend that much money on us. He never even met us." Roland looked Lu squarely in the eyes, his handsome face close to hers.

"Roland, you good looking hunk! How could I stay mad at you? Just a few days ago we were trying to get Zoe to let us share you while our husbands were away."

"I hope she said yes!" he said laughing.

"She is one selfish woman." Lu winked at Zoe.

The helicopter was in the air and heading towards the coordinates Lu had given Bonte. They had about three hours left before sunset, so they had to find the place or set down in a clearing and wait for sunrise.

The big Bell helicopter could do almost three hundred miles an hour, which gave the group hope they could reach their destination. Lu started passing out sandwiches and drinks. She asked Roland to give out the food to the Neanderthals guarding the small arsenal at the rear of the craft.

About an hour into the flight, Lu looked down and saw a large field where a helicopter and a single engine plane were preparing to take off.

Chapter 22

Quarry Landing

In order to translate, Modesto placed himself between Devil Man and Jackie in the helicopter. The noise level was so high, little conversation occurred during the flight. Chris and Mit were sitting next to a Congolese doctor who spoke some English and wished to be called Dr. Devine. He spent most of the trip with his nose in a *Native Congo Diseases* book. Rounding out the passengers on board was a geologist, riding shotgun. For Peter Vuuren, this was an adventure of a lifetime. A recent graduate, the ink on his Master's degree was still wet. On previous field trips to South Africa, he had mainly been to the DeBeers mine for a tour that anyone could book. His background included touring a gold mine, where cyanide leaching had taken place for almost a hundred years. The area around the gold mine looked like the surface of the moon. Peter had eagerly anticipated this trip to an almost inaccessible area of the Congo, where danger lurked behind every rock and tree.

Sony and Carol were on the helicopter with another archeology and anthropology specialist from New York City named Charlie Summers. She looked like a Charlie, wearing baggy jeans and a camo inspired bush jacket. Her face looked as though makeup might not do any good, but her clothing and hairstyle made it hard to tell if she had good features or an attractive body. Her hair was cropped short and pressed down by a floppy jungle hat. She wore huge sunglasses and smelled like she fell into a vat of Deep Woods Off. No one had seen her smile. Since she was packing what looked like a 9mm, and a huge knife that Jim Bowie would have lusted after, most were afraid to talk to her. If something feminine existed, most suspected it was hidden in her G.I. Joe boxers.

The other three passengers consisted of a mining engineer from the Democratic Republic of the Congo by the sole name of Jemi, and two geologists: Darley from Haiti, and Rick, hired by Haiti from Cal-Poly in California. Both were older and experts in their fields.

The third helicopter was more of a supply craft with two mechanics onboard from Haiti: Patrick and Junior. Since Bruny was aboard this was considered the lead chopper. Loaded to the point of bringing down the helicopter at any time, its contents included tents, food, cook stoves, mining equipment, generators, fuel, cots, sleeping bags, scuba tanks, air compressor and tools—both electric and hand-held. This craft would make runs back to Kisangani for more supplies as needed.

All three copters had spotted the huge walled structure and were picking places to land. Everyone knew if they landed on the black pitchblende, they would have their asses scorched, so they steered clear of that spot. The copters landed about one hundred feet apart, leaving ample room still available in the massive enclosure which was about 1000 feet in diameter.

Slowly, people emerged from the aircrafts, bending down as if the whirling blades might decapitate them, though they were ten feet off the ground. If, however, the pilot were to droop the blades by turning off the engine, one might possibly run into a blade if walking up an incline. The biggest danger was walking into the tail rudder blades. The pilots kindly warned all the folks leaving the plane.

Bruny started to tell everyone where he wanted the tents set up, but his first order of business was to put Devil man and Jackie on the wall by the front gate. He instructed the two mechanics to cut some trees outside the enclosure and build ladders for the inside climb to the top of the twenty foot walls. Snakes were everywhere, and the killing began with machetes whacking away at cobras, bush vipers, and other deadly serpents. Snakes were especially numerous close to the blue hole in the middle of the quarry. No one set up tents anywhere close to the water.

About twenty miles away the caravan of trucks and Humvees had reached the end of the logging trail. The men exited the vehicles and adjusted the loads in their packs for a two day trek through wet jungle. Most of the men, except for a few guides and language experts, were military types. The military men from the Congo and the para-military men from Haiti could communicate a little, but Creole was a problem for the Congolese. French was a somewhat common language. Two Congolese were assigned to lead the group through the jungle to the Aruwimi River. One could speak some of the dialects of this part of the Congo, including the difficult pygmy language. Rishi held a degree in social studies from a college in Kinshasa and had also spent a year living with local tribes. Isaac, the other guide, had survival training from the DRC Army.

Isaac was the leader and established his dominance by having everyone fall in and come to attention. He barked out orders for the hike and warned about elephants and natives with shot guns and poison arrows.

"I doubt we will see any of the Efe tribe of pygmies, and if we do, hopefully, Rishi can talk to them. We brought gifts to keep them happy. Keep in mind they have lived in this jungle for 50,000 years or more. This is their home. If they decide to attack and anyone gets an arrow, we will treat you with an antidote and antibiotics. If you were in the Kalahari Desert, there are tribes that make their poison from a beetle dust that will kill an elephant and has no known antidote," he said in an attempt to make them feel good about pygmy poison.

On that happy note, he pulled a compass and GPS from his pocket. Then he pointed them in what he felt was the direction of the river, leaving two guards with the vehicles. Rishi walked next to him and kept his eyes peeled for anything that moved. Everyone had guns strapped to their shoulders. They had a few hours before sunset and really wanted to make some distance on their first day.

The group walked single file most of the time because of the thick jungle growth. With packs and guns weighting them down, coupled with rain, their progress was slow. Isaac had to declare rest periods far more often than he wished. He could pinpoint where they were on the trail by using his GPS tracker. Without the tracker, they probably would have circled back on themselves and spent the rest of their lives waterlogged and confused. As dark approached they found a place in the jungle where the trees were spaced more generously. Isaac laid out the camp and posted guards in shifts. He called Bruny on a sat phone and gave his position and likely time of arrival the next day. The men were happy to have small pup tents and to get out of wet clothes. They built fires and put clothes on sticks in a futile attempt to dry them out. Shortly after setting up camp a herd of forest buffalo showed up to bed down at their favorite jungle hotel, only to find smelly humans had taken their spot. Several shots over their heads convinced them to find other lodging.

Most of the tents set up at the quarry were two-man styles with sewn in floors. Bruny had a large command tent that held six cots, and there was a big supply tent that protected supplies from the relentless rain storms that came and went almost every day. Chris and Mit shared a tent. Modesto bunked with Rick James, the California Cal Poly Graduate. They had California in common.

Charlie had no other female to share a tent with, so she agreed to stay with Peter Vuuren, who would have shared a tent with Big Foot to be a part of the expedition. Neither was married or likely to mate with anyone soon. Peter was a geologist nerd who was also a Trekie and a Star Wars fan. Most hot girls walked long paths around him to avoid his type.

Charlie was a male want-to-be, a sort of a non-sexual androgynous female. Neither Peter nor Charlie seemed to have joined the normal human race. They seemed unlikely to break through any time soon. However, they spoke to each other. They had a realization and a bond, like a secret society of misfits. Like pandas in a zoo, there was the off-chance they might notice they were different sexes. Peter was unfolding a Darth Vader poster to hang in the tent, when he noticed the sound of a helicopter.

Bundy ran out of his tent and yelled at the two Haitian guards to be on alert. Both were standing in the front of the gigantic iron wood doors, watching the men construct a ladder. Rather than exploring, everyone was putting up tents and stashing supplies. Bruny had ordered everyone to set up camp first.

The Bell helicopter set down some distance from the other three, and kept the blades moving while seven people exited the aircraft. The two Rambo types stood out front, hoping they could shoot somebody. Behind them, emerged Lu, Angel, Gretchen, Zoe and Roland. The pilot stayed put, wanting no part of whatever was going to happen. There was a déjà vu feeling of the gunfight at the OK Corral, like the first wave of men hitting the beach on Guam.

Chris was the last out of the tent and saw Modesto and Mit walking towards the girls. He saw Lu in the distance, and knew his ass was in for a chewing. Possibly, she would just shoot him. He would have to listen to the lecture. She looked really pretty, in tight camo pants and a tan cotton sweater that allowed her shape to stand out in its glory. Her long black hair was tied with a ribbon that was…yes—it was camo too. But beyond how beautiful and color-coordinated she might appear, there was a look on her face that said "death to everyone."

"Chris! You sorry sack of monkey shit!" With that statement she slapped Chris in the face, something she had never done. He turned his head and appeared to be shocked but didn't try to stop her. "You lying snake fucker!" She struck him again across the face so hard that blood seeped from the side of his mouth. "You deceitful weasel dick! How could you keep this from me?" She then slammed her fists into his chest and began to cry—something she rarely did.

Chris knew there would be retribution for not telling her about the expedition, but not this severe. He tried to hug her, but she pulled away and walked over to the edge of the stone cottage crying uncontrollably. If Chris tried to get close to her she pushed him away and screamed at him. He had known her for many years and he had never seen this side of her. Chris knew her temper had an extraordinarily long cooling time—but this was beyond his comprehension. He slid down the wall of the stone house and sat near her, but saying nothing. Chris was lost and no matter how many times he said he was sorry, it didn't seem to help. Their friends backed off and let them have their space. After what seemed like an hour, but was really just several minutes, she turned in his direction.

"How do you expect me to trust you again? The one sure thing we had in our marriage was trust."

"Lucero, my God, I'm sorry. I am asking you to forgive me. I don't ever want to see you like this again." Chris was grappling for some words that would work.

Lu slid down the wall of the house and set next to Chris, but at a distance. Slowly, she began to talk in short sentences, and Chris answered her questions in a calm voice. He never showed any anger towards her. After a long time, Chris retrieved her luggage and took it to his tent. They were not seen again that night, and it was for sure no one was willing to get in the middle of the fight.

The other two men took their butt-chewing in stride. Soon Bruny came over to find he had eight more people to house and feed. Angel explained they had brought tents, sleeping bags, and some food.

The sleeping arrangements were undecided, but it was clear, had there been living room couches, the three men would be on them tonight.

In the distance, Bruny heard a sound. He pointed to a southerly sky. There was a small helicopter and a single engine plane. They both buzzed the enclosure and flew north.

"Who the hell was that?" Bruny asked.

"Barbos and his family of rat fuckers would be my guess," Angel said.

Bruny quizzed the group and learned about a man who would strike when he felt everyone had their pants down and steal everything that wasn't nailed down. Bruny told everyone to finish setting up camp and sent the two new military men to trade the watch with Devil Man and Jackie. Once they met each other, there was a lot of yelling and loud talking. They had been friends back in Haiti.

As soon as the last tent was staked down, darkness fell. New relationships were created and old ones were healed—some more slowly than others.

Chapter 23

UCFF Plans

The truth is strange. Many people believed that the Lord's Resistance Army, led by Joseph Kony, had a religious purpose. Kony and his forces have no agenda—no goal—no moral excuse for what they did, except power over anyone they encountered. Murder and rape placed Joseph Kony at number one on the world's list of international criminals. Most countries didn't care about him, as long as he didn't interfere with a needed supply of oil, natural resources, cheap labor or goods. Kony was just a bad guy in the jungles of far-off African countries, which may change their names every year or so.

Joseph Kony was an unhappy man. He was that way most of the time, but when two of his good men failed to report on a timely basis, it meant they were dead.

Kony didn't have any forces in the part of the Congo where all these people congregated, but he did have contacts within a rebel faction operating close by. Rebel groups are as numerous as start-up businesses. A group of natives get their hands on some guns and call themselves liberators, while they steal, murder and rape their own people. Not much different from a bunch of guys in the hood, deciding to get together and hold up a liquor store.

If they were good as rebel combatants, others joined. If they weren't crafty and clever, the DRC military would wipe the jungle floor with them. The rebels Kony knew included ex-LRA members, along with soldiers from the Hutu "Democratic Forces for the Liberation of Rwanda," and the Rwandan backed M-23. Primarily the rebels had been in conflict with the Allied Democratic Forces-National Army for

Liberation of Uganda Islamist forces that had some ties with al Qaeda and of course the Congolese Government troops, along with some United Nations Organization Stabilization Mission to the Congo or MONUSCO UN troops. Although the names of an opposition might change through the years, there was very little variety in the small wars they fought. Decades of conflict had made "warring" part of the landscape in Africa.

The "Ituri Conflict," occurring in the northeastern region of the DRC, was the scene of many battles among rebel groups. About one hundred miles upstream from the quarry, the Aruwimi River ran into the Ituri River and smack dab through the war zone. On the other hand, thick jungle and lack of military targets kept the quarry section of the Aruwimi River free of fighting.

Hordes of scientists awaited the end of conflict to begin exploring most of the Congo basin, eager to discover and classify yet unknown plant and animal life. Pygmies reported a new giant chimpanzee, large enough to kill a lion. Natives still speak of the elusive Mokele-Mbembe, or dinosaur they claim to have seen. Undoubtedly, surprises were in store for experts to examine.

The group Joseph Kony contacted was called UCFF, an acronym for Union of Congolese Freedom Fighters, not to be confused with the UPC or Union of Congolese Patriots, to whom some of the group had migrated. Unlike most rebel units who wore uniforms and combat boots, the UCFF wore T-shirts and tennis shoes. Most dressed in camo slacks, commonly available, but some UFCC even wore shorts. Why not be comfortable while shooting, killing, and raping? Kony told his followers that untold riches awaited them if they ambushed an expedition on its way out of the area.

The UCFF, aware of the Sony group from a source in the DRC army, felt they could attack the expedition's vehicles as they left the quarry. Kony wanted a squad of men to move quickly from the Ituri region. Twelve UCFF men were given orders and directions. Part of their trip would be by truck and the rest by foot. Kony instructed that fifty percent of the loot be sent to him by courier after the encounter. The UCFF officer hung up, and laughed at the audacity of a man hidden in the jungle, changing locations every night and demanding proceeds from an unfamiliar raid. However, Kony felt he had the same power he had held in his so-called glory days. Since UCFF was cash-strapped, they proceeded with the raid. They had no intention of sharing with anyone—especially Kony.

~~~~~

Sony and Carol heard the ruckus, and poked their heads out of their tents to see the girls arrive on the helicopter. They both exclaimed all four girls were drop dead beautiful. Carol noticed Roland's movie star looks but kept most of her comments to herself. She didn't want to dampen the mood inside the tent. A battery-powered lantern on a makeshift table, made from a flat board laid across a camp stool, cast the only light in their tent. To say they were "enjoying themselves" would be an understatement.

"I don't see why I can't be on top. Is it because I'm a woman and you need to—like dominate another human?" Carol asked. She started stripping off her clothes.

"Wait…wait! I want the perverted pleasure of slowly undressing you myself," Sony said. He removed her hand from her blouse and starting the unbuttoning process.

"Is this going to be like a Harlequin Romance where the 'get ready' lasts for most of the book?" She smiled and watched him fumble with her buttons.

"Don't tell me you read those things? My grandmother reads them."

"Is your grandmother a horny old lady?" Carol positioned her smiling face under his gaze, and kissed him.

"That has not been a part our conversations, but on her 95th birthday, I'll be sure and ask her."

"Sony, we have two flimsy cots and a couple of thin foam pads. Where are we going to consummate our jungle marriage? I was thinking of a brass bed under a banana tree, with monkeys watching from above. I love monkeys watching me have sex—don't you?"

"Of course, dear. Are your medications nearby?"

"Are you going to use one of those rubber socks during sex? I take birth control pills you know," she said. The top part of her body was exposed. He was feverishly working on her pants but couldn't master the fastening device on the front of her slacks.

"Are these pants or a chastity belt? I won't use a condom, if you promise you don't have a disease where I wake up in the morning and find my dick has fallen off."

"Honey, I don't think my germs are that strong—at least when the doctor gave me those antibiotics he felt everything would clear up in a few months," she said. He overcame the fastener and removed her pants. His hands were on her lovely lace-fringed Victoria's Secret panties, and he couldn't resist asking a certain question.

"You cannot have sex with me unless you give me this answer. I'm sure they tell you girls when you buy things there. What is Victoria's Secret?" He lowered her last undergarment. Gracefully, she stepped out of her panties. She was indeed a beautiful naked lady. Sony couldn't help staring at her, up and down.

"Sony, are you ready for this? Victoria was a man! It's true. He had an operation. All of his junk removed, and now he has a makeshift vagina. Well, he was a fashion designer named Victor and even though he is a she, there was a need for cool women's underwear—so voilà—it was he/she to the rescue, " she said. Both hands undressed Sony, who rolled his eyes and smiled at her ability to make up stuff on the fly.

"And Carol, again, where do you keep your crazyass meds.?" Sony was now completely undressed. Carol didn't mess around with slowly relishing button after button.

They decided to move the pads and sleeping bags to the floor of the tent. Sony gladly let Carol get on top. Just as Sony suspected, she proved to be a fun lover. Recalling an earlier conversation, she told Sony his size was fine, and her ring size was six and a half. If she made a serious statement, the purpose was to set up a punch line later. They consummated their phony jungle marriage that night several times and would be very sore the next day. Neither one cared.

A few yards away, tension completely filled a different tent. Lu and Chris sat on their cots and looked at the ground, saying nothing but breathing heavily. Lu had moved from the melting point to somewhere around just simmering. Chris fidgeted like a young boy who had a porno site going on his computer when his mom came into his room for a sit down chat and had just enough time to turn the screen away but couldn't remember if the sound was turned off. Any minute the boy and his mom would hear, "Oh yes, fuck me! Oh my God! Yes!" and his life would be over.

Lu waited for something to come out of Chris's mouth that would make everything better. Maybe some words from him that would explain the deceit. Technically, he hadn't lied to her. He really did go on a lion hunt. He and the other guys just left off a few details about the aftermath of the great hunt. The side trip was a big deal omission. If they had gone to a titty bar and had drinks, that would have been something guys do and would have garnered a small ass chewing. If they had snuck in a golf game or took in a football game, all would have been forgivable breaches of conduct. To fly to another country and meet up with an expedition that had taken five lives the last time around and held the possibility of injury or death, well, he knew he had stepped over the line.

"Lu, I love you. I made a promise to be with you until I die. I plan to do just that. I also made a promise to Plato to help find what Papa Doc had hidden from his country and to help the earthquake victims of Haiti. Plato held the key to that mystery in a second log he had in his possession. All the gold Papa Doc secretly mined in Haiti went to the BIOA bank in the Ivory Coast. That gold would be sold off to help the Haitian people. Even more important to the people was the result of the 1966 Cole expedition. What Cole found was a long lasting funding source and a boost for the economy of the Congo as well—we believe. Our expedition has the twin purpose of exploring the potential value of mineral here and creating a plan to mine them that's acceptable environmentally. Surely you don't have a problem with these lofty goals." He stared right into her eyes that were red from crying.

"Don't call me Shirley." After the short bypass to tired humor, she verbally let loose with all guns a blazing. "We had something special, Chris. It's called trust. You just shit all over that and left me in the position of picking up your dead body in the Congo and telling your son, Reid, 'Daddy's not coming home anymore.' Do you think he wants to lose his daddy? What in the fuck were you thinking?"

"Lu, I'm sorry I didn't tell you, but if I had you would've refused to let me go. We're here now—so deal with it!" Lu sensed the frustration and anger in Chris' voice, which somewhat calmed her down.

"So, what are we going to be doing tomorrow—besides killing snakes and swatting tsetse flies?" Lu realized that she had sufficiently chewed on Chris. Further talk would be counterproductive.

"You and the girls can...what is that sound?" Chris said. Something hit the roof of their tent.

"Is it rain or hail?" Lu said.

"Arrows! Lots of frigging arrows!" Chris and Lu could see the points protrude in some places on the sides of their tent. Arrows stuck to the top of the tent. A rain fly prevented them from entering the tent. The couple pushed their cots together. Chris shielded Lu's body as best he could.

Bruny yelled, "Move your cots to the center of the tents. Don't touch the arrows—they are most likely poisoned. Stay inside. Guards stay behind your shields and fire rounds into the trees."

The expedition leader was glad he had told the guards to take the wooden shields that lined the interior wall of the enclosure. Tomorrow, he would have everyone place the shields on the outsides of their tents.

The big Barrett .50 caliber as well as the M-16 could be heard firing off rounds into the tree line around the enclosure. Jean-Jean and Osse were shooting wildly as if to say, *We are armed and we'll kill you dead if you come out of hiding."*

After a short while, the two Haitian brothers stopped firing. No more arrows came over that night, and snuggling in the middle of tents became very popular. Many slept under their cots. Most did not sleep at all.

Chapter 24

Pygmies

Rain—very heavy rain with thunder and lightning greeted everyone in the morning. The tents leaked around the arrows. Dr. Devine was the only one allowed to remove them since he wanted to study the poison on the tips. Expedition members began patching where the arrows had been and placed more shields on top of and next to the tents. As the rain continued, the mechanics worked to knock loose rocks on the side door to the cottage. The cottage's front door opening to the blue hole appeared to not have been unsealed in a hundred years. Since divers would be using the steps, this large door was also being put to use.

Except in Bruny's command tent, the activity was subdued because of the downpour. He had called the two anthropologists, Carol and Charlie, to discuss strategy on dealing with the area natives. Everyone was in agreement the quarry was a sacred site to them, therefore the group needed a proper method of showing respect for native beliefs. Bruny had been in contact with the land forces cutting their way through the jungle, and expected them to be at the quarry before dark. The interpreter for the Efe tribe, who was with the expedition, could hopefully call together a meeting with the natives. Bruny had brought with him a small loud speaker system. He was curious about the beliefs and habits of these forest people who had tried to kill everyone the night before.

Bruny inquired, "Tell me why you think the Efe are so protective of this place and how many different tribes of natives are we dealing with?"

"Two tribes. The Efe who are pygmies and the Lese who are normal sized natives. The Efe are one of the oldest races of humans on earth. Some say Efe bones go back ninety thousand years. Not much is known about their religion, but we can safely guess it is primitive. What I've read says they have a God, "Tore," who created them, lost interest, and went off to live in the sky. Once they die their "Borupi," or rhythm, is taken by a fly to Tore. They also recognize a jungle spirit they call "Jengi," Charlie said.

"From what I know, this spot is a source of great danger. First on my list are the snakes around the blue hole and the pitchblende. I believe sometime in the past, natives tried to live here. They may have built huts right on top of the pitchblende, with devastating results. I understand they believe in witches, so they left the quarry to rid themselves of the witches. Maybe they fear anyone who enters is firing up the anger of a badass witch. The non-pygmy Lese tribe, who work in a symbiotic relationship with the Efe, believe pygmies have the power to find and dispose of witches. Maybe we could use the angle of telling the Efe and Lese we are removing witches from inside the quarry," said Carol.

"Will you have to ride out on a broom and a pointy black hat to prove they're leaving," asked Sony, who had come in to listen. Carol smiled and gave him the finger.

"Keep that idea in mind for your sit-down pow-wow with their chief," Bruny said. He dismissed their meeting to start another one with his mechanics about the equipment in the cottage.

Unless the steady rain slacked off, the men hiking through the jungle would not reach the quarry before dark. The geologists, in rain coats, were taking samples and heading back to their shelters. Carol and Charlie ran to collect shields, dolls, spears, and artifacts lining the walls. Both grabbed some objects to study and ran back to their respective tents. Everyone predicted the rain would not stop, as a foot of rain in a day was not abnormal for the Congo. Dry inside the stone cottage, the mechanics worked on a 180-year old steam engine that no one doubted these guys could fix.

~~~~~

Several miles upstream, Barbos Vieux had found a large clearing and had set the helicopter and plane down without incident. He had a total of eight people with him and four could pilot a plane, but only he and one other of his men could fly a helicopter. Flying the copter and plane in the best of conditions was tricky and most certainly impossible in a driving rain. The group of nine had set up small tents they had carried in their knapsacks. All were cramped and tired of a diet of energy bars and water. Barbos didn't really have a plan other than to ambush the expedition when they were vulnerable. He did not have a specific time for the attack, and he would have to take into account the four vehicles he saw parked at the edge of the jungle plus all the people from the large helicopters. They had seen a few natives in the area and assumed there were more. He and his men couldn't do anything in the rain except lie in their sleeping bags.

He thought about his brother and how they had worked together during the glory days of their drug empire. Jon Jon Vieux had been arrested the same time as Barbos when U.S. DEA agents infiltrated the ring and caught them at an airstrip in the Everglades right after a huge delivery of cocaine. The two Vieux brothers weren't at the airstrip but were captured in Miami making a drug deal. Since there were no drugs on them, a conspiracy charge held up in court and they each got ten years. Jon Jon escaped without spending any time in big boy prison. He had a prison insider mess with some paperwork which resulted in his name being left off the list in the transfer from Dade County lock-up to the Florida State Prison bus. He walked out of jail and took a friend's boat back to Haiti.

Barbos was locked up at Bay Correction Facility south of Youngstown, Florida, a medium security prison vastly overcrowded and prone to excessively liberal early parole policies. In two years he was out and on a boat back to Haiti. He arrived a few months after Lu killed his brother, and Barbos began to piece things together. Although he had spilled much blood wresting back firm control, he ended up in the Congo jungle having no idea what he was doing. Maybe the rain would quit and he might figure out the best plan of action. Ideally, if he could find out when the Sony expedition was leaving, he could attack when they'd be carrying booty from the quarry. Posting someone as a look-out to radio him might work, or doing fly overs once a day, but those options would spook the members of the expedition. Also on his mind was the possibility of Kony sending men to retaliate for killing two of his soldiers. A long shot, he thought, and he couldn't dwell on wild speculations. The sleeping bag in his tent had managed to stay dry so he inched down and went to sleep.

~~~~~

Pygmy tribes had guarded the quarry ever since the wall had been built and for hundreds and maybe thousands of years before then. The Efe had been in the area for at least fifty thousand years and possibly close to ninety thousand. Scientists believe the Efe are direct descendants of the oldest human race on planet earth.

In the last seventy or eighty years some forest natives were encouraged to move close to roads in a government attempt to develop a market type economy and modernize the natives. However, when roads were not maintained, trade stopped and the natives moved back to surviving in the jungle. Amidst all the civil unrest, rebel and government forces took over food supplies, then killed and raped the native tribes. A few tribes held out in remote areas and remained largely unchanged since the beginning of recorded time in the Congo. Such was the case for ten Efe pygmy and eight non-pygmy Lese tribes along the banks of the Aruwimi River upstream and downstream from the quarry.

The elderly leader of the largest tribe of the Efe was Bok Ande. He was no longer able to raid honey trees and shoot duiker antelope in the forest. Bok Ande was wise and experienced with the old ways and had some knowledge of things modern. Many years ago the Efe traded for shot guns, but they laid them aside, because of the expensive shells, in favor of the bow and arrow. He kept a few shotguns and shells for protecting the village if needed. To Bok Ande, possessing those weapons was similar to having nuclear warheads in a bunker.

The pygmies maintained a strong relationship with the Lese natives, providing meat in trade for vegetables and fruit. The complicated relationship was one of mutual dependence in order to survive. Kombutu, chief of the eight Lese tribes, stood over a foot taller than Bok Ande yet neither appeared to have power over the other. As the expedition helicopters landed in the quarry, both tribal leaders knew they had to meet to decide their next steps. After runners from both villages carried messages to the chiefs, the leaders called a meeting the next day at Kombutu's village. No arrows would be sent into the quarry that night since a large group of men were moving in from the jungle. The natives wanted to see how many would stand guard on the big wall and where would be the best place to shoot poison arrows.

~~~~~

Isaac and Rishi had reached the river across from the island but the heavy rains had made the river swollen and rushing very fast. They decided to put their inflatables upstream where the river was wider with fewer rapids. Their goal was to transport all the men and equipment to the island before dark. Isaac led the first party and had to fight to stay out of the currents that would have pulled them into a series of deadly cataracts. Thankfully they landed safely on shore. The men on the island waded into the river and grabbed the other rubber rafts to pull them to safety. On shore they could hear chain saws cutting a trail through the heavy growth of trees. Several people from the quarry came to help the men up the wet bluff by hanging ropes over the side. All the ground forces made it ashore, scaled up the slippery cliffs and hiked through the forest to the quarry.

Rain continued to pelt the men as they set up their tents. Bruny greeted them by giving orders to stack shields against their tents. Isaac and Rishi would be welcomed to Bruny's tent with a strong glass of scotch. Everyone would begin their assignments the next day.

No one knew what to expect when Rishi announced by bullhorn that he wanted to meet with native leaders. Rishi would fill the jungle air with native tongues emanating from a mysterious loudspeaker. Sony and his large group planned to find out the results the first thing in the morning.

Chapter 25

Bundy is in Charge

Captain Ismael Bahati and his UCFF had only tarps or shelter halves to sleep under during the rain storm. Several men tried sleeping under the truck, but streams of fast flowing water forced them to climb into the covered truck, where sleeping was limited to an awkward theft of a few winks. Inevitably, a soldier would fall over on a comrade or crash to the floor on a pile of soggy troops. They were tired and hungry when the sun rose, piercing the mist and fog with rays of smoky, defused light. The day was going to be humid and hot— to the point where breathing would be hard. They should be used to air that could be cut with a knife, but at best they learned to adjust their breathing. Lasting much longer would require food and fresh water. The convoy of one truck was still a couple hundred miles from where the expedition had parked their vehicles.

Ismael ordered all to board the truck and headed southwest at a fast clip. "Fast" was a relative term, since maintenance had stopped decades ago. Now, the highways were mostly dirt and gravel, with rare pavement where it survived the DRC's failed economic experiment. One hundred inches of annual rainfall had turned the roads into obstacle courses. Very few villages existed along the so called highway, since most natives had moved back to the rivers. One of the few large villages left, Bandgadi, was about a three hour drive from their present location. Everyone in the canvas covered truck looked forward to arriving there and having some real food, even if it was bush meat and wild fruit. Village residents would, in all probability, not share their enthusiasm when they saw this pack of rebels show up in their town—especially the women.

~~~~~

The Dominican Republic gang decided to get together for breakfast. The two mechanics, who did a little of everything, had a fire going. They were cooking eggs in skillets placed on rocks at the edge of the flames. Several steaming pots of coffee showed black stains halfway up the aluminum sides. The group had arrived with metal plates and cups and grabbed camp stools for seating. Roland and Zoe had joined them, bringing the number to eight. The Haitian couple had no specific jobs, but neither did Lu or Angel. Since Gretchen was a doctor, she could easily be put to work. Chris and Mit would be the primary divers. Modesto was a great diver too, but might be better utilized as Bruny's assistant, in a military or translation role.

The men tending the fires began to pass around the coffee pots, and scrape eggs out of skillets. A Dutch oven lay in the middle of some heavy white coals. More coals laid on the lid. A metal hook lifted the lid handle, and revealed large homemade biscuits. Mit asked the mechanic if he would marry him. He received a weak smile in reply.

Angel elbowed Mit in the ribs. "Hell, you haven't married me yet! Here you are two-timing me."

"If you could make me biscuits like those…well, it might push me over the edge."

"When are you guys getting married?" Lu and Gretchen spoke in unison.

"Soon, and if you behave yourselves you may be invited," Angel said.

"Define 'behave ourselves,' and does this little side trip count against us?" Chris asked.

"I will look at everyone's body of responsible work before sending out wedding invitations," Angel said.

"We're screwed!" Zoe said.

"Count our ass cooked," Chris said. Modesto shook his head from side to side.

When they heard the end of this conversation, Carol and Sony sat down across from them. "I'm sure we will screw up sooner or later, and we have no real body of work. But…assuming you guys like us later—we'd love to attend the wedding," Sony said. Then, he introduced himself and Carol.

"Sony and I had a quick jungle wedding before we got on the helicopter. According to Sony, it can't be undone unless I'm taken as a slave by a pygmy chief," Carol said. She poured a cup of black coffee. "Is there any half and half and Splenda? Oh shit—I forgot. We're in Africa."

The whole group laughed at this crazy couple, and started asking questions. Sony didn't have to say a lot, since most everyone had read his mother's journal. They were in awe of his parents.

Carol explained she was an anthropologist from France, but had studied in the States. She now lived in a tent in the jungle with a large primate. The group hoped that the natives with the poison arrows found her amusing as well.

Bruny stopped by to say, "Hi," and explained that the supply helicopter was leaving shortly. Anyone having an emergency could go with it to see a doctor in Kisangani.

"Mr. Bruny. I have a request for half and half and Splenda. Hurry, my coffee is getting cold." Carol laughed when she made her request.

"Hot and black! Just like your men. It's Africa! Live it! Love it! You and Charlie get ready to meet your natives soon. Rishi will start calling them any minute," Bruny said. He marched off to give orders elsewhere.

Chris, Mit, and Modesto had met these people briefly before their departure, but the girls and Roland had no idea who they were—except for two coal black Haitians who had climbed down from guard duty. When Devil Man and Jackie saw them, they ran for the girls and picked them up, swung them around, and accepted kisses from all of them. They knew a little English now, as Modesto had arranged schooling for them. They certainly knew when Lu called them names for not letting them know they were part of this expedition.

"Big damn secret, Miss Lu. Could tell nobodies. Not safe here. You girls go home," Devil Man said. He grinned and accepted hugs from Angel and Gretchen.

"The only safe place I've ever been with you, Devil Man, was at my wedding," Lu said. She grabbed his huge arm and squeezed it.

"Much fun. Someday Devil Man gets married. You welcome to come," he said. He smiled down from his six-foot seven inch frame and locked on Lu with his one good eye.

"You no speaking to me?" Jackie said. He also picked her up and hugged her.

"Always, my love. I see you have taken good care of the Devil Man," Lu said.

"Must keep him out of trouble. You made us famous," Jackie said.

"You can blame Modesto for that. He got you dual citizenship, passports and a little restitution from the Italians who owned the batey, or let's call it a sugar cane prison in the D.R. and your pictures in all the papers," Lu said.

"We must go speak to the others," Jackie said. He went over to shake Chris, Mit, and Modesto's hands, even though he had talked to them at the airport. Chris had to practically drag Zoe and Carol over to meet Devil Man. He still had a hideous scar. It ran down the front of his face through an eye that was white, to an ear that was severed in a couple places. He was a giant of a man, with huge muscular arms marked by battle scars on most of his exposed skin. Roland spoke to both men and explained how important their role was for the Haitian government. Modesto overheard, and found that he and Roland had similar roles in their respective countries. They had met before at the Abu Camp Lodge, but had never really gotten into their occupations in any depth. A fast friendship began, and they forgot the spying incident.

The sun was unobstructed and blasted the small army of humans scurrying around in the quarry to find their positions in the new tent city. The supply helicopter lifted off, carrying one of the Congolese military men who had developed a fever after marching in the rain. Then, there was a laundry list of requests from everyone, (Splenda and half and half were missing.) The chopper would be back before dark. If it weren't storming, it would make this run almost every day.

Bundy Jean-Baptiste ran a tight ship. He made sure the military men took shifts around the wall and at the gate. Some were stationed in the jungle and others on the bluffs as lookouts. All had radios and orders not to shoot anyone—not just yet. The geologists were roping off the pitchblende area with crime scene tape that was found in abundance in Kinshasa. They took mineral samples from all areas of the old quarry. Human remains and artifacts were turned over to the two anthropologists. Chris and Mit worked with the mechanics to get the compressors ready and to study the compression chambers built into the old cave structure. The stone cottage now opened directly into the water.

Gretchen introduced herself to Dr. Devine. He was pleased to have the young beautiful blond German doctor assisting him. They both made sure they prevented mayhem by regulating sanitation and mosquito control. There could be no standing water. The blue hole was not a problem, because mosquitoes would not breed in such cool water. Latrines were a major concern, and they made plans to build better ones with lumber brought in by the chopper. Showers were also a part of the cleanliness profile. Bruny stuck his head into the medical tent and volunteered to shower with the ladies as a water-saving measure. Gretchen complimented him on his sense of humor and sent him on his way. Bruny and the other twenty or thirty men in the compound noticed there were at least five drop dead gorgeous young women wandering around in the quarry. Maybe more if they looked a little harder..

Several people went with Rishi to make his call out for the natives. A script had been created by Carol and Charlie with Bruny's approval. He would use languages he had learned when he lived with natives in the area. They had spoken their own indigenous language for thousands of years, but the slave traders in the mid nineteenth century had used a Swahili dialect that became pretty much universal in central Africa. The two women could read and translate Swahili, but neither could speak it fluently.

The announcement was simple and took a minute or two to read aloud. Rishi read the announcement three times, standing at the edge of the bluff facing upriver, at thirty minutes intervals.

"We mean you no harm. We will remove the bad witches from the inside of the sacred place. We have gifts for you, and wish to sit and talk to you peacefully. We hope to find minerals that will be valuable to us. If we do—then there will be jobs for you. You will not have the bad seasons when the Lese cannot grow crops and hunting is poor. We do not want to move your villages to the roads. You can stay where you are. We would like to send one man and two women to speak to you tomorrow. We hope we can speak to the chiefs of both tribes. They will cross the river and wait for you by the bank at midday. They will have two guards with them. One of the men has lived in a native village before. Do not shoot your arrows at us tonight, as we do not want to kill any of your people. Thank you."

There was no rustling of the jungle foliage, no covey of birds that flew out of bushes, no squawking of monkeys, just silence—which the expedition leader felt was a good sign.

Chapter 26

Efe and Lese Tribes

Bok Ande had just entered Kombutu's Lese village when he heard the blare of the first bullhorn. The villagers made so much noise, he couldn't hear everything. Kombutu came out of the chief's hut, and asked the crowd to be silent. Both chiefs sat in chairs made of vines and woven palm fronds, and listened intently for another blast from the loudspeaker. After Bok Ande heard enough of the first speech, he spoke to Kombutu.

"We are asked to meet with them. Do you think it is wise, my friend?"

"It is a risk to meet and a risk not to meet," Kombutu said. He tried to sound wise.

Although the language was not a perfect translation for Bok Ande and Kombutu, they understood each other quite well. They sat in silence for quite a while, until they heard Rishi's voice.

"They do not understand our witches," Bok Ande said, laughing.

"Yes, they are within people, not spirits in the blue water place," Kombutu said. "The diggers do have an idea of our seasons for food."

"We must not let them dig for diamonds in the blue water place. It has been sacred for our people since the beginning of our time on earth," Bok Ande said.

"My friend, should we let all our people die because they want to dig there?" Kombutu asked.

"They have big guns and now twenty more soldiers. We have arrows and old shot guns with very little shells. There is no one to help us. We lost many men when the white men came a long time ago and their numbers were small. I was just a child, but I heard the women cry for their sons who were killed," Bok Ande said. He recalled all the gun battles that took place when John Cole's expedition came through, now forty-four years ago.

"We have the numbers on them. We know the jungle, but if they place guns around the bluff, we will lose many men," Kombutu said.

"If we are patient, they will take what they want from the blue water place and then leave. It might take many years, but we have seen abandoned mines before," Bok Ande said.

"Go back to your village and talk with your elders—see what we should bargain for. The young men will surely want to fight, so only talk to the older wise men of your villages. You and I will meet with the diggers tomorrow by the river. Let us have large fish for them as gifts. See if someone can catch some," Kombutu said. He bowed to Bok Ande and stepped back into his hut.

Jemi, the mining engineer, called a meeting after lunch for all the geologists and divers. In attendance were Darley Konte, Rick Lasiter and Peter Vuuren to represent the geologists. Chris, Mit, Modesto and Angel registered themselves in the group as divers. Lu came as an alternate diver, and Sony also attended as an owner and engineer. Where on earth Jemi found a flip chart and easel, no one knew. He started with a drawing of the entire enclosure, with mineral deposits marked in a color coded motif. He used blue for diamond ore, orange for uranium, black for pitchblende, yellow for gold, silver for coltan and green for copper.

"Gentlemen and ladies, thank you for your time and your bravery for accompanying this expedition. As you can see from this crude drawing, we have many valuable minerals in a small space with a huge blue hole dead center. Some of the minerals here I believe to be of limited mining value. The gold is of poor quality, as is the copper, manganese, zinc, and bauxite. That leaves us with excellent diamond, uranium, pitchblende, and coltan assets. We have to ask ourselves, can we mine these minerals simultaneously or one at a time?"

Jemi really wasn't looking for an answer.

"We have an ancient wall that is of obvious archeological

importance It can't be damaged or weakened. The coltan ore runs directly next to the wall. I suggest we mine coltan last. Pitchblende is the most dangerous, so we need to mine it quickly. Our preliminary test indicates the deposit narrows at about fifty feet below the surface. However, the uranium ore is extensive and of remarkable quality. Any questions so far?"

Before anyone could form a word, Jemi continued.

"The kimberlite is the richest I've ever seen and must be mined first or at least at the same time as the pitchblende. Of course, the difficulty will be getting to the bottom of the 135 foot blue hole without killing our divers. We know they tried building a pressure chamber in the 1830s and recovered a huge load of stones, but the members of that earlier expedition died for their efforts. We would like to avoid that.

"Amen!" Mit said.

"Can I ask a question…or maybe a couple?" Chris said.

"How do we take large quantities of ore from this cliff to be processed without roads?" Before Jemi could answer, he continued. "And what kind of equipment can you fly on top of this bluff? Do you have a big Chinook that could pick them off a nearby road and put them here?"

It appeared that Jemi didn't have all the answers to the questions. "Yes, on the helicopters. Big Russian ones are for lease in Kinshasa. They will bring small front-end loaders and other earth moving equipment. Ore—not sure if we will process on site, or partly process it and fly the ore out in containers. We can't pollute the river, and the rapids mean we can't use a barge. Great deposit of minerals—horrible place for them. Might as well be on the goddamn moon," he said.

"Uh—that road is about twenty miles away. Can the choppers carry a load that far?" Sony said.

"I guess—they carry stuff into combat zones, don't they?" Jemi said.

"Maybe it isn't our initial problem. Can we focus on the diamonds for now?" Rick asked. He took volumes of notes. A few members of the group suspected he might be writing a novel.

"Since the water naturally washes the walls of the blue hole, the diamonds drift downwards," Jemi said. "The first part of the operation will be underwater suction dredges—much like what is used on ship wrecks or gold placer mining in California. We'll clean the bottom and then start up the sides. The inside chambers hold great possibilities but also the dangerous risk of getting bent. Chris and Mit, how do you think we can handle the dredging operation?"

"Mit is the engineer," Chris said.

"We can make a few mixed gas dives to get started," Mit said, "but keep in mind that any screw ups and the nearest decompression chamber is in Namibia. The permanent answer is a remote submersible with suction capabilities. However, you are limited to working the walls, the bottom and then some distance from the blue hole. Puncture the walls and it might flood this whole quarry. We need to understand where the blue hole gets her water. Springs? Geyser?" Mit added.

"Well," said Jemi, "We have a Keene 8 inch Dredge with 150 feet of hose. We should get a lot of diamond material when the dredge brings light gravel to the surface. If we really want everything off the bottom, we could use a closed system dredge and bring the thing to the surface to be cleaned out every few hours. My suggestion is to try the long hose first and switch to the closed system. One diver will use the dredge hose and the other will take manual samples. Let's dive two at a time and put long intervals between repetitive dives. Who wants to go first?"

"Lu and I will go first," Chris said. "We will only do one dive a day, stay on the bottom ten minutes and then hang at ten feet for fifteen minutes for our safety stop. If we have to be flown somewhere, we can't go over 1000 feet in altitude. This will be the rules for every diver. You guys got that?"

Jemi nodded his head in the affirmative.

"I see why scuba will not be a practical mining alternative," Jemi said. "Unless we used mixed gases and actually decompressed. Or maybe hardhat diving utilizing the pressurized chamber below us. And I know the first words out of your mouth—we would need a chamber on site." He turned to Mit with the knowledge that a lecture on decompression diving was on its way.

"Jemi," Mit said, "I'm not saying it couldn't be done, but you need professional hardhat divers for that work. You need expensive heliox and various outgassing mixtures along with suit warmers, since the helium sucks out body heat. A shit load of expensive equipment. Most hardhat divers have an entire frigging surface ship to assist. I'm not even going to talk about surface-supported air supplies, except to say there are dead people in that chamber now who did that for a while. You might be better off with a good submersible with suction capabilities. The other problem is you don't have unlimited mining surfaces. When you do the sides and bottom—what's left?" He walked over to help Lu and Chris suit up for their dive.

"I have a lot of bottom and a lot of sides to do before I worry about that. The blue hole is a hundred feet across. Cleaning all that will take forever, and then it will be time to start all over again," Jemi said

Modesto and Mit helped the two mechanics start the dredge. They dropped the metal pickup valve in the water and fed the hose out until it was on the bottom. At the end of the sluice box, where the material is pulled up and run across a series of riffles and carpet, there was a fine nylon capture cloth in case the riffles missed anything. The motor had gone to idle, so only water flowed into the sluice box.

Chris and Lu floated on the surface. They faced each other and gave a thumbs-up, then let the air out of their BC's and began the descent. The water was an indescribable deep blue, contrasting with the pale green kimberlite walls. Lu and Chris smiled at each other. They hadn't been on an adventure since Reid was born. This was something that made them both feel alive again. Chris was glad Lu came to find him. At some point, he hoped she might even forgive him.

As soon as they reached bottom, they set their bottom timers for ten minutes. Lu started holding the metal intake along the bottom from the edge of one of the rounded sides, and started working a grid. Next to her grid, Chris manually scrapped the bottom with a trowel, and put the material into a fine mesh bag.

Both timers indicated ten minutes had elapsed—time to surface. As Lu laid down the hose and took Chris's hand to start her ascent, her regulator started free-flowing air. As they went up, she took the regulator out of her mouth and banged on it—didn't help. The free flow of air could quickly use up a diver's tank, a fairly common occurrence with poorly maintained rental equipment. Instinctively, Lu reached over to unhook Chris's second stage spare regulator, but he was already moving it towards her mouth. She blew in to clear it and then took a breath. Chris stopped her descent, so that she didn't move up while holding her breath. Once he saw she was okay, they ascended to their fifteen foot safety stop.

Through the clear water, Mit could see she was sharing air, and jumped in with a fresh tank and regulator. He swam down to her. After he helped exchange the regulator, he hooked the tank on a rope tied to a float on the surface. Lu and Chris probably had enough air to share for fifteen minutes, but Mit was not going to take a chance. His instincts were correct. When they surfaced after fifteen minutes at the safety stop, Chris had only 300 pounds of air.

"Where did we rent those fucked-up regulators?" Chris demanded.

"Bruny had someone get them in Kinshasa at a big dive shop," said one of the mechanics.

"Piss poor maintenance could get one of us killed!" Chris said.

"I will test all of them before the next dive. My guess is they didn't service these at all. Hey, somebody dies—who in the hell do you sue in Africa?" Mit said.

Modesto suggested a spare tank and regulator be tied at the fifteen foot level at all times. Mit and Angel had no problem during their dive, but when Gretchen decided to dive with Modesto, she had a free flow right after she entered the water. She had to change gear to complete the dive. The divers took two regulators out of service. Everyone hoped there would be no more trouble.

After the first dive, Jemi and Rick came by to sort the material. They cleaned the riffles and the mesh bag in a big tub. The amount of diamonds was immense and even more so for the scraped material that Chris had put in the bags. Roland and Zoe were called to help with clean up. It wasn't long before Charlie, Peter, Carol and Sony stopped by and were put to work. They sorted by color, size, and clarity into plastic collection bottles.

Once the diamonds started piling up, everyone wanted to help. They wanted to see them. Devil Man came by, held a large yellow one in his hand, and laughed like a little kid. Diamonds had that kind of effect on everyone.

Chapter 27

Skinny Dip

When the satellite phone buzzed, Barbos was eating a meal at his campsite.

"Mr. Vieux. This is Charles at the airport in Kisangani. You said you would pay me for information on flights from the expedition."

"Yes, Charles, I will. What news do you have?" Barbos anxiously awaited something that might assist in making a plan of attack.

"Their supply helicopter is here. They are loading lumber and unloading a sick soldier. The pilot told someone here that he would be back almost every day to resupply and bring people in for errands. Just thought you might want to know. You can pay me when you come back to the airport. You remember I work on the refueling truck," Charles said.

"Charles, keep your ears to the ground. I will see you soon, and thank you," Barbos said.

Barbos Vieux had a huge smile on his face. He felt that the rich girls poking around in that dirty quarry would make any excuse to go into town sometime soon. He put in a call to a friend he met in prison. Barbos's friend was from a Rebel force that operated out of a strange city in the jungles of the Congo—a place where Mobutu built an airstrip for the Concorde and three huge palaces. The palaces had been looted, but the airstrip was still in place and would easily accommodate a small jet. He alerted his pilots to fire up the aircraft for the return to Kisangani. He would find a nice hotel there and wait for the prey to come to him. Sitting down next to his helicopter pilot, he issued an order. "Find out everything you can about the condition of the airstrip in a town called 'Gbadolite.'"

~~~~~

With the day's diving done and clean-up from the sluice box completed, Angel suggested a party—not just any old party, but, rather, a racier kind of festivity. Years spent as a Jansen swimsuit model left Angel with a fearless disregard for clothing.

"Let's have a skinny dip party tonight! We'll drop a couple of dive lights in the water, and pull all of the stashed booze we can find out of hiding. Who's game and who's a chicken?" She laughed and searched the group of young people. Two tried to sneak away from the crowd. The two nerds, Charlie and Peter, soon learned they were doomed.

"Those who do not show up here tonight will be found in the compound and will be dragged here kicking and screaming—stripped and thrown in the water. Best to comply with the invitation to Angel's party now, to save further embarrassment," Lu said lacking any modesty on her part as well. Many times Lu had changed clothes on the deck of Mit's boat without a second thought. Wetsuits and swimsuits were fair game to strip off on the deck of a boat. The guys felt eyeing a naked girl was a bonus for the danger of diving.

"Will there be a gun battle?" Gretchen explained how they were attacked by pirates while she was changing out of a wet swimsuit on Mit's boat. She fought the entire battle completely naked, and patched everyone up without a stitch of clothes on her body.

"Ahh, I remember that time fondly," Chris said. Lu poked him in his ribs.

That night after dinner, the group began to arrive. Osse and Jean-Jean were assigned snake guard duty, should any snakes try to come at night to spoil the party. Some were concerned they might be watching the party more than seriously patrolling for snakes. Devil Man and Jackie were on wall duty, which was fine, since they both would have been embarrassed to have seen their friends naked. Blown-up surgical gloves and condoms made perfectly good floats to hold the dive lights. Someone had tied up and knotted all the fingers on the gloves except for the middle finger.

A small boom box showed up along with CDs, which leaned a little too heavily towards hip-hop music and rap for some of the group. No one minded when excessive amounts of booze materialized around the blue hole. With the dive lights dancing in the crystal clear water and the old lanterns burning from inside the stone cottage, the setting for a party was magical. Blankets and towels encircled the water, and couples began to undress and dive into the water.

Sony and Carol were the first. As soon as Carol quit screaming from the cold water, Sony was compelled to tell the story of his mother and the snake. Carol had not read that part of Vikki's journal entry. She hugged him as he described the giant snake trying to kill his mother. When the rock python attacked his father Zuka shot it in the head. Sony loved the feel of Carol's warm nude body against his in the water. After a few minutes the temperature felt perfect.

Angel's swim suit body was next, with Mit doing a cannon ball right after she got in the water.

Soon Zoe's fashion model body was in the air and she hit the water with a yelp from the cold shock. Roland dove in and while in midair, several female admirers adopted full gawking mode. Lu jumped in after Chris and displayed her large breasts that appeared unfazed by motherhood.

Peter and Charlie showed up—the moment everyone was waiting for. They knew if they didn't come to the party, they would be kidnapped and tortured, so they stood with towels and blankets wrapped around them. No one could be sure in the dark, but Peter appeared to be wrapped in a towel decorated with a picture of Captain Kirk. Charlie had her floppy hat pulled down tightly and what may have been combat boots loosely placed on her feet. Peter undressed first and uncovered a tall slender body with a large tattoo of Princess Leia on his chest. He was surprisingly well endowed, which caused some of the ladies in the water to smile and whisper.

For some reason, Charlie came out of the cottage through the door that led to the steps and into the water. Light flooded this area more than any other spot. Two Coleman propane lanterns sat at the top of the steps and one on the roof of the cottage, not at all a place for a shy nerdy girl to take off her clothes to go skinny-dipping. Charlie took off the floppy hat, stepped out of the combat shoes, and unwrapped her "save the whales" blanket. Only the towels remained. She edged closer to the water and down the steps. Meanwhile, the boom box blasted an obscure but appropriate song by Yelawolf called, "Looking for Alien Love."

Charlie dropped the towels, and smiled as though she had fooled everyone. Under the baggy clothes she had worn and the camo this and that's, was an incredible woman displaying a body no girl there could match even after a good day at the gym. Her soft round shoulders set off the most beautiful breasts that had a perfect upturn capped with erect nipples. Her stomach was flat with a concave long run of cleavage around her navel. Her pubic hair was groomed into a small heart-shaped area above her hidden vagina. Her legs were long, smooth, toned perfectly, and tanned leading down to small sexy ankles. She turned and exposed buttocks that stuck out from her body and couldn't have been any more shapely. Had there been a gaping mouth contest, Peter would have done well. He also had an erection and no one blamed him.

Charlie stepped into the water slowly, as a princess might proceed into a crowd of her subjects. After somewhat ignoring her for the last couple of days, all the women moved in to talk to her. They also blocked the men from getting close to her. The party lasted until the excessive booze no longer warmed them and a chill set in. Peter was happy to walk Charlie back to their tent. She knew he was a friend when no one else cared to be. In the tent, she went over to his cot and took care of his erection by climbing on him. She clawed at the Princess Leia picture on his chest until he came. Later, she told Carol that he was enormous.

The buzz around camp the next day was mainly about Charlie's body, but beyond that was the meeting with the natives at noon. Carol, Charlie and Rishi compared notes and prepared gifts for the natives. No one was sure that the natives would be there, yet there was reported activity of natives near the meeting place from the soldiers on the cliff. Both chiefs would receive a solar panel with a light attached for their huts. Also canned meat and a sack of potatoes would be provided. Isaac had agreed to go in place of one of the guards, but they decided Isaac would be more useful leading and supervising the twenty soldiers he led through the jungle. Devil Man and Jackie would be imposing giants for the pygmies and the Lese to respect, if not downright fear.

At the agreed time, the small group lowered themselves over the cliff assisted by two guards. They loaded the inflatable rafts and the two guards paddled swiftly downstream and across the river. Two natives came out of the forest, grabbed the raft and helped pull it ashore. Rishi and his group would need to walk the raft upstream when they left to hit the opposite shore at the same spot where they began.

Devil Man and Jackie brought four folding chairs for the girls and the chiefs. Rishi and the two guards would stand. The two chiefs emerged from the jungle with the same two natives who had helped with the raft. They were dressed in furs made from monkey skins and headdresses made from feathers and crocodile skin. Bok Ande stood in front of Carol and Charlie, and he offered his right hand upward to them. He was about four foot five inches and looked like a child, except for his wrinkled face. The Lese chief, Kombutu, stood at about five foot six inches and was almost eye to eye with Carol and Charlie. Carol was tall at five eight and Charlie was only slightly shorter at five seven. Their book ends were Devil Man at six-seven and Jackie was six-two. The two guards for the natives looked as though they had just been birthed by two huge men who were opposite them. The native guards could hardly wipe the terror from their faces—especially the pigmy across from Devil Man. Carol and Charlie worked hard to keep from laughing.

The chiefs were surprisingly friendly and names were exchanged with much hand shaking. Their guards offered several huge river fish, which Devil Man and Jackie carried to the raft. The two ladies thanked them profusely and offered their gifts. The solar panels puzzled them, but one of their guards explained how they functioned. Solar lights and panels were actually quite common in Africa, since kerosene was expensive and many had gone to cheaper renewable sources of energy. River settlements had seen very few forms of new technology. The canned meat and sacks of potatoes lit up their faces a great deal. With those pleasantries completed, each took a seat. Rishi stood behind the ladies and a native stood behind the chiefs. A large mahogany tree provided shade for the group and a cool breeze blew in from the river. The Aruwimi produced low gurgling sounds, serving as soothing background music. It was a beautiful place for the crucial assembly.

"Chief Bok Ande and Chief Kombutu, we wish to thank you for meeting with us today," Carol said. She waited for Rishi to translate. Their native standing behind them chipped in with some additional translations. Rishi and the two women hoped at least a few words found their mark.

"We do not wish to make war with your people as we both would lose lives," Charlie said.

Again the exchange of strange dialects and some clicking sounds. The chiefs said nothing and waited for more from the ladies.

"Why do you shoot arrows at us in the quarry? Is it a sacred place? We need the minerals to sell for food needed by our country. They had a great earthquake which took down their houses and their work places," said Carol and then she realized she had said more than probably could be translated.

Rishi asked Carol to repeat her words to him. There was much back and forth talking and quizzical expressions on both chiefs. Rishi repeated everything as best he could, which started a clicking frenzy among the natives. The pygmies likely had a different click from the Lese, but finally they settled down. Kombutu spoke first, not a surprise to Carol and Charlie. They had heard the Lese considered the pygmies to be more savage and less intelligent.

"The blue water place has been sacred from the beginning of time. Many diggers have come in the past. We have killed them or sent them away many times," Kombutu said, with a swift translation by Rishi. Bok Ande looked up at Devil Man and appeared to shudder. The natives may have feared a race of giants had taken up residence in the quarry, an assumption that could have affected their decisions.

"We have small weapons compared to you. We have more men but like you we do not wish to trade lives. We will allow you to dig but we ask for food for our people. We cannot work in the blue water place since it is sacred ground," Kombutu said and the translation war began in earnest, with Rishi clicking as well.

"We ask to come and visit you there and wish for you to come to our villages to visit. We want peace," Kombutu said. He stood up along with Bok Ande, bowed and shook hands with the ladies.

Kombutu and Bok Ande agreed to meet on the island that same day to visit their sacred place and have dinner with the diggers. Charlie believed they wanted to see if more men like Devil Man were in the enclosure. Not one native could look in his face. If he walked close to them they bowed and froze. Devil Man just wanted to be friendly but they did not reciprocate in kind. Carol and Charlie would visit the native villages the next day. The men hoped the girls would restrain from skinny-dipping in front of their new friends. The natives would never let them return if they did.

Chapter 28

Bahati

The middle-aged woman would not stop screaming. The skinny soldier struck a back-handed blow to her face. Her sobs and whimpers pleased the soldier, although he encountered some difficulty in his attempts to enter her. She was naked except for the dress bunched up around her waist, which had been pulled down from the top and pushed up from the bottom.

"Play with her anties while you fok her. You mompie—stick you piel in de poes," one of the soldiers said while he held the village woman down.

Rapes occurred in two other huts in the village of Bandgadi, and screams could be heard, if anyone cared to listen. Captain Ismael Bahati lacked concern, as the scene was commonplace and one of the perks associated with being an African soldier. It mattered little if you were a soldier for the government forces or one of the numerous rebel factions. Rape was part of the payday, regardless of which side you were fighting on. Soldiers seldom earned real money. Food and water were scarce, but a soldier could always count on having sex with anyone he could catch.

It was time to load the captured food and water into the truck and continue to find the parked vehicles of the expedition. Captain Bahati ordered the men to pull up their pants and load the supplies. Some of the men complained that none of the women were young and tight. He laughed, and told them they had to be fast to catch the young ones.

This attack wasn't the first assault against the women, so they knew the drill. At the sound of a truck, the young women and girls would run to a hiding place in the jungle. Middle-aged women sacrificed themselves to protect their daughters and granddaughters. In many cases, those same daughters were the result of rapes from soldiers in the past, from forgotten conflicts led by forgotten groups of pseudo-soldiers. It cycled itself infinite times.

Bahati talked to his soldiers while the truck rattled down an African red dirt road. Dust mushroomed from the rear of the big truck and painted the leaves of the jungle. Foliage slapped the sides of the vehicle. Daily torrents of rain would cleanse the forest from the military truck's abuse.

"We will be nearing the site of the parked vehicles soon. We don't want to engage them before dark. The guards will check in, but not be expected to report until morning. I expect two guards. We can kill one, but need to question the other. We may need to move toward the main force during the night. They will call the guards when they don't hear from them. Maybe we can answer for them—maybe not."

Bahati was an experienced military officer. He might have been part of a rag tag group of soldiers, but he had fought successfully in conflicts from Rwanda to the DRC, and won most of his battles. He was an expert at taking small forces on surprise attacks against superior numbers of personnel.

At this point, had he known his enemy would be on top of a five-hundred foot cliff, with weapons pointed down at him, he might have reassessed his aggressive plan of attack.

~~~~~

The camp was preparing for a visit from the natives that evening. Long ladders were constructed to allow the natives to scale the heights of the bluff. Climbing the bluff had never been a problem before, but the chiefs were older now and not so agile. Charlie had asked them what their favorite foods were, yet they wanted to try the food in the camp. Just in case, Carol and Charlie compiled a list of native foods. Grubs, monkey meat, snakes, lizards, and various insects were marked off as impractical. Two of their favorites remained on the list: honey and pork.

Bruny made a call to the supply helicopter, and made requests for the items needed for the feast. Carol stood next to him and took the microphone.

"Look, while you are in the store, grab some Splenda and half and half. I'll pay you back." She smiled at Bruny and kissed him on the cheek. He didn't say a word, and grinned like a circus clown.

The two anthropologists found a table that had been removed from the stone cottage and pulled up some folding chairs to plan their trip to the villages. Part of that plan required Charlie to loan Carol some of her baggy, manly clothes.

The two mechanics were working on the steam powered compressor. They succeeded in getting it to sputter a couple of times.

Sony, Mit and Modesto were discussing and examining the first round sealed door on the pressure chamber. Once the old compressor was working, they wanted to test the chambers.

Lu and Chris were on a dive, and Zoe and Roland were supporting their efforts. Zoe and Roland were recreational divers who had no desire to die at 135 feet. Gretchen was working with Dr. Devine on the latrine and shower foot prints, and had a team of people digging holes and placing rock footings. Construction would begin as soon as the supply helicopter was unloaded.

The geologists were digging test holes and screwing an auger into the ground for core samples. They were also using new sonar equipment to measure the depth of ores and the formation of rock below, and had plans to meet later and share data.

The military types under Isaac's direction had built sand bag bunkers on the wall, and at the edge of the cliff. To be more accurate, the sand bags were filled with various ore samples. The section of the enclosure wall opposite the entrance gate had the least amount of guards, but featured a shear bluff that dropped straight down five hundred feet to rocks and the river.

Jemi had contacted the rental agency for the Russian helicopters and also for a couple of back hoes and front end loaders. He had them on the way on a flatbed truck. They would arrive late tomorrow, as would the big chopper. Jemi was in contact with other uranium mining operators in search of lead-lined ore containers. Most likely he would not find them and would have to use nuclear waste containers.

Pitchblende was an exciting find. Yet, since the days of the Manhattan project, mineral processing facilities had little experience with pitchblende. Most operators would simply add more protection for the workers.

Jemi had also contacted local diamond mines about processing kimberlite ore for a fee. They were willing to consider taking on the project, but they more commonly received huge loads of ore delivered in dump trucks. Small amounts of ore in containers on flat beds made them crazy. Mostly he heard, "Process it yourself. Build a wash plant. At least get it down to the fine materials before you send it to us."

Out of all his contacts, he received the most positive feedback on the coltan ore. Coltan was a red hot mineral now, needed for computers all over the world. When mining operators found they were on a cliff, on an island, on a non-navigable river, in the middle of the Congo, the excitement faded. Operators sought him out to deal with these kinds of problems. Jemi had started up mining operations in all kinds of conditions. There were gold mines in Alaska, Siberia, the Amazon, and all over Africa, and copper, manganese, iron, and silver in Australia. He had a working knowledge of deep rock, placer mining and cyanide leaching. He didn't do oil and gas, but probably because no one had ever asked him. If there ever was a perfect man for mining on a mountain surrounded by a river in the middle of a jungle—Jemi was your man.

By late afternoon, a large fire circle was completed and lit. A large tarp was erected about the seating area. Shortly, a delegation of ladies in baggy clothes would go to the edge of the cliff to welcome the guests.

The sound of the incoming helicopter generated a great deal of excitement among all the residents of the camp, because most had ordered special supplies. Rum for Chris, facial wipes for Lu (or so she said), and a long list for the doctors. Not everyone would get what they wanted, but Santa and his sleigh wouldn't have received a better welcome.

Bodyguard brothers Jean-Jean and Osse were the first to get off the chopper. They started passing out lumber to anyone who would carry it. No sooner was the lumber stacked near the latrine and shower area, power saws and the generator made prearranged cuts. Sacks of nails, braces, and other hardware quickly found their way to the workers. New regulators and other equipment were delivered for the divers. Pilot Bonte Ballo had made the market run, also making a lot of friends with his purchases. Lu got what she wanted and also financed the entire grocery run, with a huge tip for Bonte. Money talks. Carol got Splenda and several types of creamer and real cream, but half and half didn't exist. She was happy with her loot. With Lu laying down the cash, a collection of booze was brought from the aircraft. It would keep many people happy.

Most importantly, the food for the dinner party was off-loaded, including a whole piglet and raw comb honey. Natives drink a form of palm wine, where berries or dates of certain palms are fermented into wine. A few bottles of the local wine were found, but Bonte also captured some Cabs, Merlots, and Chardonnays. The pig was put on a spit for the long roast. Charlie and Carol decided to leave the noisy arena and go to the cliff to wait for the natives. As they walked out the gates, Devil Man and Jackie climbed off the wall and fell in behind them. Both ladies held small note books in their back packs, and had confiscated a bottle of South African Chardonnay to kill the time. The long walk through the forest to the edge of the cliff was much easier, now that a large trail had been cut and trees felled with chain saws, used to make ladders and even miniature log cabins for the soldiers.

Jackie walked quickly to Carol's side and offered to carry the wine. She gave in but scolded him to make sure she got it back. After thirty minutes, they came to the edge of the cliff. There were four soldiers in two different bunkers made with sand bags and cut logs. One of the soldiers gave them two camp stools to sit on. The girls moved where they could get a good view of the beautiful river and jungle. In the distance, they heard an elephant and remarked how lucky they were to be there. Neither felt good that they were disturbing the natives from their normal routines. They sat in silence, while Jackie opened the wine with Carol's corkscrew. She smiled and thanked him. Digging in her purse, she produced a couple of clear plastic cups She poured Charlie a cup of the golden wine.

"Carol, did you read Jean-Pierre's Pygmy Kitibu?" Charlie asked.

"Of course. It was required for my anthropology class," Carol answered.

"Then you know, as I do, the Efes don't have chiefs. They do have elders and are certainly respected. I think the Lese do, so Kombutu is allowing him that honor," Charlie said.

"We won't expose the deception. That would only shame him. You know they're not a warring people. Very gentle and loving among themselves. Peace is easy for them, and the times they had to fight must have been difficult." Carol pulled the hair off her lovely face, blown by a strong breeze rushing up from the river.

Both sat silently sipping the wine and taking in the sound of the jungle.

"Carol, what I love about their people is how they let their kids learn from example and trial by error. They don't spank them. Their babies don't cry much, since someone is always there to hold them and nurse them. Sometimes for five years," she said, feeling very emotional.

"Yes, that is amazing. Much like Native Americans. Beyond all that is the skin contact. The mothers may carry the babies in pouches either in the front or back, but the baby's naked body is always against her skin. They sleep in the huts with the girls skin to skin by their mother, and the men and boys skin to skin on the right side of the huts. They hug a lot and hold hands. We could learn a great deal from them," Carol said.

"If I get married, I always want to sleep in the nude. Skin to skin next to my dude," Charlie said with a huge smile.

"I sleep that way with Sony and love it!"

"Peter and I did last night, and he was okay with it. He's just so new to having a hot bod next to him," Charlie said laughing.

"Wow! What a tremendous figure you have. You had all the guys drooling, and the girls so jealous of you," Carol said.

"Quit it. You guys looked like Sports Illustrated swim suit models. Angel was one, remember?"

"Some lucky guys in that water, huh?" Carol said.

"You bet your ass!"

They had just finished the glass of wine when they saw movement on the river.

There was chatter from the soldiers. Someone said, "Here they come!"

Bok Ande and Kombutu got out of a dugout canoe. The group came in one boat; the same five they had met with before. At the top of the cliff, the ladies greeted them. The girls knew enough of the language to make short simple sentences, but would need Rishi after they sat down for dinner. Carol and Charlie put their arms through the arms of Bok Ande and Kombutu, and walked the entire distance to the quarry that way. The men wore sincere smiles all the way to the gates of the blue water place. Soon they would meet the diggers.

Chapter 29

Natives Visit

For the natives, the Tent City Tour started at the stone cottage. They briefly walked in, looked around and left. They saw where the black pitchblende had been roped off. Rishi joined the group, and explained that dark material put off rays that were harmful. He further stated why animal bones grew near the black soil, and not vegetation. The natives did not say much.

Bruny introduced himself, as did everyone except the military men. Isaac introduced himself using the pygmy language he knew and found, to his surprise, the natives understood much of what he said. The expedition had constructed a long table at which the guests were seated. Bruny poured a plastic cup of palm wine. The guest sipped the wine, and smiled at the vague attempt to duplicate their homemade brew.

Before the hosts served the meal, Bruny talked to the natives through Rishi. He said he was pleased the natives were going to allow mining of minerals there. He spoke of wanting peace, with assurances of providing whatever food they needed. Bruny proclaimed he did not want to pollute the river, disturb the villages or their way of life. He asked how much food they needed and how they would want it delivered.

Kombutu explained they would need help at certain times of the year when there were no crops and finding food was hard for them. Between the two chiefs, together they represented nine villages and over one hundred natives. Bruny said if the chiefs approved, he would deliver the food at the riverbank, once a village representative came with a request. Bruny proposed constructing a log house on the opposite bank, that he would keep supplied with canned goods and other items. Both chiefs thanked him, but declined the offer.

Charlie and Carol frowned when Bruny offered the constant supply of food, but smiled when the native chiefs refused the offer. There was a genuine desire to help them, but an intrusion into their life styles would surely affect the natural order of things. The natives realized the offer was more than they needed or wanted.

The pork and honey was served to their delight. They tried baked potatoes, corn, sliced tomatoes, and a salad with spinach and other greens. They appeared to like everything, especially the wine. When they left, all had to be helped down the ladders, and the canoe ended up being paddled in less than a straight line. The natives carried a lot of food back with them and agreed to come back if invited. They were looking forward to Charlie and Carol's visit. Both ladies were worried that the support already given and future deeds would diminish their unique jungle culture.

As always, the group from the Dominican Republic met around the table, drinking as if they were fraternity partygoers. Lu spoke up first.

"Charlie, we have seen your beautiful body, and now we want to see your gorgeous face come out of hiding. Sooooooo—you are going to get a makeover in the city compliments of Lucero Zacharius," Lu said.

"You don't have to do that," Charlie said.

"We need an excuse to get out of Fort Apache and be pampered. Even though Kisangani isn't California wine country, we have found a beauty shop and spa attached to a large hotel. We are going to raid it day after tomorrow in a helicopter. You do know I am supposed to be on vacation," Lu said, waving her arms around like she was going to round up cattle but meant to imitate a helicopter.

"I completely forgot about the vacation thing! Do we still have a room at Abu camp?" Angel asked.

"It's for sure as hell I don't have a room," Zoe said.

"Bitchy little spy. You are going with us. My treat," Lu said.

"If you've got a minute, Lu and I want to talk to you and Roland,"

Chris said. He put his arm around them both, and took Lu's hand. He moved the four of them over by the water, so he could talk to them in private.

"We want to help you with your hotel. You are missing a marvelous business opportunity with all the workers there. And believe me, they will be there for frigging ever," Chris said. He pointed to the water still lit by dive lights.

"Oh, my God!" Lu said.

"Shit. We left those blown up rubber gloves giving everyone the finger, and the inflated condoms, floating right in front of our native guests," Zoe said.

"I think they were too sloshed to notice. Anyway I hope so," Lu said.

"Roland, what do you think?" Chris asked.

"Chris, you have no concept how much I appreciate your offer. Zoe and I were idiots to have accepted a spying job. We were desperate to get back to normal. If you help us, it will only be a loan. That is all I was asking for at our bank. The place was doing well before the earthquake and will do well for a while. We might sell it in the future, but either way you will be paid back in full."

"Good. That's settled. Now, Zoe, when do I get to borrow Roland?" Lu said, laughing. Chris put her in a headlock then kissed her on the back of her neck.

"To get started, I will call my bank in Santo Domingo tomorrow, and they will call your bank in Port au Prince," Chris said. "I'm guessing they have all the construction plans you presented…name of the contractor and all that?"

"Barclays has it all," Roland said.

"Perfect. This will be easy—I use Barclays too."

"Want me to get involved and get everyone off their asses?" Lu said.

"No way! Roland and Zoe might need these people in the future." He knew Lu would rain down fire on anyone not moving ninety miles an hour.

"Hey! You guys planning a revolution over there?" Mit yelled as
he moved towards a make shift bar.

"Yes! We just enacted a non-German zone around the bar," Lu said
not realizing that she was assisting in the breaking out of somewhat
dark German humor.

"Too late. This Nazi has arrived to enforce the selective drink rule.
I select who drinks and who doesn't. Right now, you must have been a
part of a country ruled by Hitler, or a former Jansen swim suit model.
No one else is qualified."

In a strong German accent, Mit apologized with weak sincerity.

"Ha! In diesem fall mein Fuerhrer sie dick kopf bitte mix mit
dieser hure einen woodka tonic," Gretchen said. She had now broken
through enemy lines and apparently joined the Nazi party, in order to
get her drink.

Mit became unglued and laughed so hard, he could barely fix her
drink. Gretchen had a slight smile on her face, but really needed a
drink after helping build showers and latrines all day.

"Okay. My German is weak, what did she say Mit?" Angel said.

"In this case, my Fuehrer, you dick head; please fix this whore a
vodka tonic."

There was general laughter, which continued into the night. Carol,
Charlie, Peter and Sony joined them, and Gretchen had to repeat her
famous line for them. There were snacks left from dinner and plenty of
booze. They did not really feel, at least on this night, that they were in
the African Congo. Rather, they were at just another party with good
friends.

~~~~~

Creeping along the narrow logging road, Bahati's men were
in the truck that led to the spot where the four expedition vehicles
were parked. He had been told they stopped at about nine miles in,
and he wanted to give a two mile sound buffer before he sent his two
commando types ahead. Finally the truck stopped. The driver nodded
to Bahati and pointed to the odometer. From somewhere in the truck
two men emerged with night vision goggles, flak jackets, and sniper
rifles. They disappeared quickly in the darkness. Bahati had his men
take a knee and wait either for their return or a radio signal.

Isaac left two of his men to guard the vehicles. Since nothing happened other than forest buffaloes marching through their campsite, they had relaxed any pretense of being vigilant.

One of the guards was asleep in a tent. The other sat in the rear truck, snoring and slumped over his weapon. One of the intruders reached up, put his hand over his mouth until he made no sounds, and slit his throat. The other attacker went to the tent, unzipped it, and poked the soldier encased in his sleeping bag.

"What de fok!" he yelled, before he realized he was under attack. Since he had an automatic rifle pointed at his face, he didn't bother to grab his weapon.

The commando was joined by his partner who had called in to Bahati. They tied up the guard, and put him in a folding chair in the beam of the headlights of one of the trucks. Not long afterwards, the leader of these UCFF forces stood over this man, asking questions. They spoke a common language, so Bahati assured him he would not be harmed if he cooperated. The soldier knew he was a dead man, whether he talked or not. He wouldn't tell them anything for a while. Bahati's men removed the car battery from one of the trucks, and hooked a jumper cable to the battery. They instructed the soldier to stand, pulled down his pants and underwear, and forced him back into the chair. They tied the man to the chair, while others poured water on his groin area.

"Mr. Soldier, do you like your balls? How about your dick? If you tell me what I want, you may keep these items. I need to know where these soldiers went—how many—their weapons. I need to know what they are mining for and what they have found. You know these things because you have a radio. Will you tell me now?" Bahati held the cable and the spring loaded clamps and clicked them together, sending enough sparks to briefly light up the jungle. The truck was started, so the full voltage ran freely through the clamps.

"Fok you," he said, and screamed. Two clamps tore into his testicles, sending burning voltage and amperage through his body. He almost fainted, but held on.

~~~~~

This was taking too long for Bahati. After the second shock, he decided to remove the soldier's fingers one at a time. A bloody affair, but usually effective. Bahati asked which finger he wanted cut off first. The soldier had a look of horror in his face." We will start with the little finger," Bahati said. "Jambi! Bring me a wooden board."

Bahati pleaded with the soldier to give him some information, so he wouldn't have to cut off his fingers. The soldier was well aware of the game. He would endure all he could, give them the information they wanted, and then there would be a bullet to the brain.

"If I give you the information, can you just turn me loose in the jungle?" he pleaded.

"Of course, that would not be a problem. A leopard will eat you for breakfast," Bahati said.

"I don't believe you. I will tell you nothing."

The board arrived. After the third finger was severed, he fainted. The tormentors threw water in his face, and he came to, begging to tell what they wanted. As soon as he told Bahati everything, one of the men shot him between the eyes. For the poor soldier, the bullet was a blessing.

"These are our problems to be solved. We have twenty miles of jungle to go through, and most of it tonight. Once we get through, we have a river to cross. Then, there is a 500 foot cliff with two bunkers, maybe three, at the top of the cliff. After that, there is a forest with a freshly cut trail that goes for about three or four miles, to a rock wall that is circular and twenty feet tall with soldiers in bunkers. Once inside, there are armed workers. There are thirty or forty of them and twelve of us," he said, smiling the whole time.

The group discussed each problem one by one. Because the soldiers they had encountered guarding the vehicles were inept, they assumed all were poorly trained. The soldier did not tell Bahati there were four Haitian commandos at the quarry, and no one had brought up the subject of the natives.

The main reason Bahati wanted to risk his life to gain access to the quarry was the information the tortured soldier gave up. He told Bahati about the large amount of diamonds found in the quarry, as reported over his two-way radio. Had it not been for the diamonds, Bahati would have turned his troops around and gone back.

Captain Ismael Bahati started that night through the jungle, having charged the hopes and dreams of his men with the promise of an equal share in the diamonds. During their difficult trek through the wet forest and entanglements of the Congo, that promise was all they had.

Chapter 30

Visit to Natives

Fog, mist and a suffocating heat contributed to a morning of misery. Water dripped everywhere. Insects woke up to a brand new day of attack. If they could bite long enough, they just might use some unsuspecting person for a nursery ward for larva of some disgusting insect species. Then there were the tsetse flies, whose bite is guaranteed to kill, if not treated or rendered harmless by a vaccination.

A large smoky fire was a welcome refuge from most insects as well as the damp coolness of the morning. During the night, Devil Man and Osse killed snakes when they came under the gates. Just before the natives arrived, Jemi killed a rare green mamba outside the gates. All the snakes were pitched into the forest where creatures, bacteria and fungi waited to devour anything.

Charlie, Carol, Sony, Peter, and Rishi had packed up to make jungle visits to various villages of the Efe and Lese tribes. Devil Man and Jackie would tag along, because the natives' screams would provide unlimited entertainment for the little safari. The two girls asked if Gretchen would accompany them, both for medical assistance and for study of the two native tribes' natural remedies. Modesto offered to go with her, but she waived him off, as so many projects demanded attention in the quarry. Bruny and Isaac asked the group sitting around the fire pit to take pistols with them.

"Carol, where is your pistol?" Sony asked, while he showed off his weapon. "Mine is a .40 caliber Glock," he said, as he proudly slid the receiver back, and pushed a round from the clip into the chamber.

"It's in here someplace, dear," she said. She dug deeply in her purse. After handing Sony a package of tampons, lipstick, her birth control pills, and what looked like a century old package of Rolaids, out came a tiny stainless steel automatic pistol.

"Is that a gun or a cap pistol?" Sony said. He held it by two fingers, as though it was contagious.

"It wasn't cheap. It's either a Beretta Bobcat, or Alley Cat. It has little bullets like a real gun. I put them in myself—about seven or ten—can't remember. They have a number like—twenty something."

"Twenty-two maybe? This gun might be good for the wilds of Iowa, but not the Congo," Sony said.

"I don't think there are wilds in Iowa," she said.

"Exactly my point."

"I'm not wagging some Dirty Harry gun around. I have you to protect me with your forty caliber cock," she said, smiling up at him.

"That's a Glock!"

"Whatever you want to call it, dear," she said and watched the rest of the group almost fall into the fire laughing.

Everyone had breakfast and assembled by the gate. Charlie and Carol had large expensive digital cameras to record the visit. Gretchen had a small medical bag. Devil Man and Jackie had AK-47s in case the natives got restless. Everyone had small knapsacks loaded with food items, in case they weren't fond of the particular insects of the day on the native menu.

The safari of eight climbed down the ladders to the bottom of the cliff, and took one of the larger inflatables to cross the river. Three pygmies met them on the other side and led them into the jungle. The small natives were perfectly built to weave in and out of the overhanging vines and limbs. The group had to ask the natives to slow down several times, since the pygmies' bodies could handle the heat and humidity better than larger humans. Gretchen was anxious to study the reasons why they rarely died of jungle diseases; however, they did have high rates of mortality from pneumonia. She believed living in almost one hundred percent humidity took a toll on the lungs. She had read they died from forest hazards such as falling trees, snake bites, and other accidents, rather than sickness.

"Can we take a break?" Carol said. She was having second thoughts about borrowing baggy clothes from Charlie. Gretchen made everyone drink water. As they stood in the jungle on a trail used by natives for maybe a hundred thousand years, the hikers realized that stopping meant letting the insects catch up or at least make their attack. Ants began to move up from the ground. Other insects landed, while others dropped from hanging foliage. Slapping and cursing was followed by jumping and stomping. The natives were laughing so hard they actually rolled on the ground.

"I'm glad somebody is enjoying this," Carol said. She had just slapped herself in the face to kill something.

"They say it is better to keep moving," Rishi said.

"If you stop, you die—if you go on, it's a heat stroke—you die. Sony, it has been fun being your jungle wife," Carol said, trying to adjust to one of the most inhospitable places on earth.

"Hang in there, dear—it will only get worse."

Walking did help in escaping non-flying insects. Ones with wings saw a good meal on the hoof and, like fighter pilots, dove and attacked at will. Insect repellent may have actually worked on some insects, but many were attracted to it. Finally, the ladies put insect nets over their heads and stopped the nonsense. The number of insects that collected on the netting shocked them.

The men certainly shared in the attack from the insects, but beards and male scent were less attractive. The ancient trail went inland, and followed very old paths that avoided elephant and large game trails.

The first village they came upon was on a slight ridge above the river. Bare dirt was exposed all throughout the village, and a large fire was going in the center. Children were playing, and women were holding babies in cloth pouches around their necks. All stood up and greeted them, with hugs or holding of hands. They seemed to be a very loving tribe. The smell of the village was strong, coming from bodies that live in a jungle and rarely bathed. When they did, they went in the shallows of the river, without soap. Charlie and Carol said strong smells may repel some insects. Gretchen felt that harboring so many bacteria made them immune to their harmful effects.

"Are you saying I'm not nasty enough?" Sony asked.

"Something for you and Carol to work on," Gretchen said.

Carol and Charlie had Rishi ask if they could take pictures. Given the okay, each woman would get photos of all the people in the village, and with Rishi's help, record discussions.

Gretchen asked to talk to the village's healer and found that most of the older women shared duties. Two elderly Efe women took Gretchen's hand and walked her into the jungle. The rear view was of a mother holding hands with two very old grey haired children. Rishi followed, as did Jackie. Questions were asked about different illnesses and injuries. As Gretchen would ask about an infection from a wound, the women would harvest different leaves, vines and tubers. Gretchen took notes as to how they should be prepared and put the botanical items in a Ziplock bag. These remedies actually worked and had been used for thousands of years. The natives told Gretchen if they didn't work, they wouldn't use them. Although they didn't have a cure for cancer, they had a very strong opiate to ease the pain. Gretchen collected samples of the opiate. Cancer was not commonly contracted by the pygmies. Gretchen thought either diet or the environment were factors. The women did provide her with a plant medicine that helped types of skin cancer. She was thrilled with that information. The problem was, many of these plants were only indigenous to a small part of the Congo. When possible, she collected seeds, spores, and tubers.

Back in the village, all the kids and young girls were standing around Devil Man, giggling with their heads bowed. He was like a giant black God to them. He didn't like them being afraid, so he sat on the ground and put his rifle in a sling on his back. Then he opened a bag of hard candy, smiled and held them in his hand for them. Some of the brave children came over for the candy and a few even looked in his face. Soon he was a mountain for the kids to climb on, which made him laugh out loud. He had transformed himself from one of the most feared to the new rock star of the village.

They traveled to a Lese village next and found it a little more structured, with a chief who had to approve everything done by the group from the quarry, including photos and interviews. This village had a formal healer, who was reluctant to reveal his healing methods. He was interested in pneumonia, which had taken a lot of his people. Gretchen worked out a deal for his skin cancer treatment. She would conduct a couple of full treatments for pneumonia in exchange. She warned a few people might have an allergic reaction to the drug, and explained how to deal with possible reactions.

At the next village, they found the traditional combination of Efe living adjacent to the Lese. The Efe would provide meat and help with the crops, and the Lese would produce vegetables for the Efe. The anthropologists believed this had been the way for thousands of years. At this point, they shared a meal prepared by both tribes. Both tribes prepared a meal centered on a small antelope they had killed and cooked on coals. Rounding out the dinner were several types of plantains, tubers, forest beans, bananas, and of course, grubs and insects. Clay pots held forest honey with huge pieces of combs—some with the larva of the bees in them. The entire group enjoyed the perfect meal and the visit—not the typical place to be on vacation.

They thanked everyone and more gifts were given by the group— practical things like non-stick cooking pans and canned meat, including sardines and bottles of raw honey. Also, the group gave them another solar light for the village, which Sony and Peter installed.

The walk back to the quarry would be long, and they would have to get there before dark. Jackie and Rishi led the way. Devil Man was the rear guard.

~~~~~

Bahati's dirty dozen only had a few miles to go before they reached the river. The night march had not been without incident, because an elephant trail was in use when they crossed it. A few blasts from their automatic weapons scattered the elephants. Captain Bahati had a plan to stay at the edge of the jungle until after dark. The first play would be to launch rocket propelled grenades, to take out the bunkers on the cliff. He would have people positioned on the ladders rush in, to become snipers in trees that overlooked the enclosure.

After the snipers had done their work, his main force would

attack. Although hauling the rocket propelled grenades had slowed them during the night, these powerful weapons would be an equalizer in the fight against forces far outnumbering themselves. The snipers in the trees would use the powerful weapons to rain death down into the quarry. As they neared the river, Bahati had his men rest on a trail, while he sent two men ahead as scouts. When they sat down to recoup, insects started to take them apart. The best they could do was pace around in a stupor.

As the two scouts emerged from the jungle and stood on the banks of the river, two natives eased back into the vegetation, unseen. Bahati's scouts quickly backed up to hide when they saw people on the island. Expedition members were returning from the village tours and unloading their gear from the rubber raft. The scouts watched as the small assembly crossed from the shore to the ladders, where the men took most of the gear from the women. They observed the soldiers who manned the bunkers standing up to assist the people making the climb. Of great interest were the two large Haitian guards who looked like monsters next to the rest of the people. Having taken notes on distance and placement of personnel, they eased back into the jungle.

Chapter 31

The Attack

When the two Efe natives were sure the soldiers had returned to the jungle, they pulled a dugout into the river and landed on Binza Island, named for Dr. Parke's tent boy. It was still light, but a half-sun hung in the shadows on the horizon. The tiny natives waved at the men in the bunkers, and started up the ladder. One of the men stood up and greeted them when they reached the top. The guard could not translate what they were saying. He escorted them to the enclosure, and radioed ahead. Rishi, Isaac and Bruny met them at the gate and ushered them inside to sit by the fire.

Since Isaac had not heard from his vehicle guards all day, the entire camp was on alert. The news that soldiers had been seen across the river was unwelcome, but appreciated. The description of a rocket on both soldiers' backs was more bad news. Since Isaac's Haitian troops had only two of them and ten rounds, RPGs sent the odds over to the invader's side,

"Radio the men and have them move out of their bunkers as soon as it's dark," Isaac said. "They will be the first to be targeted. Have them find secure positions at the edge of the bluff and pull all the ladders up—make them climb. Once the aggressors are on top, they can be engaged." Rishi immediately carried out the order.

Modesto rushed to Isaac's side. His battle experience and tactics were well known to Isaac, who welcomed the help. They reviewed their assets and firepower. Modesto remembered they had a Barrett .50 caliber long-range sniper rifle—but wasn't sure it had a night scope. They radioed the two Haitian brothers, who assured them they had a Star Light scope with excellent night vision capabilities and an additional five hundred rounds for the Barrett.

"These guys either miss a lot, or just expect war at every turn," Isaac said.

"I fired one of those bastards for ten rounds and my shoulder was ground beef—500 rounds and your arm would fall off. Maybe we need to know who else is checked out on the Barrett, so we can pass it around," Modesto said. Isaac instructed Rishi to get information on the Barrett back-up shooters.

"Put the Barrett on the bluff where we can see targets," Modesto said. Once the scope's capabilities had been discussed, Osse and Jean-Jean came off the wall. They were running full out for the edge of the bluff.

Modesto estimated the enemy force to be small—maybe ten to twenty.

"If they were large in number, they would have sent a patrol out to assess the area of attack," Modest said. "But we need to assume they are experienced and well-armed. What is your assessment of our troops?"

"DRC troops have seen a lot of action against rebel militias. We are down to nine, since one is in the hospital, plus Rishi. The Haitian soldiers have fought against uprisings where the opposition were poorly trained and equipped forces. Different ballgame here. The four Haitian mercenaries are game changers. Each is worth five to ten men out there. They need to be in the mix, and we need to keep them safe," Isaac said. "You, Mit, and Chris have been in some fire fights. You are our aces in the hole."

"Don't discount these girls. Gretchen fought it out with a bunch of pirates. Bullets were buzzing all around her, and she nailed at least one while she was buck naked," Modesto said.

"I hope you don't get mad when I say I wish I had seen that gun fight," Isaac said, laughing. "Right now they've just got pistols, and hopefully, we can keep them out of the fray."

The two natives asked if they could leave, as there was very little light left. Bruny couldn't make them stay. Rishi told them to be careful, and they were gone in a flash. Shortly after they left, darkness fell heavily over the tent city. The night was cloudy and threatened rain.

A few wooden buildings had been constructed: a men and women's latrine with a center divider, a set of showers built along the same design, two showers on each side, with a cistern on top to collect rainwater and one large building, still under construction. This multipurpose building had a plywood roof and sides, but at this point, no doors or windows. All the rooms were divided and chopped up spaces. At completion, this multipurpose structure would have an equipment room, lab, computer room, communication room, a medical clinic, and ammo storage. The diamonds were located there, as were the quarters for Bruny, Isaac, and Dr. Devine.

The helicopter had delivered construction supplies. A couple of the other helicopters also made runs, even though they were not set up for large deliveries. A huge Russian helicopter would arrive the next day to carry a front end loader from a nearby truck. Bruny wished he had ordered a small army to be placed aboard the big chopper.

In rapid succession, the three bunkers on the edge of the cliff exploded. Debris sprayed several hundred feet. The flash temporarily blinded anyone who had been looking in that direction. Clearly, the two natives had saved several lives by scouting out the incoming enemy soldiers. Ringing ears and terror paralyzed everyone's mobility. The men on the cliff's edge hunkered down and prayed there would be no more blasts. More random explosions dashed their hopes. Basically, the insurgents were carpet bombing the top of the bluff. So far, the RPGs had scared the men from the quarry and locked them down in their positions.

The defenders lacked leadership and decisive action. Osse and Jean-Jean rushed out of the smoke, carrying assault weapons and a Barrett .50 caliber. Modesto and Isaac were behind them with AKs, sharing the load of a heavy box. They all ran to the edge of the bluff, and motioned the Haitians to climb down to the next landing and set up the Barrett. They did, and Modesto and Isaac ran to each position of the soldiers who had escaped the bunker blast and gave them grenades. They were to start throwing them over the cliff where the invaders might approach. Explosions were now pretty constant, yet the RPGs still rained down on the top of the cliff. Isaac and Modesto climbed to the place where the Barrett was set up.

Osse looked through the FLIR thermal night scope and picked up on warm reddish heads coming across the river. He sighted and pulled the trigger. The head disappeared. He spotted another which went underwater. Osse was patient. Everyone around him was wearing earplugs, since the big gun can cause permanent ear damage. When the next man surfaced, Osse erased him from the scope viewer. Immediately after he pulled the trigger, incoming fire assaulted their position.

Bullets tore into the rocky hillside, and one grazed Osse's shoulder. Another went through the top of Jean-Jean's Kevlar helmet, but only hit his hair. Modesto had brought a pair of Night Scout binoculars that Peter had handed him on his way out of the quarry. Not only was Peter a Star Wars freak, he was into every new tech device he could find. Modesto started scanning, and as he looked to the left, he saw a couple of infrared images by a rocky area near the water. Before he could say anything, a blinding light went off in his eyes. Rounds started hitting all around him. One buzzed his ear and thudded to a stop on the hillside behind him. A round skidded under Isaac, and bounced into his flak jacket, leaving him breathless and bruised. Another hit the tripod on the big rifle and slammed into the dirt. Osse wasn't blinded by the round, so he turned the rifle in the direction of the fire. He spotted the image and opened up just as the image dove behind a rock.

"What happened? Did you get him?" Modesto asked, still fighting to get his vision back.

"No. He has ducked under an overhanging rock," Osse said.

"Move out to the edge, and see if you can bust it up," Modesto suggested, while more grenades exploded at the bottom of the bluff.

The .50 caliber broke off part of the rock on the first shot. More and more multiple rounds pulverized the stone. Now Osse was beginning to see not one, but two images as they ran from the rocks. The last man to run from the cover of the rock was blown into the river. The second image was running, and Osse caught him in his sights, blowing off one leg completely. The gun clicked and Osse replaced the ten round clip in lightning speed. He found his target, hopping on one leg, and finished him.

The RPGs were not raining down as hard as before, which possibly meant Bahati's men were climbing up the cliff, but there was no way to tell where they were. Isaac and Modesto guessed they had moved around to a more difficult place, where there were fewer grenades. Modesto suggested they redirect all the men away from potentially exposed flanks, if the invaders went through the forest and came at their backs in the dark. Isaac issued the orders. Soon everyone was jogging at a fast pace down the new trail towards the quarry walls.

Isaac asked if anyone would volunteer to be a sniper and got two brave takers. If they took a shot and the invader spotted them, the snipers would be at great risk of being blasted out of the trees. Some considered it a suicide mission. Isaac really wanted the volunteers more as spotters with radios, and they were only to fire if a group could be taken out quickly. He placed the two sharp shooters close together to cover each other. Still, a sniper was on a mission that few survived.

The two chosen soldiers climbed and then hid in the big date palm trees, a few hundred yards from the front gate. One sniper had a night scope and the other had infrared binoculars. The men posted on the wall could see them clearly. Being twenty feet up was an advantage for a pure frontal assault, but if anyone got as far as the wall, they were out of view of most of the soldiers twenty feet up. If the guards on the wall leaned over to see the invaders, they risked being shot. Since pouring burning oil was not an option, they would have to wait until the enemy troops were in the killing field to take them out. The tree sniper could handle that task if they were in their line of sight.

Inside the quarry, everyone had been moved to the stone cottage. The first part of the pressure chamber was open and a ladder secured, for use as a very good bomb shelter.

"I want to shoot one of those fuckers," said Lu. She patted her Rhino 357 pistol.

"Sony doesn't like my gun," Carol said with a puckered lip.

"It will just piss someone off," Angel said. "But this bugger will kill them," she said. She gripped the 9mm that saved Mit's boat from a take-over a few years back.

The geologists, mining engineers, Dr. Devine and Gretchen were in the stone cottage. Devil Man stood guard outside. Jackie was on the wall by the front gate.

The night sky was full of rain clouds. Moonlight was sparse. In what appeared to be a freak display of celestial meteor showers, the whistling trails of rockets rained from all directions.

Chapter 32

The Battle

The three helicopter pilots in the compound had been staying in a tent near their aircraft. When the shooting started, they all climbed aboard the supply chopper and laid face down on the cargo floor. It was a good thing, since one of the RPGs hit dead center of their tent. Their personal items were vaporized.

The second series of RPGs were about half as numerous as the first volley. One hit the edge of the stone cottage and blew some rocks loose on a corner. By this time, everyone was in the first chamber with the lid closed.

Isaac and Modesto instructed their men on the walls to refrain from firing their RPGs. Instead, they advised them to answer with shots aimed at the initial rocket flashes. Someone screamed from near the rear wall of the quarry. The scream probably indicated that one of Bahati's men had been blown over the edge of a 500 foot cliff.

After small arms fire became the main weapon of attack, expedition members concluded the invading rebels had used up their allotment of explosive rounds. The expedition returned fire to each small arms muzzle flash with a rocket until their ten rounds were exhausted. Insurgent AKs hit the sand bags on the gun placements around the wall, but firing upwards was not working.

Inside the enclosure, Chris and Mit assessed the damage. Their tents, along with many others, had been blown up. One rocket hit the corner of the big wooden building and blew off part of a wall. Dr. Devine and Gretchen were inside sheltered by interior walls so they weren't injured. They moved to the stone cottage fallout shelter with the others shortly after the attack began. A couple of the rockets landed in the blue hole and blew water everywhere. Several craters appeared in the kimberlite ore, but none in the pitchblende site. Since it contained the highly radioactive ore, it was fortunate that a round hadn't found it way there and spread the dangerous ore on top of everyone. It would have caused a panic.

The snipers in the date palm trees radioed that three of the attackers had moved next to walls and were working their way towards the gate. Isaac gave the snipers permission to take them out and notified the men on the wall to cover them in case they were spotted by their fellow soldiers. The tree snipers laid into the attackers with heavy automatic fire. Although the insurgents fired wildly, they didn't see the snipers until it was too late. Two of their friends ran to the date palms, looked up and started to fire. The Barrett .50 caliber struck one, penetrated his flak jacket causing him to drop lifelessly to the ground. The men on the wall opened up on the other man, but only after he fired several rounds into the palm tree. The sniper screamed that he had been hit and was climbing down. Only a couple of militia men remained, exchanging small rounds fire.

The injured sniper saw it was too dangerous to cross the space from the tree line to the wall. He slid down the tree with his rifle slung on his back, his upper leg covered in dark blood. Some two hundred feet away, a Bahati soldier stepped out of the tree line and raised his weapon to fire. Like a silent movie, the enemy soldier grabbed his throat, and then his chest. Dozens of pygmy arrows entered his body. He died an agonizing death from arrows that had pierced his skull, neck, chest and groin. For fear of being shot, no pygmies came out of the tree line. Rishi got on the loud speaker and thanked them profusely.

Although silence had replaced gunfire, everyone was on alert. Dr. Devine and Gretchen had moved back to the wooden building to attend to the wounded. The sniper was rushed into the quarry and to the makeshift clinic where medical cots had been set up and attended by the two doctors who made the sniper's bullet wound their first priority.

Inside the dark enclosure, the expedition leaders got busy doing damage assessments around camp. Chris, Mit, and Modesto came down from the wall, where they had gone to observe the fighting. Roland and Zoe followed Gretchen to the multi-purpose building to help with the wounded soldier who because of his profuse bleeding, was lucky to be alive. Lu, Angel, Carol, and Charlie climbed the ladder from the first chamber, and asked Devil Man if they could come out. He gave them the go-ahead, and walked the backside of the cottage to relieve himself. While the four girls were standing outside the stone structure, a uniformed man carrying an automatic weapon walked up to them. They didn't recognize him, but they didn't know all the soldiers in the compound.

"Hello, ladies. I trust you are all unharmed," the soldier said.

"We are fine, thank you. I don't believe I have met you," Lu said.

"Unlikely. I am Captain Ismael Bahati of the United Freedom Fighters of the Congo. I have come here to collect my share of the diamonds. Could you be so kind as to lead me to them? Then I'll be on my way," he said, while he raised his weapon and held a grenade with a finger on the pin. "I will pull this pin and take several of you with me if you don't lead me to the diamonds in the next five seconds," he said. He herded the ladies in front of him towards the wooden building where he was told by everyone the diamonds were stored when in reality they were just a few feet from him in the stone cottage.

When they walked past the cottage, Devil Man moved quickly between the girls and Bahati. The sight of the huge man with a white eye and jagged scar caused just a millisecond of hesitation from Bahati—enough for Devil Man to blast his AK-47. It dropped Bahati before he could pull the pin on the grenade.

Bahati did get off a short blast and one caught Devil Man in the mid-section of his flak jacket where he had placed a metal insert. The other rounds went upward and away, except for clipping away a piece of his one good ear. The girls ran to check him out. He loved the attention and assured them he was okay. They were not sure so they unzipped his flak jacket. They found an ugly bruise but no penetration by the bullet. Lu and Angel grabbed a first aid kit and worked on his ear.

"Devil Man," Lu said, "I will pay for the repair on your ear. It's high goddamn time you got some work done on those other scars and that eye as well. I know a very pretty plastic surgeon, and I am taking you to her when we get back. No argument," she said. Devil Man knew her well enough to know that resistance was useless.

"Yes, ma'am," he replied.

A few wounds required attention among the fighters, including pieces of shrapnel from the RPGs and nicks from bullets. They were extremely lucky that no one else was killed in the attack, except for the two vehicle guards in the jungle. The most serious injury was the sniper's leg, but even that wound would be all right in time. Gretchen and Dr. Devine were busy for a while, but by dawn, everyone was patched up. The soldiers were sent out through the forest to bring the bodies of the insurgents to the quarry. They would be buried in an area by the back wall that seemed to contain some low grade coltan ore. A cemetery already existed outside the wall, but it was reserved for those that died in the quarry. Isaac would send a squad of men by helicopter to properly handle the return of the dead guards to their families for burial. A special fund would be provided for their next of kin.

Gretchen was tired, and the other ladies had not gotten much sleep, but Lu insisted they keep their appointment at the Hotel Grand Congo for the spa treatments and Charlie's makeover. At first Gretchen was reluctant to go along.

"We will get a few rooms. Then, you can sleep over there in royal ass comfort," Lu said.

The supply helicopter transported the wounded sniper so he could be observed in the hospital. The chopper would also carry replacement tents and plywood to fix the damaged building. Lu was taking the big helicopter, which was going to be loaded with six young women.

~~~~~

Barbos Vieux was getting bored hanging around the hotel, so he decided to book a massage for later in the day. After breakfast, he stopped by the front desk, and he said wanted to book a deep tissue massage. They directed him to the spa which was located on the same floor. He smiled when he approached the pretty receptionist at the African Jungle Spa.

"What a beautiful facility you have here. Is all this new?" he asked.

"Yes sir. It is not yet a year old. What may I help you with?" she asked.

"I need a massage. How about one o'clock today?" Barbos asked.

"Sir, we can accommodate you this morning at ten. But, after that, I am booked up for the rest of the day."

"What! Is there a convention in town?"

"No sir. A lot of ladies who have been in the jungle for a few days are coming in to be saved by the spa. They have booked everything: massages, nails, hair, facials and you name it. We had to call in people from other hotels to assist," she said.

"That must be my friend, Lu Zacharius?" Barbos said.

"We don't normally give out the names of our guests. You must be a friend," she said without revealing Lu's name.

"Oh, that I am, but please do not tell her I asked about her. I wish that to be a surprise," Barbos said. He didn't want to divulge his joy at the knowledge that his prey had decided to come to his doorstep.

He knew he would have to stay hidden while the girls were there. At the front desk, he found they had booked three rooms and would leave the next day after breakfast. He contacted his men and put a plan into action. His friend in Gbadolite would make sure all the requirements were set up there. Everything was falling into place—better than he ever dreamed it would.

Chapter 33

Spa Visit

Two taxis hauled the six expedition girls to the Grand Congo Hotel. When they arrived, Lu booked three suites rather than just any old rooms. Lunch on the terrace by the pool was the first order of business, then from there—girl's day out. As they were checking in Carol addressed the group.

"Do you know what Sony said to me when I left?" Carol asked. She didn't really want a guess since she was going to tell them anyway.

"Go Kisangani. Get butt rubbed. Do girl shit. Come back. Big sex then—Pilgrim. He's now trying to be a mixture of old Sony and John Wayne...it's just irritating," Carol said with a crooked smile.

The rest of the girls laughed. They had heard Sony's short sentence routine many times.

Lunch was a fancy buffet by the pool under a colorful canvas umbrella.

"I was hoping for an open fire with a skillet sitting on a rock—but I guess I'm just spoiled," Angel said.

"Girls, I know this isn't a quarry in the jungle. We'll have to make do," Lu said.

Their luggage was sent up. While they finished lunch, they reviewed the time schedule.

"Charlie," Lu said. "You will have your facial first, then your massage, your nails, then hair color, make-up and maybe some new clothes if the shop here has your size," she announced the schedule for everyone.

They spent the day redesigning themselves. By evening, they were ready for an elegant dinner in new dresses from the hotel shop. Few would've believed that only the night before, they were dodging rocket propelled grenades.

Charlie's transformation was the most obvious. No longer a mop, her short blonde hair had been feathered around her head. With her face made up, her pretty features were outlined and radically enhanced. The ladies were sure that no one would recognize Charlie. Everyone looked and felt great, but they all knew they would return to the mine after breakfast.

Throughout the day Barbos had his men report the women's activities. He had spoiled himself by holing up, letting room service cater to his every need. He even had a hooker drop by so he might celebrate his good fortune. Everything was in place for the next day. A large van would be available to take them all to the airport.

~~~~~

The mechanics, Patrick and Junior, had the old compressor running like new so now the critical testing could be made. Mit had been a mechanical engineer before he had escaped to the Dominican Republic to establish several dive shops in the Bavaro and Punta Cana areas. He helped Sony calculate the non-decompression diving time for the bottom chamber, using measurements from the previous expedition. Now it was possible to use the pressurized compartments next to the blue hole.

Sony had become an engineer like his grandfather. He preferred engineering over geology, even though his dad, John Cole, was a geologist. He had taken management courses with his major in anticipation of the day when his dad stepped down, and he assumed the reins of Hanover Oil. None of that mattered to him as much as having a son or daughter. Even though his relationship with Carol was new, she had told him she was ready to start "cranking out kids"—her exact words.

Chris was ready to dive with Mit. After all, they had been diving together since they were in their early twenties. Several years before both had heard about a wreck dive on the *Conception* several years before off the coast of the Dominican Republic. An aerial photo of the wreck published in a magazine caught Chris's attention. He and Mit Kruger had just met while salvage diving on a freighter that went down near the Navidad Banks. Over beers one night, Chris showed the photograph to Mit. He pointed out that the bow of the original wreck appeared to be missing.

On their days off, they began the search. After a month, they found the missing section of the *Conception* and negotiated for a large share of the treasure. Mit opened dive shops and bought a large boat he later named the *Bottom Fantasy*. After his first divorce gobbled up the house Chris bought in California, he opened a dive shop in Hot Springs, Arkansas. His second divorce took his home on a lake in Arkansas. Still, he escaped both divorces with money left over, and he enjoyed considerable success on future dives. Lucero Zacharius put the brakes on much of his diving adventures. He didn't mind, since their son Reid took up a large part of his time. The huge amount of Rafael Trujillo's gold they had found on an artificial reef in the Dominican Republic had made the three couples wealthy—very wealthy.

Since it was cool at 135 feet both men donned shorty wet suits. They wanted to retain body heat in case of a decompression situation. Roland and Sony had agreed to help them inside the deep chamber, while Jemi and Peter were in the upper chamber. In the stone cottage above them were the mechanics, Dr. Devine and a couple of soldiers. Once the pressure was equalized in the upper chamber, the round submarine airlock for the lower chamber was opened. They heard a hissing sound and foul air was sucked up into the top chamber. As soon as the men had climbed down the ladder to the lower chamber, the air lock was sealed. Peter and Jemi quickly opened the top seal. Fifty years of foul air blasted through the cottage washing over the men, out the door and into the atmosphere of the Congo.

In the lower chamber Roland and Sony secured the extra scuba tanks in case they were needed for a decompression situation. Both looked around at the interior of the tunnel. Sony surmised mining had taken place there for many years. Since the mine was a vertical tunnel type, steps had to be carved for the mine to go deeper. A series of cut backs and spiral steps led to a spot where they had hit water and flooding stopped their progress. Pumping in air pushed the water out so they could mine deeper until they reached the water at the bottom level of the blue hole. The expedition did not know how many workers died because they labored in pressurized air. In the early 1800s a small number of bridge engineers knew about caisson illness or decompression sickness and worked to combat it. It could have been some of these very engineers who assisted on this project.

The four deceased men who John and Vikki Cole found appeared to have died because the air supply above them had been cut off. Possibly, the topside support group had been attacked by natives. Some workers had escaped and returned several days later. With the knowledge that the men in the lower chamber were dead, they may have regarded the room as a tomb and sealed it. Sony and his group would never know exactly what happened. A bigger mystery remained: why hadn't anyone tried to remove the fortune in diamonds in the lower chamber?

Undoubtedly, the richest and most productive of all the mining in the past came from diamonds collected from the bottom of the blue hole. Chris and Mit set their bottom timers for ten minutes and wasted no time scraping the bottom with trowels to fill fine mesh bags. Chris and Mit surfaced at the bottom of the tunnel, removed their weight belts and started the task of walking up to their support team carrying their gear and the bags of diamond ore. Both briefly examined the old diving suits that held the skeletons of two divers minus their skulls and helmets. By the time they reached Sony and Roland, they were exhausted from the climb. They decided to be safe and stay at that level for thirty minutes, to release as much residual nitrogen as possible. While everyone was waiting for Chris and Mit to outgas, the four began sorting diamonds. Although they lacked class, Ziploc bags were used to store the rough diamonds. With four people picking through the large mesh bags, colorful stones bulged inside the bags. Most were white but there were also light blue, yellow, brown, light green and occasionally even a pink stone. Chris held up a respectfully large sized pink one.

"Mit, don't you still have some rose diamonds? I know I do. The prices have gone nuts since we sold ours in Europe."

"I have a few left. Someone told me the pink ones like you're holding will go for a million dollars a karat in the next year or so. They are rare, and every new bride wants one. Most people still haven't even heard of rose diamonds." Mit said.

"I want to give our group some diamonds before you guys leave. I need to have Jemi deduct them from my share. I may stay a couple more weeks, but I guess you guys will be going home pretty soon," Sony said.

"Not home, but back to our vacation, I hope. Roland, you and Zoe are going with us back to Abu Camp. I made the call to Abu and the bank yesterday. They are working to get started on the rebuilding, but you need to be in charge of the contractors and the details," Chris said.

"Thanks. If you are ever hanging around Port au Prince just drop by. I'll give you a good rate on a room," Roland said.

"Our time looks good, Chris, if we want to unscrew the hatch. Oh, by the way, we're okay to fly in twelve hours," Mit said.

"I won't be going anywhere till the ladies get back. We'll most likely leave tomorrow sometime—if Sony can handle things now?"

"I'll be fine from here. I appreciate your help. When I get topside, I'll tell Modesto as well. He and Isaac are up there plotting to take over the world with their small army. You know men like that need a few wars to keep them happy," Sony said.

The airtight lock was released. Jemi and Peter helped Chris and Mit into the upper chamber. Jemi inspected the diamonds in the clear plastic bag with the eye of a mining engineer. "Well, yes, this will cover some of our labor costs."

"It won't take much to cover costs for Mit and me," Chris said.

"I'll bring in professional divers to work the bottom. Eventually, I'll have to figure on a washing plant. I need to get the concentrates to a level where I can either fly them to be processed or build a facility here. The question is how much we can dig here? It's so rich in diamonds, I don't have to be in a hurry," Jemi said. "I think we have gotten several pounds of them so far."

"When are the girls coming back?" Sony asked.

"Probably in a couple hours or so. I had a call from Lu before the dive. They were having breakfast, then going to the airport. I see the supply helicopter has already returned," Chris said. He watched men unloading plywood and new tents from the chopper. A giant Russian transport helicopter was also parked in the quarry. It had just unloaded a yellow front-end loader. The quarry was beginning to look like a real mining site.

~~~~~

Lu was thrilled to get a van that held her entire entourage along with shopping bags from the hotel shops. Even though they were dressed in jungle garb, their clothes looked more like designer jungle garb. African clothing designers had caught the eyes of all the ladies, and certainly gorillas and chimps would be impressed with their new duds. When they got the bills, their husbands and boyfriends would also be impressed.

The driver of the van had a co-pilot, but no one noticed until they spoke to each other in Haitian Creole. Zoe noticed first.

"Lu, those guys are Haitian," Zoe whispered in her ear.

Gretchen overheard the whisper and started to dig for her 9mm. Then, she remembered everyone had to leave their guns on the helicopter. Observing the mumbling in the back, the Haitian man riding shotgun turned and faced the ladies who were dressed as though they were going to the premier of a Tarzan movie. Carol was sitting at the extreme rear of the van almost out of the view of the man with the gun. She ducked down and went out of view of everyone for a few seconds, then sat up with a strange look on her face.

"We are pleased to have you using our van today," he said. Calmly, he pulled out a 45 automatic and pointed it at the girls. "You are taking a small side trip. No harm will come to you if your boyfriends do as we say. I am now going to ask Lucero to call her pilot and have him meet us at the airport immediately. Here is a satellite phone," he said. He tried to hand it to Lu. She refused and produced her own phone and began to dial a stored number.

"Bill! You need to get to the airport and have my jet ready. We will be there in a few minutes," Lu said, without explanation.

"What's up?"

"Can't say."

"I have to file a flight plan. Where are we going?"

"Just a minute."

"Where are we going? He has to file a flight plan."

"Tell him—Gbadolite."

Chapter 34

Gbadolite

Barbos Marcel Vieux met the eclectically dressed ladies at the boarding ladder next to Lu's plane. The Haitian van drivers already emptied the ladies' purses and removed cell and satellite phones. No guns were found on the females. The women entered the plane and allowed the men to stow their luggage. Carol had some trouble walking and a stricken look appeared on her face. The other ladies attended to her and brought her a bottle of water. Lu asked what was wrong but got no answer. Soon the plane was in the air. Barbos called Chris on Lu's sat phone.

"Chris, this is Barbos Vieux. How are you today? Listen, I have six very beautiful ladies with me. We are going on a little side trip together. Wondered if you would like to join us? We are going to a very unique place that most tourists miss when they tour Africa. It's called Gbadolite. A heavenly place, carved right out of the jungle, with a long airstrip for your little Lear jet. Be here by five o'clock this evening, or I will start killing them—one each hour. Oh, bring some diamonds and no one else except your pilot. About eight ounces for each girl—a total of three pounds. I certainly don't want to appear greedy. Got that? Good." Barbos clicked off the power in the middle of screaming and cursing from the other end of the connection.

Chris had an ashen color to his face. He told Mit, who was standing next to him, what just happened.

"What the fuck! How many times does a goddamn Vieux kidnap our women?" Mit said.

They informed Peter and Sony. All four ran to the big wooden building to find Modesto. He was furious when he heard the news but shifted gears to being a cunning military genius with global contacts. His job was to take out Barbos and his men—kill them without harming a hair on any of the ladies' heads. All the available maps of Africa were laid out in front of him and Isaac. They made phone calls to the DRC headquarters, Kisangani Airport, the CIA, back to the DRC Army and calls to numbers given to Modesto by the sources.

"Modesto, Mit and I have a problem. We can't fly until eleven hours from now because of the deep dive," Chris said.

"Can't you fly at low altitudes?" asked Modesto.

"Yes, under 1000 feet—at the most, 1500 feet. The jet can do the job, but we'll have to be damn careful and map out a non-mountainous route—fly in the valleys—up river beds," Chris said.

"Call your pilot and have him map the route as best he can. We will delay your flight so your arrival will be as close to five o'clock as possible without going over. You can outgas as much as possible, but first we have to get you to Kisangani along with the troops we are taking—like, right now."

Isaac rounded up the troops he wanted and left the majority to guard the mine. The supply helicopter and the Russian transport were loaded for the two hour flight to Kisangani. Mit and Chris rode in the smaller supply aircraft because it was easier for the pilot to maintain a low altitude. If a five hundred foot hill was in front, then the pilot would have to drop to five hundred feet to maintain the 1000 foot altitude. By five o'clock, both Mit and Chris would only have about five hours left on their no fly status. The risk would be less, but not erased. The Gbadolite airport was at 1500 feet. Neither of them would be any good to their mates if they were paralyzed or dead.

Before they took off, Modesto learned the area around Gbadolite was controlled by forces still sympathetic to Mobutu even after he left in 1997. The leader was a warlord who was seldom seen who most rebel soldiers had never met. He was another colorful character in a long line of goofball African despots. The DRC, CIA, and Rwanda had assets in the area. The swords from hell were prodding these assets from all sides. Nobody in authority in that part of Africa wanted dead American and European female millionaires. Gbadolite was a city that was already an embarrassment for the Democratic Republic of the Congo.

When someone would ask about Gbadolite, the answer was usually, "Oh yeah. That's the city that crazy-ass Mobutu built in the jungle. It's the city with palaces and an airstrip that would allow a chartered *Concorde* jet to land so Mobutu's wife could fly to Paris to go shopping. Yeah. That place." At the Kisangani airport, Isaac put on a pilot's uniform and sat next to Chris's pilot Bonte. Barbos said 'just a pilot' but never mentioned a co-pilot, so they were taking a calculated risk. There was a good chance Barbos and their men would kill them all anyway after they got the diamonds. Although Chris and Isaac would bring diamonds, they hoped Barbos wouldn't be able to keep them.

Lu's jet had landed at Gbadolite on what was once the longest airstrip in Central Africa—that was once. Now weeds had taken over, and the smooth concrete was compromised and invaded by rampant vegetation. The surface had pot holes from a combination of the jungle rains and lack of maintenance. Barbos had called some local friends to sweep away the junk. His prison inmate friend could only come up with a handful of people who appeared to be vagrants, and only two of them were armed with what looked like muskets from a distance. Barbos had images of spit and polish soldiers with pressed uniforms and superior firepower. That dream quickly faded. Bill, Lu's pilot, was shaking when the jet came to a stop. He asked the soldiers if he could check the tires and landing gear for damage. They told him to stay put. Not a good sign.

The girls were ordered out of the plane and into the back of a white pickup truck; the kind they use for war in Iraq and Afghanistan. Gretchen and Angel had to lift Carol into the truck.

"What wrong with her?" Barbos said.

"I may be having a miscarriage. I can't be sure," Carol said.

"What the fuck! That's all I need. You better goddamn well stay alive until I get my diamonds. Gretchen, you're a doctor. Patch her ass up," Barbos yelled.

Two smaller, dented, once white pickups drove to the airstrip. The rest of Barbos's men climbed in back of them along with the vagrants. They dodged pot holes and rubble for a short distance and parked next to an old abandoned reception building near the airstrip. After being looted, the building had become an outhouse for men and goats. The women and two guards were let out there, and Barbos's other forces were dropped off at various other buildings. Moanda, a small village about two miles south of Gbadolite, was the actual location for the airfield and associated buildings.

Some of the drug dealer's men arrived first, swept an area and made the ladies sit next to a wall that had been ornately decorated long ago.

Gretchen talked to the two guards. She explained they needed privacy and things might get bloody if Carol was having a miscarriage. In an instant, the guards moved to another part of the building. Barbos was in the terminal next door, planning what would most likely be the fake exchange of kidnapped women for diamonds. He had placed snipers around two different buildings to take out Chris and the pilot, in case Chris was planning to sneak in some troops. One sniper was in the old airport tower and the other was on the roof of the terminal. The three structures were lined up in a row. Behind them were hangers and maintenance sheds. Barbos's pilot had flown a fighter jet, but had not been trained in either of the couple's jets. He thought he could figure it out. His ten men with guns were spread out in the reception building, terminal and airport tower. He had four people who were only armed with the pistols found in Lu's plane. Barbos thought to himself, "I am royally screwed."

"Carol, are you really having a miscarriage? It couldn't be Sony's, there hasn't been time. He is going to be pissed," Charlie jabbered.

"What's happening, Carol?" Gretchen asked.

"I think I'm allergic to chrome!"

"Whatttttt?" Gretchen was stupefied.

"Remember the little gun I had in my purse—the one Sony made fun of?"

"So?" Gretchen asked.

"When the guys made you turn in your purses, I stuck mine little gun in my underwear, only I forgot I was wearing a thong to impress Sony. He likes them."

"So what are you telling us?" Angel demanded.

"I first just stuck the barrel part in my 'who-ha' to hide it."

At this point, Lu and Angel were pounding the floor in muted laughter. Gretchen was the professional trying to hold it together, but she couldn't resist.

"You know Carol; you give a new meaning to a "Pistol Packing Mama." At that, the whole group except Carol was in pain from holding back laughter.

"Look, doc, somehow the whole thing worked its way up there, and I can't get it out. I'm scared it's going to fire and shoot out one of my ovaries." She tried to smile at this statement.

Charlie, Lu, Zoe and Angel were useless, with the greatest comedy routine in history playing out in front of their eyes.

Gretchen was allowed her medical bag, after they dumped it out and removed all the knives. She found something like a forceps and had Carol spread her legs.

Gretchen was calmly working to grasp the gun with the forceps when Carol said, "I can't believe my first baby is going to be a .22 automatic."

With that statement, she lost the entire crowd, including herself. Gretchen was laughing so hard she could barely direct the forceps. Finally, she had a grip on the pistol. Gretchen had to say it—she couldn't help it. "Would you like a butt baby or a barrel baby—I can do either?" The other girls were finding they were barely able to breathe in between their laughter.

Gretchen removed the gun and announced it was a healthy Beretta Bobcat Inox. "Would anybody like to hold the baby?" To that, she got a lot of "Hell nos."

She wiped down the baby, took out the clip, put it back and moved a bullet into firing position.

"These guys will kill us if they get the diamonds, or if they think they've been screwed. And here we sit with a tiny pistol and a handful of little bullets. I suggest when Chris gets here, we put a bullet in the brain of the nearest guards and take their weapons," Angel said.

"Maybe we'll do that, Angel, and I will volunteer to be the shooter, but I have faith in Modesto. He knows everyone who can find embedded assets. It is possible one of those goofy conscripts who Barbos hired here is a Bruce Lee or Rambo. And, you know he has an alternate plan if it means having the Marines land on this God forsaken airport. I wish we could take out Barbos's snipers. I wish we could do something. But I say, as Angel suggested, we take out our guards when Chris lands. A .22 pistol is the favorite weapon for hit men. They're quiet—just the right caliber for a head shot," Gretchen said. Everyone listened to her since she had been at war in Afghanistan. She received a medal for killing twenty Taliban soldiers while she was wounded.

"We have about an hour before Chris gets here. Any suggestions where we hide Carol's pistol until then?" Angel said. The laughter started all over again.

"Carol, we have some suggestions for naming your baby when you really have one," Charlie said.

"Please, I am in enough pain without you guys helping."

The six ladies were all thinking, at least they got in a good laugh in before they died.

Chapter 35

A Diamond Ransom

Modesto felt exhausted. He called in every favor he had generated through the years and then some. In part, the history of the spot on the map contributed to the resistance in helping him to get where they were asked to go.

Gbadolite was an eyesore and political land mine for any public official in Africa. No one wanted to be associated with the place. The general feeling was, "let the jungle retake the city." Under the dictator Mobutu, 35,000 people lived there. Mobutu made Gbadolite a place for conventions, parties and even vacations. Schools as well as the accommodations for visitors were first class. But, the economy was artificial and destined to fail. The city was a wild dream that a wacko dictator created with stolen money from a treasury loaded with disbursements from the U.S. and Europe.

Mobutu Sese Seko would regularly fly his mistresses, including his wife's twin sister, to his one hundred million dollar Gbadolite palace. The country Mobutu called Zaire was rich in diamonds, copper, cobalt and gold. The real treasure for Zaire was the billions received in aid from the U.S. and Europe to ward off Communism. He usually kept the peace during his reign as dictator; however, he was quick to call in outside troops to stop any force that smacked of left wing tendencies. Here was another dictator much like Trujillo of the Dominican Republic and Papa Doc of Haiti, propped up as a champion against Communism. At some point, those feeding the monsters had to stop the flow of dollars. Mobutu was molded into place by the CIA, and decades later finally rejected by most of the world. The end of the cold war caused the U.S. to finally reject leaders who had atrocious human rights records. They had ignored Mobutu's strong man tactics for way too many years.

Motubu "the Leopard" Sese Seko's plane took off from the runway at Gbadolite on May 16, 1997. Finally rebel forces had made their move to take over the country, and they fired parting shots at his plane as it went airborne. Then, there was no place for his plane to land. Where would he be welcome? He went to Togo for a while and then to Morocco where he died from prostate cancer within six months of his arrival. Part of fortune he stole was still a mystery at his death and up to fifteen billion dollars were estimated to have fallen through the cracks of Zaire's accounting system. Almost immediately after he died, there were attempts to freeze billions squirreled away in Swiss accounts. Since he rarely used his name on deeds and accounts, this made finding his wealth almost impossible.

Because of Mit's recent dive, he and Modesto, Sony, Roland and Peter landed by helicopter about three miles inland from the airstrip after a low level flight from Kisangani. Devil Man and Jackie had been dropped by the same chopper, closer to the reception building, but still out of sight. Osse and Jean-Jean were situated opposite the air strip in a forested area with a good view of all three buildings across the runway. The group from the quarry assembled about three miles northeast of the airport in the actual town of Gbadolite along a wide boulevard. They met with other forces that Modesto had talked into assisting them. There was one embedded asset, but he wasn't actually part of Barbos's little army.

The airport did get some use, but mainly by small aircraft since people who lived in Gbadolite found it hard to get to the town without a flight. The majority of aircraft were commuter prop planes that pulled up to the old terminal which was usually locked. When the terminal wasn't locked, there was a small operations office at the east end where the single airport employee had an office. This man maintained the flight schedule, ordered a refueling truck from Gbadolite when needed and kept track of hanger fees. The airport official was in a strategic position to observe who came in and went out. So the lucky guy collected checks from the DRC, CIA, Interpol and anyone willing to pay for information.

Modesto had been put in touch with the man in charge on a satellite phone almost from the time the girls got off the plane. The airport employee, Thomas Habimana, had given Modesto the location of all Barbos's men and the ladies. Thomas Habimana, Rwandan by birth, had been a resident of Gbadolite since the first days of construction. He had been the airport manager when the Air France Concorde flew in to take Mobutu's wife shopping in Paris. Thomas had seen the city being built and rebels tear down most structures and loot the palaces. He longed for the good times to return. When Barbos arrived, he came out of his office and spoke to him briefly, then retreated behind a locked door. Barbos started to take him out but decided to kill him later.

Chris's jet was about to arrive, so Barbos made the rounds of his men to see the placement of his fire power. First, he checked the ladies and their guards and found the guards had moved some distance from them. Gretchen told him that Carol was feeling better, and thank goodness wasn't having miscarriage. He ordered the guards back with the women. The guards looked relieved that a bloody fetus wasn't going to be squirted out on the floor towards them. Next, he checked his sniper on the roof of the terminal building. Barbos walked to the tower and as he waved at the sniper. He knew that one sniper up there wasn't enough.

Devil Man and Jackie were going to protect the women in the reception building and put themselves, plus at least five other DRC troops, between the women and incoming fire. Peter didn't give the impression of being a commando type, but he was into high-tech weapons. Yet in order to protect Charlie, he asked for a firing position that overlooked the building. Once his group of men crossed Highway 24, he found a place on top of a hanger at the rear of the complex. The weapon he held he had bought on line and had it shipped to a dealer in South Africa. The rifle had one of the most sophisticated firing systems outside of the military. It featured a networked tracking scope that allowed a red laser mark to be placed on a target then locked in place until you could get the hairs on the scope close, pull the trigger and the gun would do the rest. The weapon was a Precision Rifle .338 Lapua Magnum Surgeon with a 27 inch Krieger barrel, and it just didn't miss. Peter began to search out targets as soon as he got in place but was told to hold off until Modesto gave the okay.

Another group of military men from the Democratic Republic of the Congo had moved into position on the opposite side of the airport tower but stayed in the forest out of sight. The main force of twenty DRC soldiers was behind Mit, Modesto, Sony and Roland. They had moved quietly across the highway and were positioned behind the main hanger, directly in back of the terminal building.

Barbos's man in the airport tower had the best view of everything but kept moving around the large outside observation deck stepping over debris. The sniper finally decided to watch the airstrip to protect Barbos as he went out to meet the plane. If Barbos could have spared two men up there, all areas could have been watched simultaneously. The same could be said for the one sniper on the terminal, since he was just watching the runway and not behind his position.

Peter had found both snipers and knew that Osse most likely had the tower in his sights from the other side of the runway. It would be a 300 to 400 yard shot for the Barrett but well within the gun's effective range. There was a good chance the DRC soldiers in the forested area also had the sniper in their sights. Peter's shot on the man on the roof was only 150 yards but a prone target with a shallow angle.

Devil Man and Jackie could see the people inside the reception center but didn't have a good shot. They would have to get closer. The two Haitian fighters noticed a wall in the back with no windows, so they crawled behind tall weeds and brushed against the wall, causing a carpet viper to slither away making a sizzling sound as its scales rubbed together. Since no one mowed or cut weeds anymore, there was plenty of cover and an abundance of snakes.

Modesto was concerned about synchronizing the action, so he had open mikes from the other soldiers to give orders as he called them. The mikes would tell Osse, Jean-Jean, Peter, the DRC men in the forest and Devil Man when to shoot. Barbos would certainly be armed. Jean-Jean, who was paired with Osse, had a powerful assault rifle across the runway. If he could get a bead, he would take a shot. If Peter could take the first target, he should have time to shoot Barbos. Or, Isaac was armed and acting as copilot, so maybe he could kill him. Nothing ever worked according to plan when hostages were involved, but at least there was a plan. Everyone predicted Barbos would make things difficult for any preplanning exercise.

Chris announced to Modesto they were approaching the airstrip and to fill him in on the situation. Modesto told him about Barbos's snipers, the men placed to counter them and where Modesto had his forces. He warned that Barbos would be very tough and, without a doubt, would kill Chris and all the hostages with or without the diamonds. "Anything can go wrong and probably will," Modesto said forcing a mild laugh.

From a distance, everyone could hear the high whine of the jet circling to come in on the runway marked 25. The jet touched down hot and used a lot of runway, then turned and taxied to the tarmac in front of the terminal building. First, Chris could see some old Soviet jets parked on the side of the tarmac. They had been stripped down embarrassingly naked and exposed to the African sun. The plane parked parallel to the building and lowered its boarding ladder. Chris could see Barbos holding a pistol with several soldiers standing behind him. Barbos turned around and parted the soldiers, grabbed the arm of a woman and started dragging her towards the plane. It was Lu dressed in brand new African safari shorts.

Chris and Isaac walked down the ladder. Isaac had on a pilot's uniform, but Chris's real pilot Bonte Ballo was hidden in a wall behind the restroom. Isaac had a gun in his belt behind him but knew it would be risky with Lu as a hostage. Chris held a bag of diamonds in his hand.

Barbos walked to the plane to talk to Chris, holding Lu who was remarkably calm and didn't have her hands bound. Two of his soldiers were just a few paces behind them. As Barbos approached, Chris knew there were snipers keyed on him, Barbos and probably everyone who was exposed at that airport. One wrong move and a lot of people died. He could only hope it was the right people.

"Barbos! Why do the Vieux brothers always have the hots for my wife? You've got money, surely you can get a date," Chris said watching every move Barbos made.

"Lu is so pretty. We can't resist trying to get something we can't have. And who knows? Maybe she has a thing for Haitian men," Barbos said as he reached for Chris's bag.

Chris moved the bag out of his reach. "I would like to see if the rest of the ladies are unharmed."

"Certainly, Chris."

Barbos waived his hand towards the reception center building, and the two guards pushed the five women out the front door with guns at their backs.

"Satisfied? Now may I look at the diamonds?" Barbos took the bag. For a second he let go of Lu's hand as he stuck his hand into the three pounds of uncut diamonds, letting them run through his fingers. When he looked up, Lu had a small pistol in his face, and she started firing as fast as she could. Chris grabbed her, threw her to the ground and pounced on top of her. Isaac had his gun out but splattered blood and torn flesh flew off of the two soldiers, so he didn't need to shoot. It seemed that hundreds of rounds were going off all around them. Devil man and Jackie had rushed around from the back of the reception building, let go with automatic fire on the two guards and then pushed the women back inside for safety. Several DRC soldiers followed them in and shielded them from gunfire.

Peter killed the man on the roof with his first shot, then rose up to pick off one of the soldiers running out of the terminal. Osse had the first shot on the sniper on the tower, and the fifty caliber blew him off his perch all the way to the ground. Jean-Jean had taken out one of the men with Barbos, and the other shot had come out of the woods someplace. DRC soldiers poured out of the woods and from behind the hangers and rushed the terminal, killing or wounding the rest of Barbos's men.

It was finally over. Lu got up and stood over Barbos Vieux's body. He had two small round holes right between his eyes. His eyes were open, staring with a strange shocked expression on his face.

The women all raced out to see Lu and to make sure she was alright. They hugged her and said she was very brave to stand there and shoot Barbos in front of his soldiers.

"I'm sick of being kidnapped by those asshole brothers. Are there any more of them?" Lu asked.

Modesto walked up to Lu and hugged her. "Lu, you didn't wait for my signal to shoot, but then you didn't know about the plan. And you know what? Your plan was a whole lot better than mine. You are my hero!" He kissed her lightly on the mouth and turned to look for Gretchen.

Sony and Carol came over to Chris and Lu. "Can we come with you guys on safari for a few days?" Carol asked. "Because we have earned a vacation."

"You can, Carol, but you have to screw on the back of an elephant. Can you and Sony handle that?" Lu said.

"Elephant-back sex. On our way. Got camera. Got good woman. Point to camp," Sony said, who may have combined Sony, John Wayne and Tarzan of the apes.

Carol saw her pistol lying on the tarmac next to Barbos's body. Chris went over and picked it up. He clicked on the safety and handed the little Beretta to Carol. "I don't know how you guys were able to sneak that little pistol past the guards, but you saved the day with it."

"Chris, why don't we just say I hid it in a very special place?"

The End

Epilogue

One Week later-Abu Camp-Botswana

With both jets parked at a nearby airport, the group was packed and ready to end their vacation. The entire group was sitting around a large breakfast table, sipping coffee and Bloody Marys. An eventful week had passed since they left Gbadolite.

Lu had paid for Charlie, Peter, Carol and Sony to spend a week at the camp with a night elephant ride a requirement. No one complained, which was obvious, since they took those rides almost every night.

The surviving members of Barbos Vieux's small troop had been rounded up and eventually sent to a Congolese prison. Modesto thanked his friends from all the intelligence agencies he had tapped for information. The former airport manager had been the key and was compensated most generously by the group. Flights still came into the airport at Gbadolite, but now there was a remodeled reception center and terminal, thanks to the group. The Chinese Palace became a project for Lu, who felt it would make a nice restaurant for tourists and locals. She made part of the Chinese Palace inexpensive for lunches and prepared another section where dinner was a little fancier. The chef who cooked for Mobutu was still in the area and gladly took on the job of supervisor. The city of Gbadolite was slowly coming back, because, as within many parts of the DRC, minerals had been discovered nearby.

One of the most thrilling events at Abu Camp was Angel and Mit finally announcing their wedding date. The location would be Austria at their mountain retreat in one month. They actually had been secretly planning the wedding for some time to be held at their large cabin, where a new lion skin rug would be a focal point of the spacious den. Angel had been trying the whole time they had been in Africa to get pregnant so she could tell everyone her baby was conceived on the back of an elephant. It may have occurred given the popularity of the resort's night time "elephant" high club. It would take a while to find out for sure, and she may have not been alone in the effort.

Chris and Lu had also been discussing having another child. A matching birth date and conception might have been traced back to a nighttime ride as well. Their son Reid had been calling them almost every day. He was, however, having a great time with both sets of grandparents. Trips to the beach, pony rides, fishing and time spent with his Dominican friends playing video games kept Reid quite busy. His parents had installed an arcade room at Grenade Land. They nicknamed the old army base Chris had bought a few years back for the munitions once kept there. At one time the base was a testing site for weapons, but Chris had the compound completely cleaned and fenced in. He built bunk houses for Reid's little friends and their parents so they could stay at the estate that was several thousand acres in a remote part of the Dominican Republic. Soon they would go to Lake Hamilton in Hot Springs for a couple weeks where they had a house and one set of grandparents and then back to Boston for Reid's pre-school. The fall and winter would include a trip to Mit and Angel's wedding, and another wedding soon in Texas.

Sony and Carol were not waiting any longer. They wanted children and yesterday wasn't soon enough. They had only known each other for a couple of weeks but couldn't have been any more suited for each other. Modesto and Gretchen understood only too well since they had a similar experience a few years back. Carol's parents and friends were coming from Nice, France to Austin, Texas, where Sony lived. He could afford to foot the bill with the new share of diamonds alone. The entire twenty five percent would be credited to the Cole Family Trust each month and divided among his parents, sisters and himself. The quarry was slowly being converted into an actual mining operation under the guidance of Jemi and his crew. They had found an underwater submersible robotic system, plus he had contracted with professional hard hat divers. Jemi had shipped uranium in nuclear waste containers, and he was investigating other methods. Joint efforts were underway with other uranium mines in the DRC. Sony was not needed at the mine but promised to come back and visit often.

Carol would not be needed at the quarry since Charlie would be the acting anthropologist. Charlie and Peter planned to spend a great deal of time there and were going back to the quarry from Abu camp. Charlie would act as liaison for the Efe and Lese tribes and make sure they were taken care of properly. One anthropologist was enough for now, but the expedition had sparked interest in visits from all over the world. Charlie would sort through and mete out the groups that were allowed to visit the natives. She felt it would be impossible not to have some change in the natural lifestyles of the pygmies, but she wanted to protect their wild and primitive way of life as best as she could.

Peter was a part of the African geological team, along with Rick Lasiter and the Haitian geologist, Darley Konte. All were to stay on at the quarry for a while to monitor and do testing for the Haitian government. A wooden building had been constructed for Peter and Carol in their absence. Not everyone understood what a beautiful woman like Charlie could see in Peter, but never was there a happier lady than when she was with him. Although he was not particularly handsome, he was brave and had proven so at the airstrip in Gbadolite. He was highly intelligent and had a boyish charm—an innocence that made Charlie feel totally comfortable. Their lovemaking was passionate, and she wasn't shy about telling the other girls how size really did matter. They talked about marriage with a causal assurance, as they were young and fresh out of college and, therefore in no hurry. Both were doing what they loved to do with the person they loved right beside them.

Zoe and Lu would become best friends. Lu had forgiven Zoe for being a spy and welcomed a new running buddy close by in Haiti. They had already planned to get together on Lu's next trip to the Dominican Republic. Lu's father, T.J. Earnhart, was getting on in age, and Lu wanted to come often to check on him and let Reid visit him and his grandmother Allie.

Roland and Modesto had hit it off, as they held similar positions in their respective side-by-side countries. Both traveled to each other's country several times a year, which made a great excuse for a party. Gretchen and Zoe would complement each other. Zoe would take on the role of shopping for clothes for Gretchen, who was always too busy in her medical practice. Zoe and Roland had held off having children since they were busy with the hotel but now that financing was strongly in place, they didn't have an excuse. Both were, of course, invited to Sony's and Mit's wedding, with all expenses paid.

For the country of Haiti, the gold stored in the Ivory Coast bank was being sold off as needed for reconstruction. With the estimated value in the billions of dollars, the treasure would go a long way to fund public projects. That is, if the government would keep their hands off the revenues for their own perverse uses. A gold "czar" was put in charge to sell gold as needed and keep much in reserve, as the price was still trending upward. Now that Roland knew about the treasure, he would keep an eye on those who wanted to fund political campaigns, build cities in the jungle and charter jets to takes politicians' wives and girlfriends on shopping sprees.

Revenues from the Aruwimi mine would slowly build and be a long-term solution to the funding of many public projects. Haiti had so much need, many people thought the country was too broken too ever be fixed. Roland and Zoe didn't see things that way. They had seen the people survive on almost nothing and given the right help with the right leaders, they were confident progress could be made using micro-loans from the government and banks that were protected by real assets.

Roland, Zoe and the others who went on the expedition to the Congo were heroes to the Haitian people. News had trickled in that Haiti had discovered hidden gold and also owned a diamond and uranium mine in the Congo. Chris Zacharius found his way into the headlines as the person who never gave up the search for Papa Doc's gold. Plato received praise for finally turning over the journal that exposed the hidden gold and the quarry.

Everyone had a fabulous time at Abu Camp, and the ladies may even have forgiven the men for sneaking over to dive at the quarry. Chris, Mit and Modesto were sitting at the table while the rest had gone to finish checking out. Chris had something on his mind.

"Did you know that Mobutu was worth between over five and fifteen billion dollars in the 1990s. He robbed the Congo blind and much of the money came from the U.S. The CIA paid him to supposedly stop the spread of communism. What I find interesting is no one knows where the billions of dollars went. We know there were Swiss accounts where some of it was hidden. He had jillions of kids from marriages and mistresses, and they didn't get the loot. He first flew to Togo and then to Morocco, where he died of prostate cancer. I guess he wore the damn thing out. Anyway, I wonder where he hid the billions of dollars that didn't go into Swiss banks?"

"Don't know, and I don't care," Mit said.

"No interest," Modesto said.

"No interest in what?" Lu asked as she rolled her small suitcase up to the table.

"Lu, would you like to go on vacation with me to Morocco," Chris said.

"Oh no! Not if you're going on some fucking treasure hunt?"

"Five—maybe fifteen billion. A couple of camel rides away. Nice meals in a sultan's palace. Maybe a side trip to the pyramids and Petra. Any bucket list items there, dear?" he said with a devious smile.

"Chris, there may be a bucket alright—full of shit dumped on your head. You want me to crank out another kid while you ride a damn camel through the Sahara desert waving one of those curvy knife thingies. Forget it, asshole!"

"Is that a maybe?" Chris said.

Lu stomped off to join the other girls to tell them another treasure hunt was being planned and to keep their eyes peeled for indications of a real plan taking shape.

Mit and Modesto sipped on their Bloody Marys without looking up. When they looked at Chris, they saw a familiar far off distant stare. They had seen if before and knew there was no cure for it. It was a sickness and there was no medicine to treat it. They knew in the next year or two a plan would be laid out in front of them. It would be an exciting adventure with unbelievable rewards and dangers that no sane person would tackle. He would make it inviting. They would say no, and the women would revolt. But, in a way, they all wanted to see what he would come up with next. Not that they had any interest in it, of course.

Charles L. (Chap) Harper

Chap is a native Arkansan and attended the University of Arkansas and Little Rock University. After working for a large Insurance Company for twenty-one years, he retired as a Vice President. Chap moved from California to a house on Lake Hamilton in Hot Springs, Arkansas and began to write. His first novel was *Once Upon a Reef* published in 2012. It was inspired from his visits to the Dominican Republic and other Caribbean Islands. The story idea concerned billions of dollars of gold stolen by the now assassinated dictator Rafael Trujillo and a group of scuba divers looking for the treasure. Chap's love of scuba diving was evident in this novel and the one to follow.

Later in 2014 he wrote *Once Upon the Congo* which was a follow up to the first novel but certainly stands on its own since several new characters joined the ones in the first book. This book has been published by Smoking Gun Publishing Company and will be available in May of 2015. The story will remind the reader of great stories like King Solomon's Mine and those stores about great white hunters in Africa. Chap inserts humor, romance, danger and adventure and creates a story that blends history with dynamite fiction.

Currently he has just finished *Beer, Bait, and Ammo* and hopes to have it published in 2016.

Other Books by This Author
Once Upon a Reef - 2012
Beer, Bait, and Ammo - 2016